Ready or Not

Ready or Not

THE LOVE GAME: BOOK FOUR

ELIZABETH HAYLEY

This book is an original publication of Waterhouse Press.

This is a work of fiction. Names, characters, places, and incidents either are the product of the author's imagination or are used fictitiously, and any resemblance to actual persons, living or dead, business establishments, events, or locales is entirely coincidental. The publisher does not assume any responsibility for third-party websites or their content.

Cover Design by Waterhouse Press
Cover Images: Shutterstock

ISBN: 978-1-64263-269-9

To the Fugees,
because once our editor heard it,
none of us could un-hear it.

Chapter One

TAYLOR

"I think he's seizing."

My best friend, Sophia, followed my gaze to the dance floor. To Ransom Holt, more specifically.

She hummed before saying, "Pretty sure he's dancing."

"His whole body is . . . vibrating."

Her eyebrow quirked. "You know, Taylor, if I didn't know better, I'd think you were just a teensy bit obsessed with how that boy's body moves."

I flashed my eyes to her, my bitch face showing just how unimpressed I was with her comment.

She merely smirked, the asshole. "Someone's testy."

"I just don't even get why he's here," I muttered.

Here was Sophia's boyfriend's—scratch that—her *fiancé's* bar. Well, not Drew's per se, but the one he'd gotten up and running and continued to manage. It was actually a deck built off an existing bar, but they ran the Yard as a separate entity. And despite it being part of a dive bar, the Yard had a younger, funner vibe going, with backyard games sprinkled around the lawn it overlooked, cozy seating, and friendly staff.

Sophia looked at me like I was being ridiculous. Spoiler alert: I was. But I couldn't really help it. Something about Ransom . . . bothered me.

"Because he's friends with Brody," she said slowly. "And pretty much all of us by this point. Except you," she added pointedly.

Brody was Sophia's brother who seemed to collect strays like he was a septuagenarian living alone in a double-wide. Unfortunately, he was unlikely to experience an SPCA raid anytime soon. He'd brought Ransom around a couple of months ago, and the guy had been a fairly regular fixture in our group since. The others had warmed to him quickly. I hadn't.

I wasn't a big enough douche to try to tell myself that my not getting close to him had anything to do with him. It was all me and my fucked-up emotions. The guy was attractive: tall, athletic, light hair that sparkled against his tan face, and a wide smile that he flashed easily. He was a bit of a goof, but it was actually kind of endearing. There didn't seem to be any pretense with Ransom. What I saw appeared to be what I'd get with him. But I'd been wrong before. Very wrong. And that was what kept me away.

"He's, like, undulating now. Does he think he's a wave?" I asked rather than acknowledge her comment that I was the only nonmember of the Ransom fan club.

"Pretty hot wave," she muttered.

I scowled at her. "I'm going to tell Drew."

She shrugged. "Go ahead. Even he's said how hot Ransom is."

"Hot as in sweaty? Because he's doing the sprinkler now, so that should probably cool him down."

Sophia snorted. "You're the worst." She stood up, taking her glass with her. As she shimmied between our stools, she leaned down and whispered, "You're also not fooling anyone."

With that, she walked away to go mingle, her dark, wavy hair brushing across her back as she went. She sidled up next to her fiancé, and he pulled her into his side without even looking over at her, like he instinctively knew she was there.

I tried to push down the swell of jealousy that rose up by taking a gulp of my 7 & 7. I didn't begrudge Sophia for her happily ever after. I was so freaking happy that she'd found someone who complemented her so well. But watching her have the dream I'd stupidly convinced myself I'd found almost a year ago only to have reality come calling in a nightmarish fashion made me a little envious too. Not that I'd ever tell her that.

There was a lot I never intended to tell her, which made me feel like the shittiest best friend in the world, but it was what it was.

"Hey, you not dancing?"

I jolted at the sudden intrusion of the deep, out-of-breath voice. Looking over at Ransom's stupidly handsome face made my hackles rise before I could temper myself.

"Not sure I'd call what you were doing dancing."

His smile only got wider at my bitchy tone. "I'll have you know I get a lot of compliments on my moves."

"From who? Strippers?"

I was joking, but his face shuttered at my words, his smile disappearing as he stepped back from me. He shrugged. "All kinds of people. See ya." And then he bolted away from me like his hard, perfectly sculpted ass was on fire.

As I watched him go, Brody's girlfriend, Aamee, came

and stood next to me. She was in her official the Yard uniform of jean shorts and brightly colored polo, but she'd tied hers so it cinched tightly around her trim waist. The fact that Aamee, Sophia's ex-nemesis and ex-sorority president, was working as a server in Drew's bar still blew my mind a bit, but I couldn't deny she was damn good at it.

"Wow," she said. "Even I've never gotten a guy to run away from me that fast. Good work."

I rolled my eyes. "I didn't even do anything."

"Hmm... Must be your complete lack of charm, then."

"Don't you have a drink to serve or a demon to summon or something?"

She scoffed. "You sound like Sophia."

"We are best friends for a reason."

"Lack of better prospects, huh?"

"The summer's almost over. Aren't you supposed to move so you can work for your mom and begin your career in nepotism? God, how I'll miss you." The sarcasm dripped from my words so heavily I was surprised I wasn't drooling.

"Believe me, pet," she replied as she patted my hand. "The feeling is very mutual." She smoothed her hand down her shorts. "Okay, I'm bored with talking to you. I only came over here to see if Ransom needed anything, but you sent his hulking six-four frame fleeing in terror before I got the chance." She gave me a once-over. "It was like watching Chucky kill Rambo."

"I think Thor is a more accurate comparison."

She put her elbow on the back of my chair and rested her chin on it, smiling at me. "Oh, is it now? Have a little Chris Hemsworth fetish, do we?"

"Ugh, what does Brody see in you?"

Her smile grew even more gleeful. "I honestly have no idea."

We laughed together for a second before she asked me if I needed anything. When I said no, she left, but not before telling me to stop sitting alone. It evidently made me look like a spinster.

I spun around a bit so I could survey the bar. Sophia was still chatting with Drew and whoever they were talking to, Aamee had gone over to flirt with Brody as he cleared tables, Xander—another member of our weird little group—was pumping out drinks like he was attempting to medal in bartending, and Ransom was . . . watching me.

His eyes narrowed slightly, and I immediately tensed, his dark look making my breathing quicken, and not in a good way. But I couldn't look away because fuck that scowl. Who did he even think he was?

I was so busy returning his glare, I didn't register the man who'd sidled up beside me until he brushed against me on his way to the open seat at the high top I'd commandeered when I'd arrived. I jolted like a lunatic, my attention dropping from Ransom immediately and focusing instead on the smiling man who was sitting so close to me his knees touched mine. I scooted back as he extended a hand toward me.

"Hi. I'm Roger."

I stared at his hand like he'd just tried to hand me a viper. While I'd been caught off-guard by Ransom's stare, this guy's infiltration of my space was making me squirrelly.

At my silence, his smile dimmed, and he dropped his hand. Onto my knee. And fucking squeezed.

"Shy, huh? That's okay. I like 'em that way." He winked, not bothering to remove his hand.

And I . . . sat there, gaping like a fucking fish. I willed the Taylor who'd inhabited my body twelve months prior to show up and rip this man's testicles from his body, but she was nowhere to be found.

Come on, girl. Get it together. I was nearly through with my mental pep talk, and totally on my way to verbally eviscerating this smarmy interloper when a deep voice spoke.

"Hey, there. I'm Ransom." Ransom stuck his hand out, which required Roger to let go of me in order to shake it.

"Hi. Roger."

"Nice to meet you, Roger. You mind telling me why the fuck you have your hand on my girlfriend's leg?"

Roger blanched as Ransom closed in on him a bit, making sure to loom over the other man.

My eyes widened, and my mouth might have dropped open a little. Ransom in his full alpha-male glory was a sight to behold. Most of the time, his slight awkwardness and goofiness made him seem harmless. But I had a feeling I was seeing the Ransom who used to run people over on the football field.

Yes, I'd watched clips of him on YouTube. Sue me.

"I, uh, I didn't, I mean . . . She never said—"

"I think it's time for you to go, Rog," Ransom said as he picked Roger up by the scruff of his shirt and pushed him away from my table.

Roger stumbled a bit, but when he regained his footing, he whirled around on Ransom. "What the fuck, man? You can't touch me. Do you even know who I am?"

"You're Roger."

"Yeah," Roger, who was becoming an alarming shade of red, replied as if it meant something.

"Glad we cleared that up," said Ransom. "Hit the road."

"I, you, this . . ." Roger spluttered.

"I think he's going to stroke out," I whispered to Ransom.

"One could only hope."

"What's going on over here?" Drew's voice boomed across the space as he positioned himself in front of me and beside Ransom.

Brody was there a split second later, flanking Ransom's other side. Aamee and Sophia slid in behind the boys, our whole crazy little crew shifting into pack mentality.

Roger evidently missed the clear show of solidarity. "This douchebag put his hands on me and told me to leave."

Drew turned to Ransom. "You did?"

Ransom pushed his hands into his pockets. The move looked too casual, as if Ransom wanted to appear more confident than he felt. "Yeah."

"Okay." Drew turned back to Roger. "It's time for you to leave, then."

Oh boy. The red rooster named Roger looked like he was about to blow like an atomic bomb. "You've got to be kidding me. This roided-out freak can't tell me what to do."

"No?" Ransom asked as he took a step forward, causing Roger to leap back. The moment could've only been made better if Roger had shrieked.

"See?" Roger yelled. "He can't threaten me like that."

Brody stepped forward. "You're right, sir."

Straightening out his shirt, Roger calmed a little at Brody's words. "Damn right I am."

Moving to Roger's side, Brody put an arm around him and turned him around. "It's of the utmost importance to us that our customers feel safe."

"Finally, someone with some sense," Roger said, clearly not realizing Brody was slowly walking him away from us.

"Yes, I *do* have a lot of sense. Thank you for noticing."

Brody looked back at us over his shoulder and stuck his tongue out.

Fucking Brody.

"And you know where I think you'd be safest?" Brody asked in a concerned voice.

Roger looked at him like Brody was about to tuck him into bed and tell him a bedtime story.

Brody dropped his arm from Roger's shoulders. "In your car. Driving away from here." Sophia's brother's voice was icy now, and the look on his face brooked no argument. Brody might have been a man-child, but he could sure dial up the mad face when he needed it. "Enjoy your night."

Roger spluttered and looked around, seemingly just then realizing Brody had walked him to the stairs that would take him to the parking lot.

"I'll ruin you for this!" Roger shouted.

"Wow, what an original threat," Drew deadpanned.

We all laughed, now able to find the threat of his deck being shut down funny, even though it hadn't been a few weeks ago when the jerk at the marketing firm Sophia was interning at gave the name the Yard to a famous client, making us all worry Drew would face repercussions for operating with the same name.

Roger lobbed a few more threats around, but I tuned him out, instead focusing on the group that had rallied around me and stood up for me without even needing any details. *This* was what I needed in my life. And it was exactly what I didn't have back at school. The thought made dread lodge in my sternum.

Everyone had moved a little closer to where Roger was standing except Ransom. He still stood directly beside me, glaring at Roger with eyes as sharp as lasers.

“Girlfriend, huh?” I said quietly so only he would hear.

“Huh? Oh, yeah, sorry. I just said whatever came to mind.”

I smiled at him. “Thanks. I’m glad you noticed I wanted him gone.”

He rubbed a hand over the back of his sand-colored hair. He kept his hair a bit on the long side, and the strands swayed with the movement. “Oh, uh, I didn’t really notice that to be honest. I just saw the way he was looking at you before he came over. When he was standing behind you.”

Ah, so it hadn’t been me Ransom was scowling at. “Well, either way. I’m glad you were here.”

“Yeah, me too.” He gave me a small smile before he began to shuffle away.

I reached out and grabbed his arm. He looked back at me questioningly.

“I’m sorry. For whatever I said earlier that upset you.” And I was. I’d been sorry the instant I’d seen his smile disappear, even if the way it made me feel was unwelcome. Well, maybe the *feeling* wasn’t unwelcome, but the desire to act on it was. Whatever. Semantics could suck a nut.

“You didn’t upset me. No worries.” Ransom then turned and walked away quickly, leaving me to stare after him, wishing he hadn’t just shown himself to be a liar.

“Well, that was dramatic,” Sophia exclaimed when she reached me. “What the hell happened?”

I pulled my eyes off Ransom and looked at all the expectant faces looking at me. Even Xander had joined us. Of course they were all curious, but they looked concerned too.

And that was when I knew.

Zeroing in on Sophia, I said, “I can’t go back to school. I can’t go back to that campus.” Emotions made my sinuses burn, and I felt my eyes fill.

Sophia, always knowing what I needed, drew me into a big hug. "Okay, Tay. We'll figure it out."

"My dad is going to lose his shit."

She rubbed soothing circles on my back, and I gave in to it, allowing myself to be reassured by the person who knew me and my relationship with my family better than anyone else in the world.

"Nah," she said. "He'll understand."

"I don't understand." My father looked at me like I'd just asked him to solve advanced calculus.

My dad and stepmom had been trying to get me to come home for a family dinner since summer break had started, but I'd used every excuse in the book to avoid it. So when I called yesterday and said I wanted to come home for a meal, one would've thought he'd have figured out something was up. But the man looked positively gobsmacked.

It had been a week since the incident at the bar, and Sophia and I had spent all our free time putting things in motion for me to complete my final semester of college online so I could stay close to my friends, all of whom had become my support network. We'd also discussed how this conversation with my dad was going to go.

It wasn't going how we'd planned.

For one, I'd wanted to have this discussion *after* dinner, when I could get him alone. This wasn't a conversation I wanted to have in front of my two younger half-siblings. And I never wanted to have *any* conversation with or in front of my stepmother. But she'd just *had* to ask me when I was going back to school, which had really thrown me off my game. My stuttered answer of "never" had been a severe lapse in judgment and decidedly *not* part of the plan.

But I hadn't wanted to lie when she'd asked. Who knew being honest would turn out to be such a big mistake?

"I transferred to online classes for the fall," I explained. I pushed food around on my plate to avoid eye contact with anyone, which I was sure really highlighted my maturity.

The sound of my dad's utensils clattering against his plate made me wince. "Why on earth would you do that without discussing it with me first?"

I took a deep breath. Sophia had talked me into telling my dad the truth about why I didn't want to go back to school. But blurting out that I had a stalker since last October that I hadn't told him about wasn't something I wanted to get into with my brother and sister in the room. It was important to tell him what was going on, but I didn't want to scare Lila and Sawyer.

Casting a quick glance at them, hoping my dad would get the message, I asked, "Can we talk about this later?"

"No, we cannot. We don't keep secrets from each other in this family."

Really? Because I distinctly remembered Rita being on the brink of giving birth before they'd told me I was going to be a big sister. As if I hadn't noticed she'd grown a bowling ball in her abdomen.

"Besides, maybe the younger kids can learn something by seeing you be so irresponsible with your future."

Wait... what now? "How am I being irresponsible?"

My father shook his head. "I knew I shouldn't have let you move in with Sophia this summer. You always let her get you into trouble."

"I'm not in trouble. And what does that even mean? You've always liked Sophia."

"Of course I *like* her. She's a nice kid from a good family. But she's also headstrong, and you've always done whatever she's said."

I stared at my dad for a moment, unsure if I'd ever met him before. "Are you calling me a follower?"

"Now, now, let's not put words in my mouth," he said, his voice reaching a level of patronizing I wasn't sure I'd ever heard before.

"I was the chairperson of two different campus clubs this past year. I don't think someone overseeing dozens of coeds would be considered a follower," I argued, feeling the need to defend myself. I felt it especially noteworthy that I'd done a damn good job of running those clubs, considering I'd simultaneously been trying to dodge a sociopath at every turn. But the timing felt wrong to throw that tidbit out there.

"Right. And then you spend a few weeks with Sophia, and you're giving all that up to move closer to her."

"I'd already given those positions up because I'm graduating in December. It wouldn't have been fair to keep them when I wasn't going to be there for the entire year."

My mind whirled through the past few summers: my dad encouraging me to stay on campus and take extra classes and take internships close to school during summer breaks. He'd been happy that I'd finish a semester early, thanks to all the extra time I'd put into my degree during summer sessions. But now that I thought about it, he'd been decidedly less enthusiastic about my intention to complete an internship closer to Sophia this year.

The opportunity had been a good one, so he hadn't fought

me on it, but he'd been curt in the discussion of my game plan for the summer, requesting I email him a list of what I needed from him. I'd thought he'd been busy with work, but had he been worried that the daughter he so clearly thought had the backbone of a Wheat Thin would succumb to some kind of bizarre peer pressure from a girl he'd known since she was three?

It was utterly surreal to stare at a man who'd been instrumental in not only my creation but also my entire upbringing and realize he had absolutely no idea who I was. It was also more than a little painful.

"Maybe it would be better if we tabled this for another time, Dennis," Rita said, her voice somehow being both calm and condescending. The way she stared at me when she spoke made it seem as if she were implying *I* was the one who'd started this argument over her too-dry roast. Though I also could've been reading into it. Maybe the look was meant to be one of commiseration, but her face couldn't quite get it right due to all the Botox she had shoved in there.

"I don't think we need to table anything," my dad said. "As far as I'm concerned, this discussion is over."

His words made panic claw at my chest. "Dad," I started, hating the way my voice broke as emotion clogged my sinuses. "I can't go back to school."

He looked at me for a moment as if he were trying to figure me out. "Why not? Did you get into trouble there?"

I took a deep breath. I hated that his first instinct was to ask if I'd gotten myself into trouble. Couldn't I just *be* in trouble without also being at fault? I was an honors student, and I hadn't ever had to call him to have him bail me out of anything. I'd never overspent on my credit card. I'd never done . . . anything.

But here he was, blaming me for something I'd done everything in my power to deal with on my own.

I swiped at my eye, willing the tears back. "No, of course not."

He stared a moment longer. "It's a boy, isn't it?"

I gaped at him. "Yeah, but it's not what you think—"

My dad banged his hands on the table—not in anger, but more in a celebratory way, as if he'd guessed a punchline and needed his own cymbal clang. "I should've known. It's always a boy. Let this be a lesson to you, Lila," he said, pointing a finger at my ten-year-old sister. "If you want to have a successful future, you've got to keep your head on your shoulders. Being boy crazy won't get you anywhere."

I wanted to say that crazy boys wouldn't get you anywhere either, but I'd grown weary of trying to explain myself to a man who simply refused to listen. Seemed like I was having quite a bit of bad luck with them recently, and quite frankly, I was fucking over it.

My dad had been there for me my entire life. He'd pushed me to be the best I could be, he'd celebrated my successes with me, and he'd encouraged me through my failures. Then I'd left for college. And it suddenly hit me that he'd been basically encouraging me to stay away ever since I left, suggesting I attend summer sessions, convincing me to return to campus early from winter break to make sure I purchased my books and supplies in time to get a head start on studying. It was a jarring thing to realize.

Did I think the man loved me? Yes.

Did I think he knew how to show it anymore? No.

And at this point in my life, I just couldn't work with that. I picked up my napkin from my lap and dropped it on my plate.

"The student housing office said they would refund eighty percent of my housing costs for the fall. You should be getting a check in the mail within the next week."

He scoffed. "And I guess you expect me to give you that money so you can rent a place with Sophia."

I turned my head and looked at him somberly. "I don't expect anything from you. I'll give you back the twenty percent you lost too." I stood and looked around at my family. "Thanks for dinner."

When I started to walk out of the dining room, my father said, "I'm serious, Taylor. Your tuition is already paid, but beyond that, if you don't return to school, I'm not helping you with anything else."

I blinked back tears as I walked to the door and reached down to grab my purse from the chair I'd left it on. My dad had a clear line of sight of me as I walked back, withdrew my wallet, took out my credit card, and dropped it on the table next to his plate. "You want me to leave the car?" I asked, my voice ragged.

He looked from the credit card to me, seemingly stunned silent. He cleared his throat. "No. That was a gift."

I smiled, but it was joyless. "Got it. Gifts I can have. Your understanding I can't."

His mouth opened and closed as if he were trying to figure out how to reply, but I didn't wait for him to. I walked around the table so I could drop a kiss on Lila's and Sawyer's heads and then got the hell out of there.

Sophia hadn't prepared me for that conversation at all, and I couldn't wait to tell her how bad her fortune-telling abilities sucked.

Chapter Two

RANSOM

"What the fuck is on your face?"

I could see Brody's reflection in the mirror of the apartment gym, and I slowed down my run to a steady nine point five so I could answer. "It's a training mask. You've never seen one?" The mask was a black Under Armour one, and like any training mask, it covered the majority of my lower face.

"Nope. But you should probably know you look like a cross between Bane and Hannibal Lecter."

"I don't think I've ever been compared to a hybrid of two iconic villains, and it's actually not as insulting as you probably meant for it to be."

"Not an insult, really." Brody put his water bottle on the floor next to the leg press machine and began contorting his body into different positions that he seemed to think were stretches. "More of an observation. You know, in case any females come into the gym. I wouldn't want you to be reported or anything."

I slowed to a walk and pulled the mask off before wiping

the sweat from my head and neck with a towel. "Shouldn't you be the one who's worried about being reported? You don't even live in this apartment complex."

I met Brody when he was hanging by the pool, even though his girlfriend, Aamee—the one who actually lived here—was nowhere to be found. He'd also gone to a few of the events the complex had held for its tenants.

"Whatever," Brody said, waving me off as he hopped on the leg press machine and moved the pin down on the weights without really looking. "I'm here all the time. I'm sure people think I live here."

He was probably right, and I couldn't exactly blame him for spending so much time at Aamee's place because one, the property was gorgeous with high-end amenities, and two, for most of the summer, a woman named Veronica was staying at Brody's while the two of them faked an engagement so Brody's dad wouldn't think he was irresponsible and would invest money in a bar that Brody and Drew wanted to eventually open.

"I'm gonna miss this place when Aamee moves," Brody said after struggling to push the weight he'd chosen.

"The gym?" I couldn't help raising my eyebrow at him because I was here almost every day, and this was one of the first times I'd seen him.

"Yeah. Well, all of it, I guess. But the pool will probably close soon anyway. It's almost Labor Day."

"Nah, they said they heat it in the cold weather so people can use it and the hot tub in the winter if they want."

Brody gazed off into some imaginary place I couldn't see. "I forgot about the hot tub," he said slowly. "I feel like I didn't really take full advantage of it while I lived here."

"You *didn't* live here," I reminded him as I walked over to grab a barbell and load it. "So when's Aamee actually moving?"

"Saturday," he said through a long sigh. He'd stopped his reps a little while ago and was resting his feet against the platform, looking like a toddler who'd just been told he couldn't have dessert.

"You should put your feet down."

"Huh?" My suggestion seemed to bring him out of his own mind long enough for him to look over.

"Your feet. In between sets you should put them down to allow the circulation to go back to normal in your legs."

"Right," he said, placing his feet on the floor. "Thanks. What's the mask do anyway?"

"It regulates air intake so you can breathe more efficiently. Trains your lungs like you train the rest of your body, pretty much." I'd used them when I'd played college football, and since I'd found them effective, I'd made them a habit even though now my workouts were for my own benefit and not for the sake of the game. Two knee injuries had crushed my dream of playing professionally before I had a chance to make it a reality. But still, I had plenty to be grateful for.

"Oh, cool." Brody finished the last two sets of his leg presses before moving on to the machine next to him. He studied it for a second before turning to me. "You wanna work out together?"

"Sure. I mean, if you don't mind following my routine. I can walk you through it as we go."

Brody was in good shape, which, considering the way he ate and drank—and the fact that he didn't seem to know his way around a gym—probably had more to do with genetics than it did any sort of training regimen or diet.

I kind of envied him. I'd worked hard to get into the shape I was in, and I worked just as hard to keep it. There was so much in life that wasn't determined by our actions. I at least wanted to control what I could, so I'd made my health a priority.

"Sure, man. I'll do my best, but I'm sure I won't be able to keep up with what you're doing."

I shrugged that off, and we got started. For the next twenty minutes or so, I led him through a series of mobility exercises before moving on to some back squats. Surprisingly, Brody's form wasn't too bad. He definitely had more body awareness than some other people I'd seen in gyms who worked out more frequently than Brody did.

"Did you play sports in high school?"

"Baseball," he said. "That's all, though. What about you? Anything other than football?"

"Baseball and basketball. I swam a few years too."

"I feel seriously inferior right now."

I couldn't help but laugh. "Don't. I wasn't very good at anything other than football. Considering I was almost this tall as a sophomore, I should've been a ringer in basketball, but there were a lot of guys who were much better than me and were almost a foot shorter. I really just played the other sports for the fun of it." I also did anything that kept me busy, and sports were always a great way to make friends, especially in new places. But I didn't tell him any of that.

"That makes me feel a little better. But not much," Brody admitted with a smirk. "Where'd you grow up? I don't think I ever asked you."

Even though Brody's question had been a typical one, it wasn't one I was comfortable answering. At least not with full disclosure. I liked Brody. And I trusted him as much as I was capable of trusting anyone I'd met since I moved here a few months ago.

But my childhood wasn't something I shared openly. "Moved around a good bit," I said because it wasn't a lie. I'd also been careful not to say it was only me who'd moved. That would've opened up a barrage of questions I had no interest in answering. Instead, I just added, "But I went to high school in Georgia, pretty close to Florida."

"Oh, nice!"

It wasn't.

"You could've been part of the band." And because Brody probably knew much of what he said only made sense to himself, he explained further. "Florida Georgia Line."

"Oh, yeah." I was thankful for the levity Brody's suggestion provided. "You think they'd be up for another member with absolutely no musical talent?"

"Never know." Brody shrugged before taking a drink from his water bottle. "And I knew I detected a hint of a southern twang."

"No way," I told him. "Impossible."

"Totally possible. I'm like the Rain Man of accents."

I finished out the last few reps of my current set. "That's a very odd skill that I don't believe for a second you have."

"See! Did you hear the way you said, 'you have'? It was more like 'ya've.'"

"Nope."

Brody rolled his eyes but thankfully changed the subject. "Got any big plans for tonight?"

"Not really."

"Oh, okay. Well, if you wanna hang out, the gang's coming to the Yard around ten or so. There's a good band playing tonight."

"Cool. Thanks for the invite," I said, careful not to say whether I was going.

"So can we count you in?"

"Umm . . . probably not, actually. I have a party I have to go to later on."

Brody looked understandably confused. "But you just said you didn't have anything?"

"Not anything worth mentioning." I tried to focus on my workout, hoping he wouldn't recognize my lack of eye contact as my hesitance to talk about this. Which was exactly what it was.

"Uh, a party's definitely worth mentioning."

"Not this one. It's more of a . . . work thing."

"You work at a kids' sports camp. Are you spending your Friday night with a bunch of little kids? Because that's . . . weird. And maybe illegal. Make sure you don't buy them any alcohol. Drew and I almost got in some serious trouble when we accidentally delivered beer to some underage frat guys when we had our Nite Bites business."

"I'm not buying anyone alcohol. It's more of a . . ." I tried to think of any way to explain the party without disclosing my actual role there. I hated lying, even lying by omission, and I'd already had to do that once with Brody today. But that was serious. This was just . . . potentially embarrassing? Though I didn't think Brody was the type of dude to judge other people's choices, especially considering the ones he'd made during his life.

"A what?" he asked, making me remember I hadn't finished my sentence.

The more I thought about it, the more I was fine with telling Brody about my other job. But then he'd probably tell

Aamee, which was pretty much like replying to everyone on a company email when you'd only meant for it to be seen by one person. And I didn't want the whole crew finding out because I was still a relatively new addition to it.

"The party's more of a what?" Brody said again. "You're making me nervous."

Screw it. Brody was my boy. If I asked him to keep this close to his chest, hopefully he would. And if he didn't, well, then I only had myself to blame, and I could just hope the rest of the group was accepting of it.

"The party's more of a . . . place where I take my clothes off."

Suddenly Brody looked like one of those wax statues—eerily human without actually being alive.

I waved my hand in front of his face but couldn't get him to blink. Thankfully, I was certified in first aid and CPR, because there was a good chance I'd just put Brody into some sort of catatonic trance.

Finally, he seemed to move again—first his eyes and then his jaw—but it still took him a moment to find his words. "Just to be clear, are you taking your clothes off for the kids you work with? Because that's a kind of fucked-up I don't wanna be a part of."

"No! God, no! The party doesn't have anything to do with the after-school program. I get paid to take my clothes off because I'm a stripper." I should've known I'd have to spell it out for him, but it still felt weird to say the words.

The color seemed to return to Brody's face, and as he smiled, he seemed to look proud. "Dude! That's awesome. I can't believe you didn't tell me."

"I know, it was probably stupid, but I was worried you'd

think it was creepy or something."

"No way, man. I'm totally cool with it."

"I thought you would be, but I wasn't sure. And I also wasn't sure how everyone else would be. Your sister, Drew, Aamee, Taylor. Look, I can't tell you not to say anything, but I'm asking you as a friend to keep this between us for right now. It's just . . . weird. Ya know?"

"Yeah, I get it." Then Brody made a gesture of zipping his mouth shut and throwing away the imaginary key as if that would actually keep his lips closed.

"Thanks, man. Y'all are such a fun group, and I just don't want anyone to think differently of me."

"See!" Brody was almost bouncing. "That was it! The southern thing I was talking about. 'Y'all,'" he clarified. "Only southern strippers say that."

"Asshole," I said, though we both couldn't help but smile. Brody was one of a kind.

TAYLOR

I knew when I moved in with Sophia at the beginning of the summer that time would fly by, but I hadn't expected that I'd be as sad as I felt getting ready to part ways with my best friend.

Even if I were still in the area, it wasn't the same as rooming together. We'd had so much fun over the last couple of months, I'd almost forgotten the real reason I'd decided to get an internship near her college and not my own. Almost.

I couldn't forget completely. Not really. The physical distance helped, as did staying in a nice apartment complex, but it would take more than a summer away to fully rid me of the memories of Brad. Maybe I could call Sophia's friend Xander and ask him if he knew where I could score some ecstasy. A guy we went to high school with used to pop them like Tic Tacs. His drug use caused such extreme memory loss he needed to be taught to eat again.

On second thought...

"Do they still perform lobotomies?"

Over the flattened boxes I was carrying, I couldn't see Sophia's or Aamee's faces, but without missing a beat, Aamee said, "You can get any type of work done if you know where to look. What kind we talkin' about here? Ice pick or head holes?"

"What's the matter with you?" I'd known Sophia long enough to recognize she was disgusted but also slightly impressed. In the short time I'd gotten to know Aamee, I'd noticed she seemed to have that effect on many people.

Aamee shifted the boxes she was carrying as we approached the door to our building. "Nothing's wrong with *me*. Taylor's the one who wants a lobotomy."

"I didn't say *I* wanted one." Which was true because the more I thought about it, the more I'd prefer that Brad forget about *my* existence instead of the other way around. "I was... asking for a friend."

"I'll ask around for your 'friend,'" Aamee said, clearly assuming the friend was me.

"Seriously?" Sophia asked her. "You're gonna ask people about back-alley lobotomies?"

Aamee let out a sound of disgust. "Ew, no. Alleys are so early two-thousands. I've heard the trend lately is Airbnbs."

I scanned my key fob on the door and pulled it open with two free fingers. Pressing against the door so Sophia and Aamee could enter, I heard a deep "I got it" followed by some quick footsteps behind me. Thankfully, I recognized the voice as Ransom's, or I might have been more startled when the door I'd been leaning against pulled away from me, causing me to nearly fall over.

I caught myself, though barely. But I did manage to drop almost all the boxes I'd been holding in the process.

"Oh, no. I'm so sorry," Ransom said, reaching down to pick up the cardboard as quickly as he could. And since neither of us had any part of our body on the door anymore, it swung back toward the frame, smacking my ass with the glass as I bent over. "Are you okay?"

Ransom wasn't usually flustered, but this encounter seemed to do the trick. For an athletic guy, it surprised me how clumsy he could be sometimes. About a week ago, he spilled a beer—which wasn't even his own—all over both of us when we were at the Yard with Carter and Sophia. Though Drew had given us both free T-shirts with the bar's logo on them so we didn't have to go home to change. So I guess it hadn't been all bad.

Once I righted myself from where the door had thrown me off-balance, Ransom managed to collect the boxes and keep the door open so I could go inside. Apparently Brody must've gone in at some point because he was standing with the girls, holding both of the boxes they'd been carrying.

He looked more than pleased with himself. "Guess being able to lift all that weight doesn't always transfer to practical tasks," he said to Ransom with a smirk.

"Shut up," Ransom replied with a laugh.

"Were you just at the gym?" Aamee asked.

"Yeah," Brody said as if her question were ridiculous. "Were you just talking about an Airbnb? Because I want in.

Where we goin'?"

"Not us. Taylor's 'friend,'" she said, using air quotes and exaggerated tone when she said the word, "is thinking about getting a lobotomy."

"No shit?" Brody said. "That's intense. They still go through the eye sockets for that?"

"No one's getting a lobotomy," Sophia said as we all piled into the elevator. "Aamee just . . . takes things to the extreme sometimes."

"Well, excuse me for trying to be helpful. Next time any of you are about to remind me what a horrible bitch I am, remember I'm the only one who was willing to help someone get proper medical treatment." She tucked her blond hair behind her ears and reapplied some lip gloss as she stared at the mirrored wall of the elevator.

The rest of us stared at her too for a moment before I said, "Thanks for helping with the boxes. They're all for me. I have way more stuff than I realized. I swear I didn't move in with this much."

"You definitely did," Sophia said.

When the elevator stopped on Aamee's floor, Brody piled his stack of boxes onto the ones Ransom was already holding. "Well, I'm off to take a shower. See you fuckers later." Then he turned to Ransom and winked. "Well, except for Rans. Right, bro?"

"Date?" I asked when the doors closed again.

He shifted in place, and I almost regretted asking the question because really, I didn't actually *care* if Ransom was going out with someone tonight. I was just making small talk, and it seemed like the next logical comment.

"Um, not really. No. More of a party. With lots of people."

He nodded but didn't make much eye contact with me.

The elevator came to a stop again, and Ransom successfully kept the doors open without causing any sort of accident. He exited last and followed us to our apartment. After setting the boxes down, he asked, "So when's the big move?"

"Tuesday afternoon," I said, plopping myself onto the couch so I could lean down to begin putting the boxes together. "Can you toss me the packing tape, Soph?"

"Oh, okay," he said. "Well, you need any help? I'm done at the camp at three. Not sure if that's too late, but I'm happy to lend a hand if you need it."

Most of the crew were going to help since several of us were moving, but I wasn't going to pass up an extra set of hands—especially ones as strong as Ransom's. He could probably lift twice as much as Brody.

"Um, sure, if you don't mind. We'll probably have my stuff out of here by then, but I'm sure we could use your help at the new place if you wanna meet us there."

Ransom smiled, appearing almost happy. Moving sucked, so I wasn't sure why anyone would want to do it if they didn't have to, but I definitely appreciated his offer.

"Okay," he said. "Just text me the address when you get a chance, then."

"Will do," I told him with a nod that felt too businesslike for a friend.

Ransom gave me a nod back before saying goodbye to Sophia and me and heading to the door.

Once he was gone, Sophia stared at me silently.

"What?"

"'Will do?' Really, who says that?"

Chapter Three

RANSOM

I arrived at the address Taylor had texted me and immediately double-checked that I had the right place. When I'd driven into this part of the city, I thought I'd be driving through it to get to her new neighborhood, but that evidently wasn't the case.

Squinting at the numbers over the door of the gray brick apartment building, I saw that they matched what she'd sent me. Weird. Since Taylor and Sophia had grown up together, I'd always assumed they came from the same wealthy background, but I obviously shouldn't have.

Not that this was the worst place in the world. It was just kind of… forgotten. There were a lot of boarded-up businesses with exteriors covered in graffiti, the roads were full of potholes, and a lot of the traffic lights blinked red or yellow instead of actually changing.

I scanned for a parking spot, knowing her building was still a whole lot better than some of the places I'd stayed growing up, but the thought of Taylor in such a depressing place didn't sit right with me. Not that it mattered how I felt about anything. It was already a minor miracle she'd agreed to let me help her move.

After parallel parking across the street from her building, I jogged over to find the front door open. There was a buzzer system, but someone had propped the door open with a concrete block so the buzzer wasn't needed—dangerous as hell. I moved the block to the side and let the door close behind me. I hoped the concrete block wasn't a sign that the door was left open on a regular basis.

Taylor said she was on the fourth floor, so I hit the button for the elevator and waited. I was a little later than I'd anticipated due to an issue with one of the summer campers I worked with at Safe Haven, so I hoped I hadn't missed the opportunity to be useful. I'd expected to see the gang carting things in and out of the building, but I didn't see any sign that anyone was moving in.

When the elevator arrived and I got in, I noticed how dingy it was. It was covered in that thick fabric that made it seem like a freight elevator even though it wasn't. When it arrived at the fourth floor, I disembarked quickly and followed the numbered arrows on the wall until I noticed an apartment with the door wide open.

Standing at the entryway was a man peering inside the apartment. I quickened my pace, saw that the number on the open door matched the one Taylor had given me, and then glared at the guy.

"Problem?" I growled.

He instantly held his hands in front of him and scurried past. "No, man. No problem."

I watched the guy until he disappeared into the elevator just to make sure my message was received and then stepped inside the apartment.

"Hey, man, you made it," Brody yelled as he tripped over boxes to get to me and give me a bro-shake and back slap.

"Yeah, sorry I'm late," I said to the room, which held Aamee reclining on a futon as she stared at her phone, Xander moving items around, Drew's younger brother, Cody, hooking up a TV, and Sophia and Taylor sitting on the floor unpacking a box.

"No worries. We just got everything in here, so you can help unpack."

"Thanks for coming," Taylor said with a small smile.

I got lost in it for a second before I came back to myself and pushed the door closed. "Hey, you should probably keep this closed. I caught some weirdo peeking in."

Taylor stilled at my words, and while it wasn't my intention to scare her, I also wanted to make sure she stayed safe.

"And some idiot propped the door downstairs open. If that happens again, you may want to let the super know."

She cleared her throat. "I propped it open."

"Oh. Well, you shouldn't do that. Anyone can wander in."

She fidgeted with something in her hands. "I was just trying to make it easy for everyone to get me moved in." Her voice sounded defensive, and I probably should've let it go, but no one would ever argue that I was the smartest guy they'd ever met.

"Well, yeah, but you're not the only one who matters. Other people live here too."

The glare she sent me would've frosted the balls off a weaker man. Lucky for me, I'd had people look at me like that pretty much my entire life.

"I'm aware of that," she snapped.

"Okay, good," I replied lamely.

She rolled her eyes and returned to emptying the box.

"Drew went to pick up a few pizzas," Sophia said, probably attempting to break the tension in the room.

I nodded and smiled at her before asking, "So where can I start?"

"Maybe you'd like to check that the smoke detectors work," Taylor muttered.

Despite her snarky delivery, I actually didn't think that was a bad idea. My eyes drifted up to the ceiling, but a growl from the floor stopped me.

I looked down to see her glaring at me again.

Brody elbowed me. "Don't worry. I'll hold a candle up to them later to check them out."

"That's not..." I started, but he'd already walked away. I moved toward the kitchen, thinking that it was maybe best for me to begin unpacking in a different room.

"Hey, Aamee," I said as I walked past.

"Shh, I'm trying to pretend I'm somewhere else," she replied.

"You know," Sophia started, "you could actually go somewhere else. Pretty sure no one would mind."

Aamee sighed. "Brody and I have decided we're going to be inseparable until I have to move to start my new job. Right, babe?"

"Right, babe," Brody replied before bending down to press a quick kiss to her lips.

"Ugh, thank God I haven't eaten yet," Sophia said.

I actually thought it was cute that they wanted to spend time together. Not that I'd say that out loud in this crowd, out of fear of being verbally flayed.

After opening a few boxes, I poked my head around the corner so I could see into the living room. "Do you care where stuff goes in here?" I asked Taylor.

She blew a strand of her blond hair out of her eyes and looked up at me wearily. She didn't look tired of me per se, but rather exhausted in general. "Um, no? You can just put stuff wherever it seems to make the most sense. I can always move it later if I need to."

"Yup," I replied before disappearing from view and setting about the task at hand.

I worked for a while until a loud buzzer sounded in the apartment. Leaving the kitchen quickly, I saw Brody with his hands over his ears.

"Jesus Christ, is there an air raid coming?"

"I think that just took five years off my life," Cody muttered.

"Good thing you're so young, then," Brody said to him.

Taylor had jumped up and was staring at the intercom system on the wall by the door. "How do I work this?"

Xander moved beside her and pushed a button. "Hello?"

"Hey," Drew's voice sounded tinny as it filtered through the intercom. "Can you buzz me in? Someone took the block out from the door."

Everyone's head snapped in my direction. I shrugged. "I stand by my actions."

"Yeah, okay, hang on." Xander pushed something else. "Did that do it?"

The sound of a locked door being rattled filtered through the room.

"That thing has good audio," Cody remarked.

"Nope," Drew replied.

Xander pushed something else. "How about now?"

"Still nothing."

"Push the red one," Sophia said as she looked over Taylor's and Xander's shoulders.

"You never push the red one," Xander scolded.

"Why not?"

"Because it's red."

Sophia stared at the back of his head for a second before reaching over him and pressing the red button.

A buzz sounded and Drew yelled, "That's it. Be right up."

When Xander turned, Sophia was looking at him.

"What?" he asked.

"You're supposed to be the smartest of us, Xander. Get your shit together."

"Hey, I got Taylor free internet. Cut me some slack."

"Hacking into someone's Wi-Fi doesn't make it free," Aamee pointed out.

"It's free for Taylor," he shot back.

"Free for Taylor sounds awesome, just saying," Taylor added.

Sophia clapped her hands. "That's a fun slogan. We should get shirts made."

"Please do," Taylor replied. "It makes all of you sound like my concubines."

Sophia sobered. "Oh. That's less fun."

Speak for yourself. Being Taylor's concubine sounded like a blast to me.

Drew appeared a couple minutes later with the pizzas, and everyone stopped what they were doing to eat. I felt awkward taking a slice because, while all these people had been friendly to me, they still felt like Brody's friends instead of mine.

But when I returned to the kitchen to continue unpacking, Drew walked in with a pizza box and held it open to me. Smiling, I took a slice and followed him back to the living room.

"So, what still needs to be done?" he asked.

Taylor looked around. "Honestly, nothing I can't do myself. So while you're all more than welcome to hang out for as long as you want, don't feel obligated to stay."

I looked around at the hastily painted white walls and dark-brown carpet that likely hid untold horrors. The place definitely didn't make me want to stick around, but I also didn't want to leave Taylor here alone. She seemed . . . dimmer here. So while I knew I couldn't stay forever—or cart her out of here and find her a different place to live—I'd hang and try to see if I could spruce the place up. Either decoratively or with morale.

Everyone else seemed to feel the same because they all said they'd stay awhile longer.

As we continued to eat, a thought occurred to me. "Have any luck in the bedroom?" I asked with a mouthful of pizza because I was evidently a toddler.

Every head in the room slowly panned in my direction.

"What?" I asked.

"Dude," Brody gushed excitedly. "Did you just ask if she had any fucks in the bedroom?"

"What?" I asked, truly horrified. "No! Of course not. I asked if she'd had any *luck* in the bedroom." That didn't sound much better, even to my own ears. "With the unpacking!" I ran a hand over my hair, the slight length on top dragging through my fingers. "Jesus Christ."

At that, they all burst out laughing.

"Yeah, yeah, laugh it up, fuckers," I mumbled.

"Didn't your mother ever teach you not to talk with your

mouth full?" Taylor chided teasingly.

And even though I knew she was joking, I couldn't help the small pang at her words. Because no, my mother hadn't taught me that or anything else. But that was my baggage to deal with, so I tamped the awkward feeling down before shrugging. "Guess not."

For as cool as I tried to play it, I saw a slightly puzzled look take over Taylor's face and wondered if I wasn't as smooth as I liked to think.

"I'm gonna finish up in the kitchen," I announced before fleeing to the cramped space so I could pull myself together.

"Aamee, wanna go have some fuck in the bedroom with me?" I heard Brody ask.

She sighed heavily. "I get you're trying to be clever, but that's a really unappealing invitation."

"I'm nothing if not unappealing," he joked.

I heard a snap of fingers. "So that's what you two have in common." Had to be Sophia. Taylor's voice was pitched a little lower, almost raspy.

"One day, when we're sisters, I'm going to disown you," Aamee threatened.

"That's so not how that works."

I left the kitchen to watch the show. When those two got going at each other, fireworks were close behind.

"Is too," Aamee replied, her tone petulant. It always surprised me how someone as put together as Aamee could morph into a preteen prima donna so fluidly.

"It's not. I speak from experience," Taylor said over her shoulder as she moved a box.

Sophia whirled around to face her friend, all bantering with Aamee seemingly forgotten. "He didn't disown you, Tay."

She shrugged as if the topic of the conversation didn't bother her, but it was clear from the way she didn't meet anyone's eyes that it did. "He didn't support me either."

"I'm sure he'll come around."

Taylor shrugged again. "Maybe. But all I know for sure is I can't count on him." With that, she turned and disappeared into the bedroom.

Sophia gave Drew a helpless look before following her.

Once both girls were gone, Drew blew out a long breath. We were all silent for a minute until Brody spoke. "I'm not sure how to handle drama that isn't mine."

That broke the awkwardness as we all laughed quietly and got back to various tasks, though it was more to keep busy than anything else. Taylor didn't have much, and what she did have was mostly set up already.

After a few more minutes, I took a peek in the bathroom to see if I could hang her shower curtain or something. I had to walk past the bedroom to get there, and I heard Taylor's and Sophia's voices as I passed, causing me to pause. Eavesdropping was a dick move, but I couldn't help it. I knew what it was like to not be able to rely on family, and if there was something I could do for Taylor, then I wanted to do it.

"Drew already said he could get you a job at Rafferty's," Sophia said.

"I know. And I appreciate it. I'm not trying to be stubborn about it, but—"

"Then stop. You need the job, Taylor. Take it."

"I know they're already at capacity with employees. I'd be stealing hours from someone because of a favor."

"That's not true. Aamee's leaving."

"And you told me they'd decided not to replace her

because the Yard was closing for the season soon and there was no point in adding staff."

Sophia paused. "I said that?"

"Yup."

"I have such a big mouth."

"That's considered a perk in some circumstances."

Sophia laughed for a second before sobering. "We can scour job apps later."

"I appreciate the offer, but I can handle it."

Sophia groaned. "Ugh, fine. But don't be an island. If you need help, ask for it."

"An island? Really?"

"Shut up and hug me. You know I'm bad at analogies."

Having heard enough, I moved into the bathroom and looked around, though I didn't really see anything. My brain was too busy working double-time. Taylor had interned at a summer camp for adjudicated youth this summer. A bar might not be her speed, but I bet I knew something that was.

Before I could think too much more about it, Taylor barged into the bathroom, startling at the sight of me.

"Shit, you scared me," she heaved between breaths.

"Sorry. I was just . . . in here."

"Yeah, I noticed," she replied, eyeing my curiously.

I needed a good transition for how to bring up the plan I had.

Be smooth, Ransom.

"I heard you and Sophia talking, and I can help."

Her eyes narrowed at me.

Not smooth.

"Were you eavesdropping on my conversation?"

How did I answer this without being a creep? "Yes."

At the hardening of her face, I realized that was, in fact, not the way to avoid being creepy.

She crossed her arms over her chest and cocked a hip out like the angry little bee she was.

"I didn't mean to. I was coming in here and heard Sophia mention you needed a job."

She raised an eyebrow, which was as effective as a torture method to get me to keep talking because that was what I did.

"I work at a community center. We run a camp in the summer for kids. It's ending this week, and a lot of our counselors are heading back to school. But our after-school program is starting, and we need staff. It's probably not quite as intense as where you worked this summer, but we still get our fair share of troubled kids, so it's no cakewalk. They could probably use you every afternoon, and it would leave you time to do your school stuff during the day."

It had been quite a word vomit I'd released, but I wanted to get it all out there before she told me to mind my business. I did think it would be a good opportunity for her. And having an excuse to see her almost every day was a definite plus. Though I'd keep that bit to myself.

She eyed me warily, her jaw bobbing up and down as she nibbled into her bottom lip. After what seemed an eternity, she exhaled. "Why would you do that for me?"

Not quite the question I was expecting. The intent way she was looking at me let me know that my answer to this was important.

No matter how many times I'd tried to get close to Taylor since we'd met, she'd always rebuked me. Her inviting me into her space was a major step forward, but I had a feeling we'd plummet backward if I was too honest. Not that I wanted to lie, but she seemed . . . skittish. My only guess was that she wanted my offer to be genuine and not because I wanted to get into her pants—something she'd shown she was decidedly not interested in me doing.

Telling her that I wanted to help would come across like pity, and explaining that I wanted any excuse I could get to be in her presence would have her erecting a metaphorical Berlin Wall between us.

So, instead, I went with, "Because you're terrifying, so the kids will like me more in comparison."

Her smirk told me I'd gotten the answer right.

Chapter Four

TAYLOR

"Excuse me, lady. I have twenty dollars for you."

"Huh?" Hesitantly, I looked to my right, where a guy who looked to be around my dad's age, standing at the metal mailboxes in the apartment entrance, was holding out a twenty-dollar bill. "Oh, um, that's okay. You keep your money."

He was only about my height, with graying hair that needed a washing and thick glasses that were held together with what looked to be black electrical tape.

"Take it," he said. "Really. Buy yourself somethin' nice."

"I don't need it. You keep it," I said again.

I wanted to head to the elevator, but I would've had to move past him to get there. He hadn't done or said anything inappropriate, but for some reason, someone offering me money felt more insidious than it would've felt had he asked *me* for some. Like offering a stranger cash was the adult equivalent of someone rolling down the window of a nondescript white van to tell a child that they have extra candy. The only difference was the child would have more room to get away. Here, in the dimly lit lobby with peeling floral wallpaper, I felt closed off from the outside world.

The space was actually too small to even call it a lobby. It was more of a hallway that could fit either someone getting their mail or someone walking toward the elevator, but not both. I grabbed some bills that had already arrived—which made me thankful Xander had been able to at least hook me up with free Wi-Fi—and did my best to ignore the awkward man attempting to give me a handout.

By the time I got back upstairs, I felt exhausted, as if the efforts of the day had suddenly caught up with me now that I could actually relax. I appreciated everyone's help, more than they probably knew, especially since I'd only known most of them a few months. But that same fact made me feel a little strange taking their help, mainly because I hated feeling indebted to anyone.

Living independently shouldn't have been an all-or-nothing scenario, but something made it feel like that—like if I didn't have the help of my own parents, I shouldn't have help from anyone. Though logically the opposite was probably true.

Sophia had told me not to be an island, and Drew and Ransom had already offered to help me get jobs where they worked. And judging by how long everyone stuck around after I was completely unpacked, it seemed like at least a few of them wondered whether I'd make it through the night by myself.

Whether that said more about my ability to take care of myself or my choice in housing remained to be seen.

After lying down for a little while, I pulled myself up to look for something to eat. It would have to be either peanut butter and jelly or another slice of pizza, and since I'd already eaten three slices earlier with the gang, I opted for the former.

I was two bites into my sandwich when my phone rang and my mom's face appeared on the screen. She'd called once already—though not through FaceTime—but I'd been too busy to answer. I didn't exactly want to talk to her now either, but I didn't have an actual reason not to.

Answering the phone, I took another bite of my sandwich and finished chewing before saying hello. I hadn't talked to my mom in a few weeks, other than through text, which was our usual form of communication since she was sometimes in another time zone. And I knew why she was calling.

"Hey, hon." She waved, and behind her I could see the morning sun rising. "You look exhausted."

"Thanks," I answered dryly, though I was sure she didn't pick up on my sarcasm because she was already on to her next comment.

"How's everything going?"

I told her the minimum: that I was planning to stay near Sophia—though not why—and that I moved into another apartment because Sophia was heading back to the sorority house for the new semester.

"It's fine," I added. "Just a long day with the move and everything, but I had people helping, so it wasn't too bad, I guess."

"That's good. Did you have to go far?"

"A few miles away from where I was."

"Oh, I don't know why I assumed you were in the same complex. I figured you just had to move because your short-term lease was up, and they had someone lined up to move in there soon."

"No, I probably could've stayed, but the friends I made here were all moving too, so it was just as well. No point paying for a luxury apartment when I don't really need it. Other than doing my schoolwork here, I probably won't even be home too much."

"Are you continuing with your internship?" My mom looked to her right, and I saw my stepdad come into frame with a cup of coffee.

Joe handed it to my mom and gave her a kiss on the forehead. "I gotta head out to a client meeting, but I'll call you later and let you know what time to meet for dinner."

"Oh, hey, Tayl," he said with a wave, and I couldn't help but cringe at the name. It'd always reminded me of the appendage attached to an animal's butt.

"Hey," I answered.

Even though Joe had technically been my stepfather since I was twelve, I'd never actually told him about my feelings on the nickname. Then after a while, it seemed strange to bring it up at all, especially when I didn't see either one of them more than a couple of times a year.

I'd never been close with him, which really wasn't all that strange since I wasn't even that close with my mother. He seemed like a nice enough guy, and he certainly treated my mom well, but I'd never spent enough time with him to formulate a thorough opinion of the man, other than what my mom had told me.

"Where are you guys, anyway?" I asked.

"Australia," my mom answered. "Joe's company just acquired a client here, and we're staying the month."

"Looks beautiful there."

"A bit too cold, but I certainly can't complain," my mom said with a smile at Joe before looking back at me. "What's it like where you are?"

"Hot as hell."

My mom laughed, and Joe disappeared. "Anyway, you were saying about your internship?"

"Oh, right. No, that's done. I'm just going to find a job here and try to save some money. I won't have to attend classes, so I'll have more time. A few of my friends might have openings where they work, but I haven't given it a ton of thought yet."

"They must be some good friends if you decided to stay there. I thought you loved school."

This was my mom's way of probing for information about why I'd really left, because even though we weren't as close as I would've liked, she still knew me better than a lot of people. I couldn't pretend I'd simply wanted a change of scenery.

"I did." The fact that it was the truth made me feel better about saying it. I had loved school—the classes, the people. Well, *most* of the people. "It just made more sense to stay here and finish everything online."

It was hard to tell if she bought it, but thankfully she didn't ask anything more about that.

"What'd your dad say when you told him?"

She looked like she winced at the thought, and I hesitated before saying, "He wasn't exactly pleased with my decision, but I'm paying my own way, so there isn't much he can do about it."

"Paying your own way?" My mom looked like she'd been verbally slapped. "So he's not helping you with school or housing or anything?"

"He agreed to pay for the rest of my degree. I guess he was afraid if he didn't, I might not get to finish it. But he said I'm on my own for pretty much everything else."

"You don't have to be on your own, Tay. Joe and I are happy to help."

"It's really okay. I'll be fine."

"Are you sure? It looks like you could use some furniture and a few decorations." My mom knew I didn't like taking money from Joe, so even if I wasn't sure I'd be fine, she also knew I'd say I was anyway. And I was sure part of the reason she was offering to help was because my dad had refused to, which only made me want to refuse more.

"Nope. I'm good," I said, hoping like hell I would be.

Chapter Five

TAYLOR

Claymont Community Center was located in a busy part of the city and in close proximity to three elementary schools, two middle schools, a high school, and a K-12 charter school.

From the research I'd done before my interview, I'd learned that the center offered a plethora of services to the community—everything from dance classes to cooking lessons to parenting seminars to literacy instruction. They even had a person who helped with job placement. It was impressive to say the least.

With so many offerings, I'd expected the building to be larger. As it was, it looked like it might have once been a church or maybe a Catholic school. Even though the website said the center was nondenominational, it held a certain Gothic feel that made me almost expect to see stained-glass windows and a bell tower.

A woman at the front desk directed me down a long hallway toward the back of the building when I said I was there for an interview with Safe Haven. My heels clacked against the tile floors and echoed in the quiet halls. Ransom had said there was a week of camp left, but I wasn't sure where that took place because the building was almost eerily quiet.

I arrived at a door with a placard beside it that read *Safe Haven*. Taking a deep breath, I pushed the door open and immediately met the shrewd gaze of an older woman sitting behind a desk.

"Can I help you?" she asked, her tone somewhat accusing, as if I'd just barged into her bedroom.

"Yes, my name is Taylor Peterson. I have an interview with Mr. Gillette."

"Have a seat. I'll tell him you're here."

I turned toward the smattering of plastic chairs pushed up against the cream-colored wall, and then jumped a mile in the air when the woman shouted behind me.

"Harry! Interview's here."

That was certainly one way to let him know.

"Be right there, Edith," a voice shouted back.

What the hell was this place? Even a walkie-talkie would've been better than shouting between rooms. But paupers couldn't be choosers, so I slid onto a seat and gave Edith a small smile that she did not seem the least bit tempted to return.

A few minutes later, a harried-looking man hurried into the room. He looked to be in his late thirties, though his receding hairline perhaps aged him a little. But he had kind eyes and a wide smile, and when he approached me with a hand extended, I didn't hesitate to stand and grasp it.

"Taylor?" At my nod, he continued. "Harry Gillette. Not related to the razors, unfortunately. Come on back and we'll get started."

Edith tracked my movements, and when I passed her desk, she said, "Harry, you want me to call your *husband* and *kids* to let them know you'll be a little late today?"

Harry stopped short and looked at his watch before glancing up at Edith curiously. "It's only three. I don't think the interview will take two hours."

She looked at me primly when she replied. "Just checking."

I briefly wondered if I should be offended that Edith had pegged me as a home-wrecker after spending less than five minutes in my company, but it was honestly too amusing to be angry.

Poor Harry looked baffled but seemed to shake the curiosity. "Shall we?" he asked before heading into his office.

"Message received, Edith," I whispered before following.

Harry's office was small and cramped, made to feel even smaller by the fact it was covered in artwork that all seemed to be done by kids. His desk held frames facing away from me, but I had no doubt they held pictures of his family. He also had a PC that might have been built before I was born and two filing cabinets that both had drawers open. All in all, it was an endearing space that spoke of a hardworking man who was loved by many.

He gestured to a chair across from him, and I sat. He shuffled a few papers around on his desk before looking up at me.

"Don't mind, Edith," he said. "She's convinced every woman under fifty has her sights set on me. It's flattering, if not completely delusional. Not to mention"—he turned a picture around so I could see him and another man surrounded by four children—"I'm gay. But she enjoys looking after all of us, so I let her get her warnings in."

So not as oblivious as he pretended to be. That was a good sign. And I couldn't deny, knowing he humored the elderly woman made me warm to him even more.

"Okay," he continued. "Down to business. I have your résumé and already called your references—all glowing, by the way—and Ransom's told me great things, so I figured I'd tell you about the place, show you around, and you could tell me if you were interested. Sound good?"

I refused to let my mind dwell on the fact that Ransom had sung my praises to his boss. I'd already spent more time thinking about the man over the past few days than I was comfortable with.

"Sounds wonderful."

"All the elementary schools in the area have their own extended-day programs run by the city, so we don't get any young kids here. Safe Haven's target demographic is middle school kids who don't have anywhere safe to hang out after school. Either their parents are still working, their neighborhood isn't conducive to safe play, or... their home isn't a place they want to be. We occasionally also get some younger high school kids who come around, but not many. Most of them get involved in one of the specialty programs the center offers: tutoring, intramurals, things like that."

"I saw some of the programs the center offers. It seems like a wonderful place."

"It is. It's helped a lot of people in the community since it opened fifteen years ago. Now, I know you worked at a program for older kids this summer. Any problems with working with slightly younger kids?"

"None at all."

"Perfect. In a few minutes, I'll show you around so you

can get a better idea of how things run, but just to give you an idea of your schedule, kids enter Safe Haven through the back of the building so they don't have to traipse through the entire center. Some get dropped off by a bus or van, and some walk, depending on where they're coming from. They start rolling in about three fifteen, so we like staff to arrive at two thirty to set up whatever activities we have planned for the day. The program ends at five, but we offer an extended service for parents who work late. The families who qualify for that have until seven to collect their kids. Those kids head to the gym for those two hours so the janitorial staff can clean and sanitize our space, but it's our employees who accompany them. If you want the extra hours, they're yours."

"Yes, I'd be open to that." A thought popped into my mind and left my mouth before I could censor it. "Does Ransom work the extended hours?"

Ugh, stop thinking with your figurative dick, Taylor.

Harry smiled fondly. "Technically, no. But last year he almost always stayed until the last child was picked up anyway. Wouldn't let me pay him for the time, though. He's . . . something else. The kids and staff adore him."

Awesome. Like Ransom needed more ways to be attractive.

"So the pay isn't great, but with your qualifications and experience, I can bring you on at twelve dollars an hour. We pay you for an extra half hour for cleanup, which would give you five hours a day. So you can think about it while I show you around and then let me know if that could work for you."

"Perfect."

After a bit more talking, Harry showed me around Safe Haven. The bulk of the space reminded me of a cafeteria.

It was a large room with a couple of smaller areas that had partial privacy due to a low wall. That had probably once been the kitchen, and they'd turned it into spots where small groups of kids could complete activities away from the chaos that likely took place in the main space.

Harry took me out a back door and showed me where the kids would arrive. There was also a large blacktopped area with basketball nets. It was also where the summer camp was.

My eyes instinctively roved over the crowd in search of a blond-haired Adonis. I found him in the middle of a large group of kids. He seemed to be telling them a story that had them all laughing hysterically.

"I know it looks a little disorganized, but it's nearing the end of the day, so the kids get free choice of what they do. Within reason," he tacked on with a smile.

I smiled at him to show I understood and then refocused on where Ransom had been. But this time, he was looking back, a smile splitting his handsome face.

He said something to the kids and then started in our direction. I noticed quite a few of the girls watch Ransom walk toward us—and a few of the boys too. Not that I blamed them. The tight white T-shirt he wore clung to every muscle the guy had. Honestly, it was borderline obscene. Though he was so big and broad, there probably wasn't much he could do about it. He'd probably have to actively try to not look like a bodybuilder-meet-*GQ* model.

When he arrived in front of us, he looked like an excited puppy. "Hey. How's everything going?" His gaze moved back and forth between us.

"Going great on my end," Harry answered before looking pointedly at me.

I smiled. "Great for me too."

Harry extended his hand. "Does that mean we have a new employee?"

I hesitated, thinking about how even with the extra money I'd need a second job, but odds were I'd need one regardless. And at least this job would leave my nights and weekends free.

There was also something about the place, and I wanted to be part of it. So I took Harry's hand and gave it a firm shake. "Yes, that's what it means."

"Excellent. Why don't you hang out with Ransom for a bit while I get the employment paperwork together, and then you can come back to my office in . . . let's say ten minutes?"

"Works for me," I replied.

Harry nodded and slapped Ransom on the back before retreating toward the way we'd come.

When he was gone, Ransom said, "So, you like the place?"

"I do. It's . . . pretty great."

Ransom's smile widened. "It is, isn't it?" He seemed so proud and pleased that I liked it that I couldn't help but return his smile. "And I can't wait to be everyone's favorite," he added, rubbing his hands together maniacally.

I hit him playfully in the chest before I could think better of it. "Jerk. And from the looks of things, you're already everyone's favorite."

He moved next to me so he could survey the campers like a king observing his kingdom. "Yeah, I'm pretty much a god here," he deadpanned.

I instantly remembered my Thor comparison a couple of weeks ago but kept it to myself. Instead, I rolled my eyes and groaned. "So humble."

He opened his mouth to respond but was interrupted with

a kid brushing past him with an armful of water guns.

"Whoa, whoa, where are you going with those?"

The boy shrugged. "It's hot."

"So? You making decisions now? I didn't know you worked here." Ransom said the words with outrage that was clearly for show, and by the look on the kid's face, he knew it.

The kid put on a pout that could've won him an Emmy.

Ransom pointed at him. "Save that look for someone it works on, DeSean."

The boy dropped the dramatic visage and resorted to more overt pleading. "Come on, Ransom. Please. It's almost time to go home."

"Yeah, and I'm sure your dad will be thrilled to have you sit in his car soaking wet."

"He won't care. Please," DeSean said, dragging out the word.

He was cute and likely knew it. Around ten if I had to guess, he still had an innocence about his face that contrasted with the preteen mischievousness in his eyes. It was a deadly combo, and I became worried that I'd never be able to say no to these kids.

Ransom put his hands on his hips and leaned down over the boy. "On one condition."

The kid bounced on his toes. "Anything."

Ransom reached out and carefully dislodged a water gun from the pile in DeSean's arms. "I get the biggest one."

"Deal," DeSean squealed before taking off. "Hey, guys, Ransom's playing!" he yelled across the yard.

We watched him run for the spigot that was against a wall and begin filling the guns for a moment before I said, "Guess I'll leave you to it, then."

Ransom slung the water gun over his shoulder like some kind of Storm Trooper. “Yeah, I gotta teach a few lessons around here.” His eyes sparkled. “You can stick around and play if you want.”

I glanced down at the white button-down tank I’d worn to the interview and then back to him meaningfully. “Think I’ll pass.”

Ransom flushed adorably. “Oh, yeah, no, I get it. Water, white, yeah, maybe . . . maybe next time.” He looked down at himself. “Crap.”

I laughed. “It’s probably more acceptable for a guy.”

“True. Though I have big nipples for a dude, so it still—” He stopped abruptly as if his words had just registered with his brain.

I bit my lip to keep from barking out a laugh.

“Can you forget you heard that?”

“Not on your life.”

He breathed a heavy sigh. “Figures,” he mumbled. “See you around?”

“Looks that way.”

He gave me a nod before turning toward the crowd of kids waiting for him with water guns at the ready. “I hope you guys are ready, because you’re all going down.”

I watched for a second, my heart beating a little harder at the sight of this big man playing with a bunch of children who obviously adored him. Forcing myself to turn away, I steeled myself and walked back toward Harry’s office.

One thing was for sure—if I were going to make it at this job and keep my sanity, I was going to have to stay away from Ransom Holt.

Chapter Six

RANSOM

"I'm not sure if I like this place or if I should check myself for ticks when I leave," Carter said.

I looked around at the jungle-like décor—some of which I was pretty sure was from an *actual* jungle: vines, leaves, and even a tree that seemed to grow through the center of the floor. And there was a spiral staircase that led to something above, like a real tree house. Other than the wooden barstools and a few booths, most of the chairs were beanbags. And the place was adorned with fairy lights.

Brody nodded happily as he took it all in. "Maybe both," he said, sounding unusually excited about having to check himself for parasites later. "I can't believe I never knew this was here."

"Brings back memories," Sophia said, causing Drew to raise an eyebrow.

"Really?" he asked. "You have memories from that night?"

Sophia nudged Drew with her hip playfully. "Well, bits and pieces maybe."

"So what's the story there?" I asked. "Anyone planning on telling it?" I'd heard the night referenced more than once by the group, but no one ever elaborated.

"Nope," Sophia said. "No real story. Taylor and I just had a rough night, and Drew had to come pick us up from here."

"Um, I think *I* was the one who had the rough night," Drew said, laughing. "Taking care of the two of you was like babysitting newborn twins overnight."

"Every time he talks about this, the experience gets exponentially worse," she told me. "My fiancé likes to exaggerate just a tad."

"Definitely not exaggerating," said Drew as we approached the host station.

There was a little bit of a wait to get a seat, and that, combined with the crowd at the bar, told me this place was popular. I was happy for Taylor that she'd hopefully make out well in tips but also nervous she was in over her head. Not that I knew what her limitations were.

Sophia had mentioned Taylor was new to waiting tables, and since she'd only worked one other day during the lunch shift, I was concerned she might feel overwhelmed tonight. And it probably didn't help that we were all coming to see her.

I turned around when we got to the stand so that I could count all of us and then gave the hostess my name.

"Did you say Random?" she called over the din of voices. She had short, dark choppy hair with purple tips and nails so long it made me wonder how she could even click the iPad.

"No, Ransom. With an *S*," I clarified.

"Oh okay, that makes so much more sense."

I had a feeling she was being sarcastic, but I couldn't be sure and didn't plan on investigating it further. "Could we be seated in Taylor's section if possible? We don't mind waiting."

"Who?"

"Taylor Peterson. She's new. She's about this tall," I said, holding up a hand below my shoulder. "Early twenties, long blond hair, pretty smile . . ."

The girl flicked her tongue ring against her teeth impatiently before looking up from the iPad. "You just described like every college girl who's ever gotten a job here."

"Well, except you," I joked, though she clearly didn't think it was funny. I hadn't seen her crack a smile since we'd arrived. "Sorry. Isn't there like a name listed for who's in what section or whatever? We just wanted to surprise her and show our support since it's a new job."

She was quiet for a moment, but I wasn't giving up that easily.

Not knowing what else to say, I muttered, "Please. It would mean a lot."

She rolled her eyes but said, "I'll see what I can do."

"Thank you!"

She took down my number so she could text when the table was ready, and then asked us to stand off to the side or have a drink at the bar while we waited.

Since I was the tallest, I took it upon myself to squeeze into a spot at the bar so I could grab the bartender's attention. I ordered all of us beers to make it easy for him and handed them out to everyone. "First round's on me since I can't stay the whole night."

"Thanks," Aniyah said, taking her beer from me. "Where you off to? Anywhere good?"

"Not sure. I've never been to the place. Just meeting some people at a bar downtown. I don't need to be there until nine or so, though."

"Is it a surprise party or something?" Xander asked. When I didn't answer right away, he added, "Because they said you have to be there at a certain time. Or do your other friends just keep you on a really short leash?"

I knew he was kidding, but I also knew the whole thing probably did seem strange. "Just some people I haven't seen in a while, so I want to make sure I get there close to when they do."

That sounds plausible.

I caught a glimpse of Brody, who was bringing his glass to his mouth and wiggling his eyebrows at me. After he took a sip, he pressed his lips together as if to say my secret was safe with him. I was glad Aamee had already gone back home to her new job because she definitely would've picked up on Brody's reaction and asked about it later. Or now.

With our drinks in hand, we moved back from the bar a bit to allow some other people to order, and I was thankful when Drew spotted some pictures on the wall of celebrities who'd been customers. How Paris Hilton knew this place existed when I didn't was a question I'd probably never know the answer to.

"What?" I asked when Brody was still staring at me.

"Pretty smile," he said.

The fuck? "Dude, did you just say I had a pretty smile? That shit's weird, even for you."

"No! That's what you said, not me."

"I definitely did *not* say you had a pretty smile. Did you drop acid before you came here?"

"You said it about Taylor, you big, stupid idiot. When you were describing her to the hostess."

"Oh. So?" I tried not to make eye contact with him even though I'd just asked him to explain the implications of something I had no interest in hearing about.

"Sooo . . ." Brody said slowly. "You like her," he practically sang.

"You're high. She does have a pretty smile. It's an objective statement. Straight white teeth that fit her mouth perfectly. I'm sure nine out of ten dentists would agree with me."

"You like her," he sang again.

Fucker. "Would you keep your voice down, please? I don't like her, like her. I just . . ." Sighing heavily, I said, "I don't know what I feel or even if I feel anything at all, so just don't tell anyone, okay?"

"Dude, you and your secrets. I feel like I'm working for the CIA here."

"Well, then enjoy it because this'll probably be the closest you ever come to being trusted with important information."

Brody looked like I'd just slapped him. "Um, you do realize that I'd make the *best* secret agent mainly because no one would ever expect that I am one."

"Keep telling yourself that, buddy."

"I will." Then he gave me his dopey Brody grin and said, "For as long as you keep telling yourself you don't have a thing for Taylor."

TAYLOR

Other than one table of thirty-something hipsters who'd brought their newborn and toddler with them, most of the tables I'd waited on had been relatively easy. The majority of the customers were content to sit for a while without my checking in too many times. I ran the apps out as soon as they were ready and kept the drinks coming as best I could, and since I'd told everyone I was new when I'd introduced myself to each table, most were pretty understanding.

The other servers helped too by running out a few drinks here and there if they had time, so overall, the night had been going pretty smoothly. I was glad I'd been scheduled for my first shift on a Wednesday afternoon, though, because the place had still been pretty crowded. I would've been completely overwhelmed if I'd had this weekend level of demand on my very first day.

I barely had time to breathe, let alone take an actual break yet tonight, but so far I'd made some decent tips, which was more than I could ask for considering I had no experience waiting tables. I was feeling pretty confident as the night progressed, but it still surprised me that the hostess would seat a large party in my section. The manager, Jeremy, had told me he'd keep the limit to tables of four for my first Saturday night, but I'd just been given a table double that. *Fuckers.*

I grabbed some napkins and coasters from the bar and headed over to get their drinks started, praying I could keep up with the rest of whatever they ordered. From what I could tell at a distance, it looked like the group already had some drinks going from the bar and were studying the menus closely. I hoped they wouldn't have too many questions I couldn't answer, like when one person asked if we had vegan cheese for our pizzas.

As I approached the table with my friendliest smile and got ready to introduce myself, I realized why I'd gotten such a large party seated in my section on my first busy night.

"Aww, you guys. I didn't know you were coming."

Sophia, Drew, Brody, Ransom, Xander, Carter, Toby, and Aniyah surrounded the table.

"This is such a great surprise." I leaned over to give Sophia a hug from behind. "This was your idea, wasn't it?"

"Actually, no. I'm not sure who brought it up first, but it wasn't me. I'll still take the hug, though."

"Well, thank you to whoever thought of it. It's been a crazy night. Good, but crazy. So it's nice to see some familiar faces."

"It was Ransom's idea, I think," Brody said.

"Really?" I hoped my question didn't reveal my surprise, but with the exception of Aniyah and Toby, I probably knew Ransom the least out of all of them.

I looked over to see him combing his wavy, light-brown hair with his fingers. "Yeah, I figured you could use the support. We tried to come sooner, but we had to wait for a while to get seated in your section."

"What's up with that hostess, anyway?" Brody asked.

"Who? Gail?"

"Gail?" Brody's eyes were wide with surprise. "My mom's friend from college is named Gail. That chick's like our age and looks like a bitter female version of Marilyn Manson. No way that's her name."

"Yup, it's Gail," I told them. "And she's actually pretty nice. A little hard to read, but that's why she's good at her job. A lot of people come in being dicks for no reason—"

"Like Gail was," Carter chimed in.

"Was she really that bad?" This time I looked to Ransom because for some reason I felt like he would be the most objective.

"I mean . . ." He hesitated like he didn't want to bad-mouth her, which I could appreciate. "She wasn't the friendliest person I've encountered today, but we're at a table in your section, so I can't be too upset, right?"

I was about to reply when a voice from behind me got my attention. "Hey, can we order now." It wasn't a question.

"Yes, sorry. I'll be right there." I put the drink specials on my friends' table, ready to go over to Mr. Personable's table before the vein in his neck burst and my section looked like an episode of *Dexter*.

"Can you just do your job, please?"

I wanted to tell him that just because he said "please" didn't mean he was being polite, so there was really no point to the pleasantry, but there was no sense reasoning with him.

"What's your problem?" said Ransom.

The white baseball cap guy's two friends started snickering as they looked at Ransom.

"Somethin' funny?"

The guys quit laughing, and one muttered a "Nah," but the other remained silent.

Unfortunately, the asshole sitting across from them wasn't as smart. "This your boyfriend?" he asked with a nod toward Ransom.

"Nope," Ransom answered before I could. "Just a guy who's gonna teach you a couple things about manners."

Brody put a hand on Ransom's shoulder as Ransom started to stand. "Let it go."

Ransom's chest expanded with the breath he'd taken, and he held it there for a second before slowly releasing it and taking his seat again, his eyes never leaving the other man's.

"It's fine," I told him. "Let me take their order. I don't want to get a complaint from a customer."

"Sorry about that," I said to the group of guys, even though I wasn't. I would've felt bad for making them wait, but their reaction made it difficult to apologize with any sort of sincerity.

Once I had their order, I hustled toward the kitchen to retrieve food for another table and get my friends' wings going before heading to the bar to grab their drinks. I also put in a few appetizers for my friends, figuring I might be too busy to take their orders soon, and I was pretty sure they wouldn't mind some fried food arriving.

I stopped by a few times to check on a few of the tables in my section but didn't get a chance to circle back to Sophia's table until about ten minutes later. "I got some apps cooking for you guys. They should be out soon."

"Oooh, awesome," Carter said. "I hope there's mozzarella sticks involved."

"Those plus loaded fries and hot and honey wings."

He looked like he was about to begin drooling. "I love it when you talk dirty to me."

"The fuck is wrong with you?" asked Drew on a laugh, causing me to laugh too.

"So much," was Carter's reply.

"Hey," Sophia called from the far end of the table. "You think someone could get our picture? Or maybe we could just have you do a selfie or something at the end of the table if you think you can fit all of us in."

"You want a picture of me working?" I groaned but had already accepted it was going to happen. Sophia could be relentless when she wanted to be.

"This girl thinks she's a reality TV star," Drew joked, pointing to Sophia. "How much would someone have to pay you to never take another picture? Hypothetically. Like would a hundred thousand be enough?"

Sophia stared blankly at him, and it seemed like she was considering his question. "Just to clarify, am I never allowed to take a picture again, or I'm just not allowed to be in it? Like could someone else take the picture, or does that violate the agreement?"

"Both. Can't be in any and can't take them yourself."

"Oh, then no way. I can't put a price on that."

"Life-changing money," Drew added.

"Can we just take the fucking picture already?" Brody said. "I feel like I'm losing brain cells with every comment."

"I'm so glad you guys came in," I said dryly, already taking Sophia's phone and positioning myself at that end of the table. I held up the phone, my arm outstretched so I could capture everyone. "Squeeze in. Brody and Ransom, duck down a little."

The guys did what I said, and I snapped a few shots of us smiling and a few goofy ones.

I wanted to look through all of them because there was no telling which one Sophia would post, and I didn't want to look like a complete weirdo.

"Thanks," Sophia said when I handed her phone back. "And now to choose a filter."

"Jesus Christ," Drew said, dropping his head into his hands.

"I'll leave you to it, then," I told them. "I'm gonna go check on your appetizers, and then I can take your orders. Right after I do one more lap around to check on everyone else."

A few minutes later, I was back with the apps, so I quickly dropped them off before checking in on the four other tables I had. I was relieved to find that the group of guys who'd been a little rude earlier wanted to settle the tab they'd started not that long ago. I was a little concerned that their unexpected departure had something to do with my service or maybe Ransom's response to them, but it wouldn't do any good to worry about something that might not even be true.

Once I managed to get their check squared away and cleared off one of the other tables, I headed back to Sophia's table. Despite the three appetizers they'd blown through, they were probably starving. They'd been seated around seven thirty, and it was already almost nine.

"Sorry," I said, pulling out my pen and notepad. "I'm guessing you guys are ready to order some real food now since you had like an hour to look over the menu."

"No worries," Toby said. "It gave me more time to explain how macro- and micronutrients affect our energy expenditure."

"Ohhh," I said, sympathetically. "Then I'm extra sorry it took me so long to get back here."

It seemed to take Toby a few seconds to realize what my comment meant. "Hey!" he said, but then left it at that.

Noticing that the table was one short, I asked, "Should I wait for Ransom to get back, or does one of you know what he wants?"

"Oh," Brody said. "He actually had to get going. But he said to let you know he's sorry he couldn't stay longer. He didn't wanna bother to say bye while you were working."

"It's fine." I mean, it *was* fine. I didn't need Ransom here or anything. I barely knew the guy. But what I did know of him made me curious about why he was always disappearing, and usually at night. I'd already asked him about it and hadn't gotten a real answer. If I didn't know better, I'd think he was moonlighting as some kind of superhero. Which was the reason I had to ask, "Where'd he go?" I tried to act casual, like I cared less than I did.

"He was meeting some friends or something at another bar," Sophia said.

Who was he meeting? I'd never seen any of Ransom's friends, other than all of us, and since he'd just moved here fairly recently, I didn't think he had many in the area. Except that he was, or used to be, an athlete, and I was pretty sure that circle could be extensive no matter where someone lived. The guy probably had connections all over the county. "Were they old friends from college or something or . . ."

Or some other thing that was none of my business?

"I don't think he said who," Carter answered right as Brody said, "I think it was a party or something. He sounded like it was pretty important."

Aniyah glanced between the two of them. "I thought he said it *wasn't* a party."

"Uh," Brody stammered. "I think he said it wasn't a *surprise* party."

"Aniyah's right," Toby chimed in. "He didn't say it was a party."

The group debated Ransom's whereabouts for a little longer, and I wondered why Brody was so insistent that he'd gone to a party when everyone else seemed so sure he hadn't.

Had Ransom told Brody the truth and Brody forgot he was supposed to keep it to himself? Was Ransom in some guy's basement snorting coke off a dirty parquet coffee table while nineteen-year-old college freshmen twerked in the background?

I didn't think so, but I also only knew the Ransom

that Brody brought around. I had no idea what he did in his personal life or who he hung around with.

And I was torn between whether I wanted to know or not.

Chapter Seven

RANSOM

"When you shoot, try to put your fingers up in the air a little more and flick the ball up higher. Just be careful. You're right-handed, so the ball'll drop off to the right if your wrist's not straight." Manny tossed the ball up into the air from behind the three-point line toward the right of the net and turned toward me. "See, I don't even need to watch it to know it went in." The ball dropped into the net with a satisfying swish, and he smiled when he heard it.

A lot of people might feel a little inadequate getting shooting lessons from a fourteen-year-old whose voice hadn't quite deepened completely yet, but I was just happy Manny got to show off his skills, not to mention I got to learn a few things about a sport I'd never been great at despite my height. I had over a foot on this kid, but he could dribble circles around me. Literally.

"Dude, you gonna play on a team this year, or what?" I asked him.

Most of what he'd learned had been in the local

neighborhood courts from his older brothers and other guys. And now that he was entering high school, I knew how important it was for him to play an organized version of the sport if he planned to get any type of scholarship. I wished he could've played for a summer league, but his mom didn't have the time or the money for all the travel that was needed.

"I guess," Manny said, tossing the ball hard toward me. "Try the shot again."

I jumped up, letting the ball slide off my fingertips. It sailed toward the basket but didn't quite make it in. Though it was closer than my previous shot.

"Almost," he said. He grabbed the rebound and threw it at me again. "Another. Remember not to let your hand drift over."

"Aren't I supposed to be the one mentoring *you*?" This time the ball went through the net with that beautiful sound I'd heard on Manny's shot.

"Yeah, but you're doing a shitty job of it."

I couldn't help but laugh. "Watch your mouth."

"Yeah, yeah. Again," he said, tossing me the ball.

I hit the shot with an ease I hadn't felt since, well, probably ever. "Once you learn the fundamentals, you can help coach a kids' team, I bet. That'll look great on a college application."

"Why you always gotta be talkin' about college like it's the only way to do anything with my life? You startin' to sound like my mom."

Manny shuffled around me as I tried and failed to steal the ball from him.

"Your mom's a smart woman," I told him.

"Yeah, I guess," he said, though I knew Manny well enough to know he had more respect for his mom and how hard she'd worked.

Maria Gonzalez was a saint, and her boys knew it. She'd raised three of them as a single mother from the time Manny's oldest brother was five. Their father hadn't been a stable figure in their lives before he went to prison, and he certainly wasn't one now. Of the three boys, Manny was the only one who took the time to visit him, and those visits were still few and far between.

I had no idea what it was like to have a parent who was there for you from the beginning and would be until the end. The kids in this neighborhood weren't exactly lucky when it came to family dynamics, but Manny'd hit the jackpot with his mother.

A few other kids came over to get a game going, including a twelve-year-old girl named Yazmine who had some serious skills. I let them play a three-on-three and was heading over to help a few kids do summer work at a nearby picnic table when my phone vibrated in my pocket.

I pulled it out to silence it, but when I saw that the Caller ID said *Melissa*, I answered. Though we didn't talk much anymore, I'd made a promise to myself that I'd answer whenever she called. And I didn't plan to break it.

"Hey," I said, slowing my walk down a bit and plugging my other ear with a finger so I could hear her over the kids.

"Hey, Rans." No matter how infrequently I talked to Melissa, it was always nice to hear her voice. "Did I catch you at a bad time?" She must've heard the noise in the background.

"No, no, you're good." It wasn't exactly true, but to be fair, no time was ever great. I was usually either working or at school. Harry wouldn't care if I took a quick phone call, because he knew I'd only answer if it was important. "What's up?"

Melissa and I hadn't made a habit of talking unless there was a reason. I wasn't sure if that had been more her doing or mine. I did know that along with the good memories attached to her voice, there were also too many that were bad. And Melissa knew that too.

"Well, first of all, how are you?"

"I'm good, I'm good. Busy but good. Just started the fall semester of classes."

"Okay, so that's good things are good. I didn't know you were starting school. Is it a . . . What kind of program is it?"

"Master's in sports medicine. Figured that'd be the most practical next step."

Melissa laughed softly. "Listen to you being practical. I never thought I'd see the day."

"Yeah, well, a lot's changed I guess."

The Ransom Melissa had last known was a kid in more ways than I realized at the time. I'd been nineteen, had just started my freshman year on a full ride, and thought I'd play professionally. It was the first time I was truly excited about my future, and I had every reason to be. I'd vowed to myself that my past was my past—that Melissa, Matt, and Emily were more than a family I knew from my after-school program. They were *my* family—the first real family I'd ever had. Or at least the first family I'd ever had who gave a shit about me. It was amazing how five years could feel like a lifetime ago, especially since I felt like I'd already experienced more of life than most people twice my age have.

"How's Matt?" I asked, knowing the answer. It was one of the reasons I'd distanced myself from Matt and Melissa, and it made me feel like shit to acknowledge it.

"He's okay. You know how he gets."

I didn't know if that meant he was drinking too much again—not that I could blame him if he was. Losing Emily had been one of the most painful experiences I'd ever had. I couldn't imagine the hurt that came with losing a child, which was one of the reasons I never planned to become a father.

There was a long pause on the other end of the line, and I wondered if she was crying but was afraid to ask. I was such a pussy sometimes.

Her sniffle gave me my answer, though I wouldn't acknowledge it out loud.

"We miss you, Rans."

"I miss you guys too." It was true. How could it not be? Melissa and Matt had been rocks for me after I'd spent most of my childhood being tossed around in a sea of uncertainty. I'd clung to them—all *three* of them—until three had become two. Then it just became too painful. For all of us. "I don't wanna rush you off the phone, Melissa, but I gotta get back to work."

"Sorry. I'll get to it, then. Kari called us. Has she called you?"

Melissa already knew the answer to that, or she wouldn't have contacted me.

"Yeah. A few times, I think. She only left a message once, though."

"What'd she say?"

"Same thing Kari always says. She's clean. She wants to see me. Typical stuff."

"How'd she sound to you?"

"I don't know. It was a short message." I hadn't even given it much thought because I had no intention of seeing her. I didn't even know Kari well enough to evaluate her sobriety with any amount of accuracy.

"Well, she called me," Melissa said. "We talked for a while. She sounded good. The best I've ever heard her sound, actually."

"Well, considering her usual state, that's hard to believe."

A few kids had started tossing around a football, and they were waving me over. I held up a finger and gave them a nod.

"She's your mother, Rans."

I understood why Melissa always said that, but that didn't stop me from hating it. Giving birth to me did not make Kari any type of mother. Matt and Melissa had been there for me long before they'd taken me into their home. I'd aged out of the system before Kari's parental rights had been terminated and the Holts had gotten the opportunity to make me their son officially. But that didn't mean they weren't a million times better than the "parents" who'd created me.

"Yeah, well, that doesn't mean a whole lot to me."

"I feel like this time is different. I can't really explain it."

"You don't have to."

Melissa sighed heavily. "Look, you're a grown man, so I'm not going to tell you what to do or how to live your life. Your decisions are yours to make. But just remember you have to live with those decisions. I'm not saying to do this for Kari. She doesn't deserve that. I'm just saying maybe you should consider that talking to her might offer some closure for you."

I doubted it, but I understood what Melissa was saying. It wasn't in them to shut someone out because of their mistakes, especially if that person had found their way and was on a good path. And while I liked to think I could offer the same forgiveness, I knew it wasn't true. Some damage was irreparable.

"I'll think about it," was all I could offer her.

"That's all I'm asking. You know one day there'll be a time when you don't have this chance, and I wouldn't want you to have any regrets when that day comes. You don't want to leave anything left unsaid, you know?"

"Yeah."

Emily had said something similar too once. That life was too short to cut people out of it, and that time wasn't promised to anyone. It had been more of a general observation toward the end; she hadn't been talking about Kari when she'd said it. But that didn't stop me from drawing the connection myself.

"If she calls again, I'll try to answer."

"Okay. I'll let you go. Love you."

"Love you guys too."

Neither of us spoke nor hung up.

After a moment, Melissa said, "And Rans, don't be a stranger, okay?"

"Okay. You guys neither."

The words we always said to each other at the end of our conversations were more of a closing than an actual promise. As much as we all wanted to be close again, we knew the memories we shared would never let that happen.

Chapter Eight

RANSOM

I pulled up to the three-story colonial and double-checked the address before putting my truck in park and getting out. It was ten o'clock at night, and the last thing I wanted was to show up at the wrong house dressed as a police officer. You could really scare the shit out of people like that. I wouldn't make that mistake twice.

I could hear music as I approached the stone pathway to the entrance. It was a nice neighborhood, which always made me feel more comfortable. Not that I was afraid to go to bad ones. I'd been in enough of them throughout my life to hold my own, but there was something that made me feel slightly uneasy about stripping in one.

It was like taking my clothes off increased my vulnerability. Maybe a group of women would hold me hostage, bound and naked until someone agreed to pay . . . well, the ransom. The ridiculousness of it all was too much to think about, let alone actually live.

It didn't take long for a woman to answer the door, and

she had a group of ladies behind her. I'd been told it was a surprise forty-fifth birthday party, so I hadn't expected it to be as rowdy as it seemed to be. I was aware that forty-five wasn't *technically* old, but I figured it would be tame compared to most of the twenty-something parties I typically worked.

"Someone called about a neighborhood disturbance," I said. "I think you ladies better keep it down in here."

The music blared so loudly, I wasn't sure they could hear me.

A desperate housewife in leopard print approached me, curling her red hair with a finger. "Who called? Was it that bitch across the street?"

"I'm not at liberty to say," I said, guessing she wanted me to play along, before taking a few steps inside and closing the door behind me. "This your house?" I put my thumbs in my belt and leaned back casually, broadening my shoulders and chest.

"It's mine," said a brunette who'd approached from behind her.

"And it's her birthday," said another, "so don't be too hard on her."

"What seems to be the problem, Officer?" the birthday girl asked, her voice low like *she* was the one trying to be seductive.

It always struck me as odd that women were so turned on by men in uniform, especially when I took it off so quickly.

"The problem," I said, stepping a bit closer to her, "is that this party is getting out of hand, and if you don't settle down, I'm going to have to take matters into my *own* hands." I removed my handcuffs and let them dangle seductively from my finger.

All the women screamed, and a few came running in from

where they'd been pouring drinks in the kitchen.

"Take it off!" one yelled as she held up a red Solo cup that had the name *Sleazy Samantha* written on it in marker.

It made me ask to see the other cups: *Dirty Denise, Raunchy Rachel,* and *Erotic Eve*—which seemed oddly worse than the others, given the biblical allusion—were some of them, along with the birthday girl, *Wild Willow*.

I took Willow's hand and put one half of the cuffs around her wrist.

She squealed happily while the rest of her friends hollered excitedly.

"Are you married, Officer?" she asked as I took her other hand and brought it behind her so I could cuff it to the other.

"I don't think that's an appropriate question to ask the person arresting you."

Women loved when I played along and became a figure in their fantasy. I could understand it in theory, but it always felt a little weird to actually participate in the role play even though that was what I was there for. Well, that and to take off my clothes.

I grabbed a chair from the dining room table and lowered Willow into it before turning off their music so I could play my own. Then I pulled my speaker and phone out of my SWAT bag—which always struck me as funny since I was in a normal street cop uniform, though to date, no one had ever pointed out the oddity of it. A few seconds later, I had my playlist going and was moving to the rhythm while Willow blushed in her seat.

A few of the women began fanning themselves when I opened my shirt, and one even began pulling on it when I didn't take it off right away. I let it slide off my arms before swinging it in the air and tossing it to the side like a bouquet at a wedding that all the women chased after. It was cliché but always earned an enthusiastic response from the crowd.

"Look at his muscles!" the redhead screamed much louder than necessary. "He's so . . . big."

"Let's see how big he really is," called another. "Take your pants off."

I glared hard at her. "I thought I was the one giving the orders." But I began unbuckling my belt anyway, and I unbuttoned my pants and pulled the zipper down a little but left them on for the time being.

The women groaned in frustration, and I almost laughed.

I moved around Willow, grinding the air between her legs before flipping over into a handstand so my crotch was practically face-level with her.

The women hollered beside us.

Once I was upright again, I kicked off my shoes and pulled off the quick-release pants. Willow was red now, and I wondered if I was too. No matter how many times I did this, it still felt a little strange having people gawk at me while I was almost naked.

Dirty Denise and Raunchy Rachel pulled a few five-dollar bills out of their bras and slid them into the waistband of my black G-string.

I'd never gotten used to that either.

"Here," Denise said to Willow as she held out a few ones toward her. "Take it with your mouth and put it in his underwear."

"That's disgusting."

"I'm sure he's clean," Denise said. "You showered earlier, right?"

"Not him," Willow said. "It's disgusting to put money in my mouth."

"I put it in the washing machine earlier."

"That's smart," Erotic Eve told her. "You've always been such a good planner."

"So you basically laundered money so I could put it in a stripper's thong?" Rachel asked.

"Yes. But not laundered *Ozark*-style. I only did the washing part. It's not like it's drug money or something." Denise turned to Willow again while I kept dancing. "Now put it in your fucking mouth."

I tried to focus on the job I'd been hired to do, but I couldn't stop myself from wondering if this was what Taylor, Sophia, and their friends would be doing in twenty-some years.

Probably.

Willow put her hands on my chest, and as she went lower, I prepared to move them if needed. Someone turned up the music a little more, and I couldn't hear much of anything except the song.

That was until I heard, "Mom? Mom!"

I looked to my right to see a girl who couldn't have been more than sixteen standing with her mouth agape near the door.

"What's going on?"

Willow jumped up, obviously forgetting that she had her hands cuffed behind her back, and she stumbled as she tried to find her balance. "It's not what it looks like, Tione!"

"Really? Because it looks like you have some stripper's balls in your face and you're enjoying it."

Okay, so it was pretty much exactly what Tione thought it looked like.

"Does Dad know this is happening?" She was already pulling her phone out to call.

"He knows I was having a girls' night here for my birthday. That's why he went to play pool with the guys. I thought you were staying at Madeline's."

"She's a bitch." Tione's voice got noticeably more somber. "Kaitlynn told me Madeline put up a Snap about how my jeans make my ass look flat." She sounded like she might cry.

I need to get the hell out of here.

"I'm so sorry, Tione." Willow began walking toward her daughter but tripped as she approached her because she was still handcuffed.

I reached out to grab her, but as I leaned down, Willow's head slammed into my eye, causing both of us to lean back in pain. And because I instinctively brought my hand up to my face, Willow fell backward when I let her go.

"Get these things off me!" she screamed, trying to stand without the use of her hands to help her stabilize herself.

"Sorry." I crawled toward her on my hands and knees, just wanting this night to end. I liked being almost naked in front of a teenager about as much as I liked getting hit in the eye. I grabbed my pants to fish out the small key but couldn't find it.

Panicking, I stood without realizing I was under the table. "Sorry," I said again when my head hit the table and caused a few drinks to spill.

By now, Tione was crying, and I didn't know if it was because of what she was witnessing or because her friend had been an asshole.

Thank God I never planned to have kids. Parenting seemed like a job I wasn't cut out for. Like stripping.

A few moments later, I found the key, unlocked the cuffs from Willow, and did my best to help clean up the drinks that were all over the table and carpet. I wondered if the red stains would come out, but I didn't actually want to ask.

"I'm gonna go."

"That's probably best," Dirty Denise said. "Here's the balance." She reached into her purse and handed me some cash.

"It's not necessary." I pulled my shirt on but didn't bother to button it or put on my pants because snapping them up the sides would have taken too long. I hoped my shirt covered my bare ass. "This was a complete disaster. I injured the guest of honor and spilled stuff everywhere. It's okay. Honestly," I said when she didn't look like she was going to let me leave without paying me for the full night.

Finally conceding, Denise dropped her hand.

On my way out the door, I looked at Tione, who was still in tears. "Sorry you had a bad night."

"Thanks," she answered softly.

"And sorry about"—I motioned around the room—"dancing with your mom and stuff. You know, without any clothes on."

"Just go."

I nodded silently, knowing that anything else I said would only make the situation more awkward than it already was, and headed for the door. And as I sprinted to my car, wearing nothing but a G-string and an open shirt, I was thankful that at least it wasn't winter.

TAYLOR

Like every Monday since classes had begun, I'd spent the majority of my time watching lectures I would've otherwise been in class for and gathering research for presentations. While I was glad I could do all of it remotely, I didn't realize how antsy I'd get sitting at a desk for most of the day. Though that was still preferable to looking over my shoulder when I walked around campus alone.

It felt good to go out for a run after a day cooped up in the house. I could stretch my legs, burn off the large iced latte I had earlier, and watch everyone going about their business in town before heading to my shift at Safe Haven. It was the first week of school for the kids, so my routine had already changed. But that also meant some new kids, which made me feel more comfortable since I was still new too.

As I jogged in place at an intersection, waiting for the light to turn green, I looked around at the people nearby, most of whom were likely college students walking to or from class or grabbing a bite to eat at a café or coffeehouse.

Once I'd gone a few miles and had worked up a pretty big sweat, I headed back to my apartment to grab a shower and change before work. As I rounded the corner to my street, I saw the man who'd offered me twenty bucks my first night there.

He was leaning against the exterior of our building, his words coming out in puffs of smoke as he talked with another guy I'd seen around. He was younger, probably only a few years older than me, and looked gaunt in a way that made me wonder if he was on drugs or couldn't afford food. I was an asshole to think that, but chances were good it was one or the other.

When the older man saw me running toward him, he threw down his cigarette. "You okay? Whatcha runnin' from?"

"I'm fine. I just went for a jog," I said, slowing to a walk as I approached my building.

"You're fuckin' nuts," said the younger one. "Only people you see running around here are runnin' *from* somethin'."

"Not me," I said with a tight smile. "I just needed the exercise."

"You look good to me," the younger man said, and as he looked me over, I wished I hadn't elaborated.

His comment was creepy as hell, but he might just have meant it as an innocent compliment. At least that was what he'd probably claim if I said anything back to him about it.

I just went with a "See you later"—though I hoped I wouldn't—before hauling ass inside and jogging quickly up the steps to my apartment.

When I arrived at work an hour and a half later, Ransom was waiting outside, a broad smile across his face as I headed toward him.

"Hey," he said.

"What's up? Did you come out here to greet me?" I asked, only half kidding.

"That's exactly why I'm out here. That and I have to get the kids off the bus."

"Why are you out front?"

"I feel like I'm having a flashback to like two seconds ago when I said why I was out here."

"Shut up," I said, smacking him playfully on the shoulder.

I could feel how solid he was—like his skin had been injected with some sort of substance that made it impossible for anyone to physically hurt him. I wondered what he looked like without his shirt on, but I tried to push the thought out of my head since there was no use imagining something that would most likely never happen. If I'd never seen him shirtless at the old apartment when there was a pool there, I doubted it would happen at an after-school program.

"There was a beehive hanging from one of the branches on that tree near the back parking lot. Roddie tried to knock it down because he swore it was vacant and thought the kids would freak out if they saw it."

Roddie was a college student who'd been at the center for a year or so. He was a sweet guy, but he had about as much sense as some of the kids we worked with.

"I'm guessing it wasn't vacant?"

Ransom shook his head and tried to suppress a smile as he took out his phone. He already had the video cued up, and when he pushed play, my hand immediately covered my mouth. It was cringeworthy. He split the hive in two, and a swarm of bees came flying out. Even though Ransom had filmed the video from pretty far away and the quality wasn't great, I could still see the cloud of bees following Roddie as he ran toward the building. After that, the video got shaky before cutting out completely.

"Oh my God," I said. "Is he okay? Did he get stung?"

Ransom nodded, still trying not to laugh. "Like all over. I feel bad for the guy, but it's also his fault, and he's not allergic or anything, so he's fine. I mean, he went home to get some Benadryl, but he'll *be* fine, I'm sure. Once the swelling goes down." This time he couldn't stop himself from laughing, and I joined in. "So anyway, there are still bees flying around everywhere out back, so I wanna make sure the buses don't go down there and that the kids who walk know to go in through the front today."

"Okay, let me just put my bag inside and get the room ready for their snack, and I'll come back out."

"Already done."

"Really?"

"Yeah, I got here a little early today."

"Thanks," I said, smiling.

"Plus, the last few times you did snack, the kids hated it."

We were standing next to each other near the curb, looking out for the bus, and I glanced over to see if I could tell if he was serious. I couldn't.

"Stop. My snacks are fine. And it's not like I make them. I just pick them from the kitchen."

"Only a weirdo chooses yogurt or string cheese when there's still Goldfish left. I didn't want to be the one to tell you how disappointed the kids were, but they know you're new and didn't have the heart to tell you."

"Well, sorry for being health-conscious. Jeez."

"Don't apologize to me. The real victims are over there," he said with a one-sided smirk as a bus entered the parking lot.

Once the vans and buses had dropped the kids off, Ransom took them inside to get them settled while I waited for the few walkers who still hadn't arrived.

After the kids got settled and got their homework out, Ransom announced that he'd gotten pretzels and pudding from the kitchen for snack.

"Once you've washed your hands, you can come up and grab some," he said. "I got chocolate and vanilla."

After they were seated again and shoveling spoonfuls of pudding into their mouths, I felt obligated to apologize.

"Sorry about the carrots the other day," I announced.

"Why?" Gianna asked, taking a few pretzels out of her bowl.

"Because they're vegetables, and no one likes vegetables."

"I like them," Gianna said.

Her friend Emilia ate a bite of her vanilla pudding and washed it down with some milk. "Me too."

Then a boy named Kyle chimed in. "And they're good for our eyes, right, Mr. Ransom? Didn't you say if I wanna play QB in high school, I gotta eat things that'll fuel my body?"

"I did," Ransom replied. "Good for you for remembering."

I internally sighed, wanting to be irritated about Ransom playing with me and, by extension, causing me to look like an ass in front of the kids, but I couldn't muster it. He was such a goof, it was really my own fault for not suspecting he'd been lying to me earlier. Despite that, I couldn't completely let him off the hook.

I can't stand you, I mouthed to him, which only made him smile wider. "Are you gonna take those dumb sunglasses off, by the way?"

He'd been wearing them outside, which wasn't all that strange, other than it being a bit overcast so they weren't really needed. But now we were inside where it *definitely* wasn't sunny, and his sunglasses looked odd, like they were too big for his face. Or maybe women's?

"They're a fashion statement."

"I'm not sure that's the type of statement you want to make. They look like something you stole from Kris Jenner's closet."

"Who's Kris Jenner?" Gianna asked.

"She's . . ." Ransom started to explain before clamping his lips together. "Never mind." He pulled the glasses off and hung them from the collar of his V-neck T-shirt.

"Oh, damn," Kyle said. "What'd the other boy look like?"

"What?" Ransom said, reaching up to his eye, which was puffy and bruised. "Oh, this? A door got me. That's all."

"Yeah, okay," Kyle said, walking closer to check out Ransom's injury. "This door have a name 'cause I'll fu..." He caught himself before Ransom had to. "I'll mess it up."

Ransom put his hand out and rested it on Kyle's head and looked him in the eye. "I didn't get into a fight, Kyle. Just drop it."

Thankfully for Ransom, Kyle did, but I couldn't blame the kid if he was still wondering who the hell did that to him. I wondered too.

We spent the rest of the afternoon helping the group with their homework, playing card games, and bringing them out to their parents when they arrived. Once all the kids had been picked up, I walked over to the cabinet where I kept my bag.

"You're horrible at Uno," Ransom said.

It was true. I'd lost all but one game. "Not as horrible as you are at lying."

"I don't lie."

"That's a lie right there. Everyone lies."

"Even you?" he asked, his eyebrow raised.

"Even me," I admitted. Though I wasn't about to say about what.

He opened the main door for me so we could head to our cars.

"So what really happened to your eye?" I asked. "Are you in like some sort of underground fight club or something?"

"Ha! Not even close."

"Then what happened? And don't tell me you got hit with a door."

He walked a little farther, and I kept stride beside him. Finally, when we arrived at my car, he stopped. "Things got a little crazy over the weekend. It was a complete accident."

"Okay."

"It was," he said, sounding eager for me to accept that as the truth.

"I believe you," I said, thinking that now we were even because every time I'd acted like I couldn't stand him, I'd been lying too. And I was sure we both knew it.

Chapter Nine

TAYLOR

It'd been a while since Sophia and I had gone out just the two of us, and I was definitely in need of a girls' night. Between two jobs and keeping up with school, I barely had any time to hang out anymore, and Sophia was just as busy. But since one of the girls at the bar had asked if she could pick up my shift so she could earn some extra money before her sister's bachelorette party in two weeks, I figured I'd let her take my Friday so I could have a night off.

Sophia and I had tried to think of something different to do, and she'd suggested going to a lake where we could rent paddle boards for an hour or so. It sounded low key and pretty relaxing, so it wasn't a difficult sell despite the fact that I'd never gone paddle boarding in my life. But really, how hard could it be?

"We get life vests, right?" I asked Sophia as we waited in the rental line.

"Yeah, but I think you only need to wear one if you're twelve or under. I think they just strap it to your board so it's nearby for adults."

"Can we rent two paddle boards for an hour?" I asked when we got to the window of the little hut they used as their rental station.

"Sure," the girl replied. "I just need a license to hold, and you guys can pay when you return."

I handed my license over and then put my money and phone in the waterproof pouch I'd brought. It'd worked pretty well when I'd taken it to water parks and pools before and seemed to withstand getting wet, though I didn't trust it if it submerged should I fall off the board, which was likely, knowing me.

We headed down to the small beach where two tanned, shirtless guys jogged up to us so they could measure us for our paddles. They gave us some minimal instructions, including that we should start on our knees until we were out farther before trying to stand on the board.

"I might have to stay on my knees the whole time," Sophia said after we'd paddled for a few minutes.

"Well, your knees are where you're most comfortable, so I'm not surprised by that."

"Asshole," she said with a laugh.

"This isn't too difficult yet. I think I might be able to stand. I'm just gonna go for it." I brought my paddle up onto the board and laid it perpendicular in front of me. Then I shifted into a squat on my toes and popped up before I had a chance to chicken out. I'd just begun my internal celebration when I realized I'd left my paddle on the board. "Shit. I have to figure out how to get that."

"Just reach down and grab it."

"You think?"

"Yeah, you were fine standing. You can do it again."

It made sense, but I didn't consider that the board had slowed down, making balancing on it more difficult, like riding a bike that was barely moving.

So when I tried to kneel down again, I leaned too far to one side and fell right into the lake. I managed to grab the board so I didn't go under, but I was still completely soaked. After a minute or so, and Sophia paddling over to help pull me up with her paddle, I was able to get seated on the board again. Though it wasn't graceful.

"Oh, shit. I hope my phone isn't ruined. I should've tied the lanyard around the life vest on the front of the board so if I fell, my phone wouldn't go in too."

"That would've been a good idea."

I was already opening up the plastic case to see if the water had made it to my phone, and what I saw on the screen made my heart jump.

Sophia must've noticed my reaction because she said, "Is it completely broken?"

"Um... no," I said, my voice absent and detached as I stared at the screen. I scanned the beginning of the text like I was trying to take in all the words at once and make sense of them, but I had to slow down and read it all the way through.

Hey, T. Hope you're okay. You had me worried when you didn't show up to school. Don't do that again.

There was no name assigned to the phone number, but I didn't need one to know it was Brad. He was the only person who'd ever called me T, and even without that reference, there was something about the tone of the text that made me sure it came from him. I'd blocked his number months ago, but he must've gotten a new phone. Did he buy one just so he could contact me? I didn't want to think about that possibility. That had a new level of fear attached to it.

"Taylor?" Sophia's voice snapped me out of my internal monologue, and I looked up at her. The concern on her face most likely mirrored mine. "You okay?"

This time she'd asked about *me,* not the phone, and I knew she wouldn't believe me if I told her I was fine. She knew me better than that.

"It's him."

"Him who?" We were both quiet for a moment before her eyes widened. "What'd he say?"

I shook my head like the motion might get the words out of my mind. "Nothing really. Just that he hopes I'm okay and not to worry him again."

"That's . . . kind of disturbing." Sophia looked almost as freaked out as I was. "It's like he's giving you an order or something. You think you should contact the cops or something?"

"And say what? A guy I used to date texted to see if I was okay when I decided not to return to school without telling anyone where I am?" I leaned back on my board to lie down so I could stare up at the sky.

The sun was fading behind the trees that lined the lake, casting beams of light through the leaves that fell onto the water. It was absolutely beautiful. And I should've felt peaceful, calm. But instead, all I could think about was how unsafe I felt even though I was in public surrounded by water. *I guess Sophia was right,* I thought with an empty laugh. *I'm an island.*

She seemed to be thinking about my question since she

hadn't spoken. And after a few more moments, I let my head fall to the side so I could see her.

She was sitting on her board with her legs crossed, moving her fingertips through the water slowly. "Do you have any threatening texts or emails or anything from him?"

"Nope. Nothing like that. He's too smart to put anything in writing. And it's not like he tried to attack me or anything. He hasn't even *verbally* threatened me. Technically, he hasn't done anything illegal. He's just creepy and doesn't listen when I say I want nothing to do with him. He knew most of my friends at school before I did, so it's not like they'd be rushing to see my side of things. Brad's good-looking and charismatic. He's funny, athletic." I sighed heavily. "He's one of those guys that other guys wanna be and girls wanna be *with*."

"We'll figure it out," Sophia said, giving me a small smile that comforted me more than her words did. "You're my ride or die. The Thelma to my Louise."

"Does that mean you're gonna kill him and then take me on a road trip?"

Sophia shrugged. "I'm not ruling it out."

That made me laugh out loud, and I felt a little better when I pictured Sophia and me driving down some unnamed highway in a convertible. "You know the end of that movie is them driving off a cliff, right?"

"So maybe that wasn't the best pop culture reference. Hillary and CC from *Beaches*?"

I raised an eyebrow at her.

"You can be CC since she's the talented one who lives."

"Love you," I said.

"Love you too. I'm so happy you're here."

"Me too." I felt tears starting to form, but I managed to

stop them from falling. “How about Janis and Damian? Can’t go wrong with a *Mean Girls* reference, right?”

“No. You can’t.”

After a few moments, Sophia said, “Just try to forget about it for now. You’re hundreds of miles away from him.”

I hated how Sophia was always right. “I’ll try. Though that may mean extending our girls’ night to dinner and drinks with the rest of the group. I might need some antics with my alcohol if I’m gonna try to ignore what a disaster my life is right now.”

She was already taking out her phone. “I’ll text everyone now.”

RANSOM

“Whose idea was this?” Taylor asked after her ball hit a stone around the edge of the putting green and popped up into a flower bed beside the course.

“Uh, I’m pretty sure it was yours,” Sophia told her.

“That’s untrue. When I suggested we go over to the old apartment, I was thinking we could hang by the pool or the fire pit, not compete in a sport.”

I put my ball down and lined up the club behind it. “It’s not really much of a competition when there are only three holes and five people.”

“It’s also not much of a competition when most of the people playing have absolutely no golf skills,” Toby pointed out.

We’d all been hitting the balls around for the past fifteen minutes or so, and almost everyone needed a minimum of six shots to get it in the hole.

When Sophia texted all of us after she and Taylor had finished dinner, I didn't expect anyone to be free to hang out. It was a Friday night, so Drew, Brody, and Xander were working at Rafferty's, and Aniyah and Cody both had plans already, so it ended up being just the three of us and Carter and Toby.

I was happy I could make it. There were very few Fridays I was free, and this happened to be one of them.

"Let's make this interesting," Toby said.

"But it's so interesting already," Sophia said dryly. "I don't know how it can possibly get any better."

Toby seemed oblivious to her sarcasm. "A bet." He sounded more excited than the moment called for. "Guys versus girls. We'll add up the total shots it takes for every member of the team to get it in the hole. Winners buy the losers drinks at the place of their choosing."

"Okay," Taylor said. "This shouldn't be too difficult since there's two of us and three of you, and all of us are horrible."

"Yup. The catch is that if you lose," I said, "You're buying three big guys drinks, and the tab's split between two people. If we lose, we're buying two lightweight girls drinks and the tab's split between the three of us."

"I passed fifth grade math, so yeah, I understand how it would all work," Taylor said with a smirk.

"So you're in, then?" Toby asked.

"I'm in."

"Me too," I said, mainly just to spend a little more time with Taylor.

Carter and Sophia agreed too, and Toby said, "Ladies first."

Sophia set up and managed to get her ball in with only four shots, which was probably the best she'd done since we'd started. "Okay, one of you go now."

Carter was the first to putt, and even though he hit the stones in the middle of the green, he recovered and sank his in four shots too.

Then Toby went so the girls wouldn't finish their shots before two guys hadn't gone yet. With Taylor and I the last to go, the score was seven to four, with the girls in the lead. As long as Taylor didn't fuck up royally, they'd win.

"It would've made more sense if one of you had gone first," Taylor said, pointing out what the rest of us were all probably thinking.

"It's fine. Shouldn't make much of a difference. I'll get a hole in one, and you'll probably get a nine like you did earlier, and we can all go to Rafferty's to celebrate our win."

"I'm not gonna get a nine," she said with an exaggerated laugh most likely to show how ridiculous she thought my prediction was. "This is the easiest hole."

"Guess we'll see in a minute."

Chapter Ten

RANSOM

"Who eats wings naked?" Taylor asked as I brought the drumstick up to my mouth.

"I'm not eating wings naked. I'm eating naked wings."

"Semantics." She pulled off the chunk of pineapple from the small straw in her drink and took a bite.

"It's not semantics. The way *you* worded it not only sounds like I should be arrested, it also sounds extremely dangerous."

"We can get the others to weigh in if you want." She was already motioning to Sophia, Carter, and Toby, who were congregating at the bar while Xander and Brody tried to keep up with the drink orders. "Hey, Soph!"

"They're gonna take my side on this. Just want to warn you before you embarrass yourself."

"Ha! Since when have you known me to be scared of embarrassing myself?"

She had a point. "By all means then," I said, gesturing toward the bar. "Should we make another wager?"

"Why? So you can lose again?" Guess the drinks hadn't

affected her wit yet.

I leaned back against the wrought-iron chair and raised my eyebrows at her. "I'll take my chances. Sophia! Carter!"

They turned around that time, and I motioned for them to come over to the table. They'd originally sat down with us, but they'd gotten sidetracked after going up to the bar to say hi.

"What's up?" Carter asked before recognizing there was food on the table. "Oooh, wings. Thanks for letting me know." He grabbed a few napkins and a wing, but I had a feeling he couldn't eat just one.

"The wings aren't why I called you over here," I told him.

Taylor shrugged. "They kind of *are*," she said. "Settle an argument for us. What would you say if I asked you if you like eating wings naked? You too, Soph."

Carter chomped down on the chicken before answering, and Sophia said, "I'm not sure what you guys have planned for the rest of the night, but I'm gonna pass."

"I'm into it," Carter said, grabbing another wing.

"See?" I widened my eyes at Taylor. "He thinks we're asking him to participate in some weird threesome involving chicken and hot sauce."

Sophia opened her mouth like she was about to say something but instead just turned around without a word and headed back to the bar.

"Whoa!" Carter looked more freaked out, which seemed to be a first from what I'd gotten to know of him. "I didn't say anything about any sexual encounters. I can get into food play, but in the past, I've been limited to whipped cream or chocolate syrup or ice cream. I'd be willing to branch out a little from sundae ingredients, but I feel like buffalo sauce might be too risky. Sorry," he added because clearly he thought he was disappointing us.

"Thanks, Carter. You've been a huge help."

He looked genuinely pleased with himself, though I didn't know what he thought he actually did to be helpful since neither of us bothered to explain.

"Can I grab one more before I head back to the bar?" He was already reaching for the basket. "Next time get the breaded kind, though. These are a little weird."

Once he left, Taylor and I immediately burst out laughing. "So a threesome involving chicken wings and Carter," I said. "That's one scenario I definitely never thought I'd consider."

"You're considering it?"

"No, uh, no. You know what I mean." I felt myself turning red, but there was nothing I could do to stop it. My cheeks always flushed from the slightest hint of embarrassment. "I'm pretty sure having Carter eat wings while we . . ."

Since now I probably looked like a time-lapse video of a tomato ripening to its full hue, I left my comment unfinished, though I was sure Taylor was capable of filling in the missing details.

She looked down at the yellow liquid in her glass and stirred it quickly, even though there was probably no need to. "Maybe we should drink more and talk less."

"Definitely," I said. I took a long drink of my beer until it was nearly finished.

Both of us were quiet for a while until the silence seemed to be more awkward than talking. "So how are your new classes? Is it a big change to do everything virtually?"

"Yeah, I guess. I'm just not great at sitting all day. I actually got a cheap projector cart to put my laptop on so I can stand while I work."

"Smart." God, I sucked at conversation.

"How are your classes?" she asked, and I couldn't be sure if her question stemmed from genuine interest or a feeling that she needed to reciprocate. "This is your second semester, right?"

"Third if you count the two classes I took in the summer. If I take two in the spring and two next summer, I'll be finished in a year from now."

"That's good," she said, before taking a sip of her drink. Then she downed the rest of it and slid it to the edge of the table.

She was on her third... whatever that was. I couldn't remember the name of it, but it was one of Xander's creations for the Yard—the deck and lawn area Drew and Brody ran that was owned by Rafferty's.

Taylor leaned across the table, her eyes fading a bit from the alcohol. Guess she was going to get her money's worth out of her win.

"Yeah. I feel like my life had no direction for a while," I said. "I thought I'd go right from playing college ball to playing professionally. And then when I messed up my knee, my whole life kind of stopped for a little bit there. I had to rethink everything I'd planned."

Apparently I was a man of extremes, because now I was sharing *too* much.

"At least you're on track now with a plan, though. The sports medicine thing is a good avenue for you I bet."

"Made the most sense, I guess." And then I asked, "Is there a reason you chose to major in criminal justice?"

"Um, yeah, but I don't think it's a very good one."

Now I was more curious than before.

"Basically I watched like a million episodes of *Law & Order: SVU* and thought it looked like a cool job."

"That's . . ."

"Something I should never tell anyone ever again?"

I laughed but didn't get the chance to reply before Taylor said, "Hey, wanna do a shot with me?" Her eyes lit up like a child's might if they were told they could have ice cream for dinner.

"What kind?" I internally tensed, hoping she didn't say tequila or something that was straight liquor. I didn't want her to get totally trashed.

Taylor's face contorted with thought. She bit her lip and pressed her eyebrows together like she was making an important life decision. "Gummy Bear?"

Okay, at least it's something with a mixer. "Sure. I haven't had one of them in a few years."

After waiting a few minutes without the server coming by, I volunteered to go up to the bar to get them.

"What are you guys up to?" I asked Brody while I waited for him to make our drinks.

Unfortunately, Xander wasn't anywhere to be found. I considered asking Brody to go light on the alcohol since he typically overpoured, but I didn't want anyone to overhear me asking to make Taylor's drink weaker. Even though my intention was not to have her show up to her shady apartment completely wasted, she was a grown woman and could make her own decisions.

I chatted with the gang for a few minutes, but once Brody came over with our shots, I headed back to the table. Taylor's head was so buried in her phone, she almost didn't notice me sit down.

“Everything okay?” I asked as I slid the drink in front of her. She looked . . . worried. Or sad. I didn’t know her well enough to take an educated guess at her emotions, but I knew without a doubt they weren’t positive.

When she lifted her head to look at me, she smiled, though I could tell it was forced. “Yeah. I’m good. Just some annoying emails, that’s all.”

She put her phone away, and I lifted my drink. “I always feel like there should be a toast with shots.”

Though a bit lazy, her smile looked more genuine now. “To my win?”

“Eh, that’s like toasting to my own loss. I don’t think the athlete in me will let me do it.”

Taylor thought again, her mouth twisting like it did when she was deciding which drink to get. “How about to new beginnings? Both of us are pretty new here and starting new . . . stuff.”

I laughed at Taylor’s choice of words, and thankfully so did she.

“To new beginnings, then,” I said with a wide smile. *I like the sound of that.*

XO

Taylor had two more drinks before Sophia noticed her leaning over the side of the deck.

“What the . . .”

“She’s been like that for at least ten minutes,” I told her. “She said she likes how being upside down makes her head feel.” I wasn’t about to leave her alone like that, mainly because it was probably a ten-foot drop to the yard below, and she’d likely fall on her head if she tipped over completely.

"Tay?"

Sophia leaned over the deck rail in an attempt to see Taylor's face when she didn't respond to her.

"Why are men such dicks?" Taylor muttered.

I really hoped she wasn't talking about me. I had no idea what she could possibly be referencing, but since I was the only guy she'd talked to in the last hour or so, I couldn't be totally sure.

"Can you stand up so we can have this conversation, and so the gravitational pull is working on my feet and not my head?"

"It is at your feet," Taylor said.

The girl was still smart and a smart*ass* even when she was wasted.

"You know what I mean."

Taylor groaned loudly like Sophia's request would be severely inconvenient for her but complied anyway. She swayed a little once she stood upright, and I had to put my hands on her arms to steady her before she fell.

It would be ironic if she fell onto the deck instead of over it, considering she'd spent the better part of the last half hour with half her body hanging off the side.

"Would you maybe just get us a glass of water, Ransom?" Sophia asked.

I headed to the bar, where the rest of our group was hanging out, and got Taylor some water. A minute or so later, I found Taylor and Sophia sitting at the table we'd been at earlier in the night. It still had some of our appetizers on it, though neither of us probably would've eaten any more of them. I sat down across from them and put the water in front of Taylor.

"Here, drink some," Sophia told her.

"Hang on." She was scrolling through her phone, a hardness to her face that I hadn't noticed before. "Look at this."

"Holy shit. He wrote all that in one text?"

"Yeah. Well, it's not all one. It's broken up into different ones, but I never responded. He just kept firing them at me."

The two stared at Taylor's phone for a minute, and Sophia seemed to be reading the texts. I suddenly felt like I should be doing anything except hearing this conversation. I guessed it was an ex texting her, but I obviously had no plans to ask about it. It wasn't any of my fucking business, and I didn't have any intention of making it mine.

"Jesus," Sophia said. "Just block him."

"I should go," I told them. I was already pushing the chair back to stand.

"No!" Taylor practically yelled, and her voice made me stop immediately. "You can sit. I think I'm gonna call it a night. Just call me tomorrow, Soph. 'Kay?"

"Yeah, sure. How you getting home, though?"

"Walking," she answered like the question had been a dumb one.

We'd walked to Rafferty's from my apartment because it wasn't too far, but Taylor's was on the opposite side of town, and it would probably take her an hour, and it was already midnight. I hated the thought of her alone as she trekked back to her place.

"Can't you at least take an Uber or something?"

"You know I don't take Ubers alone."

I could see Sophia's frustration. "Yeah, but how is walking miles alone in the middle of the night any safer?"

"It just is, okay?" She slung her bag over her shoulder. "Or maybe it isn't. I don't know. But I'll be fine. I'll call you when I get home."

"Just wait until one of the guys gets off work. They can drive you."

Taylor looked flustered, but she steadied herself long enough to grab Sophia's hands and look at her. She took a deep breath. "I just wanna leave now," she said calmly.

"Wait a sec. I'll go ask Drew if he can take a break to drive you," Sophia said before hurrying away.

Sophia had a right to worry, and Taylor was acting like her walking alone was no big deal.

"I could walk you," I offered. "I don't mind."

"I'm really fine. You guys stay and have a good time."

There wasn't much I could do other than watch her turn around and walk straight into a nearby chair. She grabbed the back of it before it fell to the floor and then adjusted her bag on her shoulder. It was a good save, but she still looked completely ridiculous. And if she couldn't even walk out of the bar without getting into trouble, I didn't trust her to make it the more than three miles home.

By the time she made it down the deck steps and into the parking lot, I was convinced I should walk her. She'd slipped once on the steps but caught herself again. I'd just stay far behind her so I could keep an eye on her safety. She was clearly intoxicated, and I didn't trust that someone would see a drunk girl stumbling home late at night and decide they should leave her alone. She could get robbed or… I didn't even want to let my mind go there.

Without giving it another thought, I told Sophia I was going to make sure Taylor got home safely. I put money on the bar on my way out before jogging down the deck steps toward the direction of Taylor's apartment.

The area was fairly populated, though it wasn't in the

busiest part of the city. Still, the fact that it had street lights and a good amount of cars were still driving around made me feel a little better about her walking alone, but I still wasn't going to allow her to do it when I could easily make sure she got home safely.

I let her get about a half a block ahead of me—close enough that I could see her clearly and get to her if she needed help, but far enough that I doubted she would notice me. My plan worked for most of the walk until Taylor stopped to lean against a building and check her phone, causing me to have to stop as well so I didn't get too close to her.

To make myself look busy, I took out my phone only to find a text from Taylor.

Why are you following me?

When I looked over to where she'd been standing, I didn't see her. Without texting back, I jogged toward where she'd probably gone, but I didn't see her right away. Where did she go?

"How do you like being followed?" asked someone behind me.

I spun around. "What the—"

"I went into the alcove in front of the barber shop when you ran past me. Do you have any idea how creepy it is to feel like someone's following you? And then when you turn around it's a friend who you already told not to walk you home?" She let out a harsh sigh. "I'm honestly not sure if that's better than a stranger following me or worse."

"I'd think better," I offered cautiously because I could tell she was pissed. "I know you said not to walk you, but I just didn't feel comfortable letting you walk alone at this time of night, especially in your neighborhood." I felt myself cringe at the mention of where her apartment was located. *Way to insult her too.*

Taylor's expression hardened. "Since when is what *you're* comfortable with more important than what I am? I asked you to let me be alone, and you just couldn't do it. You couldn't respect that?"

"I'm sorry. I didn't mean to upset you. I didn't think it was that big of a deal. I just wanted—"

"Stop with what you want. This isn't about *you.*"

I didn't know if her anger was a result of the alcohol or something else, because this was a side of Taylor I hadn't seen before, and I didn't know what to do about it.

"I'm sorry."

Her shoulders fell a bit with my words, and she seemed to let go of some of the tension in her body. Though I could still sense her anger.

"Go home," she said.

So I did.

Chapter Eleven

TAYLOR

At Safe Haven, I kept stealing glances at Ransom even though I willed myself to stop. Evidently my impulse control was total shit.

I'd spent the rest of the weekend trying to sort through all the conflicting thoughts in my head. On one hand, I felt justified in calling Ransom out on following me home, even if I'd been drunk. He didn't have to go all covert-ops with it. That was next grade creeper level behavior.

So why didn't it feel like it?

That was the question I couldn't escape. His following me home should've had all my red flags flying, but it . . . didn't. With Brad, I was on edge as soon as I'd started seeing him around after we'd broken up. The first time he'd popped up somewhere I was, the hairs on the back of my neck stood up even though it *could* have been a coincidence.

I didn't feel any of that with Ransom. There was no pretending he hadn't willingly followed me without my knowledge, but I wasn't weirded out about it despite having acted like I was. Because it *was* weird. Wasn't it?

This was one of the things I hated Brad for most: he made me question my instincts. Everything in me told me Ransom was just being a good guy who worried about me. But I hadn't done anything to earn his concern for me, and that put me on edge a bit. What kind of guy went to that kind of trouble for someone they barely knew?

Who got them a job and vouched for them with his boss? Who helped them move into a new apartment? Who made time to come to someone's first night at a new job even though he clearly had somewhere else to be?

Obviously, Ransom did, but why? There had to be a reason, but for the life of me, I couldn't convince myself it was malicious. After all I'd been through with Brad, it was like I'd learned nothing. I should have been running for the hills from Ransom, but instead, here I was, staring at him when he wasn't looking.

Oh, shit, now he's looking.

I averted my eyes quickly and took an inordinate amount of time picking out a bead to add to the bracelet I was making with a few of the girls. We normally didn't bring arts and crafts items into the gym after the regular Safe Haven hours ended, but the girls had put on their best pouts and totally played me.

It was just after six thirty, so the rest of the extended-day kids would be getting picked up soon. I looked around at everyone's progress. "We're going to need to clean up in five minutes. If you're not going to finish, I can put your projects somewhere safe, and we can finish them tomorrow."

I received murmured "Okays" in reply, the girls unwilling to take too much attention from their creations.

I chuckled to myself. It was still hard to believe I got

paid to play all afternoon. Of course, there'd been a few trying moments since I'd started—a few arguments we'd had to mediate, some tantrums we'd had to quash, some defiant behavior we'd had to have discussions about—but overall, things ran smoothly at Safe Haven.

There was no denying that Ransom was one of the reasons things functioned so well. He was amazing with the kids. He played with them like he was a kid himself, but they also respected him—looked up to him in a way that seemed almost instinctual for the kids. Like they knew they could trust him, that he was on their side without him having to say anything in that regard.

Though I guessed actions spoke louder than words. And Ransom had been there awhile, so maybe he'd laid the foundation with many of the kids before I'd arrived. But even when a new kid started the program, they always seemed to gravitate to Ransom, hiding in his shadow until they felt safe to venture out into the group. There was just something about him that made people feel safe, and I desperately wished I didn't feel the pull of that. I simply couldn't trust it, no matter how badly I wanted to or how much my gut told me I could.

"Gina, Gina, bo-bina, banana-fana-fo-fina, mee-mi-mo-mina, Gina!" Ransom bellowed, causing everyone, even Gina, to giggle. "Your mom's here."

I smiled at Gina as she put the beads she'd gathered back into the appropriate bins. Cleaning up after themselves had been my stipulation for them bringing the crafts into the gym, and I was thankful they were holding up their end of the bargain.

"You want me to hold it for you?" I asked.

"Yes, please. I'm almost done, but I wanted to add a few more to it."

I held out my hand, and she placed her necklace into my palm.

"No problem. It looks beautiful."

Gina smiled. "Thanks. It's a present for my mom."

"She'll love it."

Her smile grew as she said goodbye to me before grabbing her school bag and hustling toward her mother. Ransom was there, and he and Gina did some kind of complicated handshake before she left. He had some kind of special ritual with almost every kid in the program, and I couldn't for the life of me figure out how he remembered them all.

Over the next half hour, all the kids had been picked up except one. Cindy was the youngest child we had in the program. As a second grader, she was eligible for the after-school program through her school, but her mother needed the extended time, so Safe Haven arranged for another bus to swing by her school and pick her up every day.

She was absolutely adorable, with blond hair she often wore in pigtails and freckles across her nose. She was very quiet and didn't usually play with the other kids often, but she loved arts and crafts. She'd been silently building a bracelet for the past hour or so, and with every child who got picked up, her body grew more and more tense.

It wasn't the first time Cindy had been the last to be picked up. Her mother had rushed in, full of apologies and what seemed to be valid excuses about having been kept late at work three other times since I'd started. Harry had spoken to her about it, and she'd sworn she wouldn't be late again.

But here we were.

Ransom approached and crouched down on the other side of the table from Cindy. "Hey, Cinnabon, how's it going?"

Cindy seemed to shrink in on herself and answered with a shrug.

She was probably the only child at Safe Haven who *didn't* react positively to Ransom, which was probably why he settled across from her instead of next to her. Ransom tried to connect with her—even nicknaming her Cinnabon because she was sweet—but he also didn't push her to interact with him. I gave him a lot of respect for that.

His eyes filled with a hint of what looked like sadness as he gazed at Cindy for another second before turning to me. "Do you have to work at the Treehouse tonight? I was going to let Roddie go home, but I can have him stay if you need to leave."

"No, I can stay," I replied. It was protocol for there to always be two adults on duty until all the kids were picked up.

"Great," he replied. "I'll go let him know."

I watched him leave because who was I kidding? Watching the back of Ransom was almost as appealing as watching the front. Maybe more so because there was less risk of him catching me staring.

As Ransom spoke to Roddie, I tried to figure him out. Ransom technically wasn't even working, but he always stayed until seven, just like Harry said. He was also the one everyone went to when there was a problem.

I hated that we'd have to tell Harry that Cindy's mother had been late again. I wasn't sure how many warnings a family got before they were kicked out of the program, but Cindy's mom had to be running out of chances.

As I cleaned up the beads Cindy wasn't using, I asked her, "Are you making that bracelet for anyone special?"

She shook her head.

"It's really pretty. I bet you could save it and give it to someone as a present. Your mom or teacher maybe."

Cindy turned the bracelet around in her hands a couple of times before shrugging and reaching for another bead.

"I used to make crafts all the time, but I never gave them to anyone either."

She looked up at me, her forehead creased a little, and I read the expression as a question she never voiced.

"I'm not sure why," I continued. "I guess I never thought they were actually good enough to hand out to anyone. So I ended up with tons of bracelets and necklaces and potholders, all kinds of stuff. I stored it all in a box under my bed. Come to think of it, it's probably still there." I huffed out a small laugh. "It's a shame when I think about it now. All these years, people could've been using them, but instead they're just sitting under my bed, doing nothing."

"Cindy!"

The young girl and I both jerked our heads toward the voice. Cindy's mom was young, mid-twenties tops. She was attractive, but she also looked exhausted. I heard her telling Ransom she was sorry, but I couldn't hear the rest of her words.

I turned back to Cindy to see her putting away the beads in front of her.

"Don't worry about it, sweetie. I'll pick them up."

Cindy gave me a small smile—which made me feel like I'd hung the moon—and then started to round the table to where her bag sat. But before she got too far, she stopped and turned back to me. She reached out her small hand, holding out the bracelet.

"Are you sure?" I asked.

She nodded.

I gently took it from her and slid it on. "Thank you, Cindy. It's the best gift I've gotten in a long time."

She smiled again before grabbing her stuff and running for her mother, who scooped her into a big hug and kissed her cheek.

"I'm so sorry, Cindy. I missed you so much today." Her mom set her down, and the two of them walked out hand-in-hand.

"It's a shame," Ransom said from beside me, his proximity startling me since I hadn't seen him approach. If he noticed, he didn't mention it. "Taryn clearly loves Cindy and does the best she can, but I don't think she has a lot of support."

"Do you think Harry will kick them out of the program?" I asked.

"Nah, Harry's a bleeding heart. I also think he knows more about their situation than the rest of us. That's probably why he moved heaven and earth to get her into the program."

My face must've shown the confusion I felt, because he continued. "It was a whole thing to arrange transportation for her. She gets out of school later than the middle school kids that take the bus here, so Harry called in a few favors to get her dismissed early."

I hadn't considered the logistics before. The fact that Harry would go to so much trouble for one family made my respect for him grow even more.

Ransom looked over at me and down at my hand. "I like your bracelet."

I brought my arm up and spun the bracelet with my other hand. "Thanks. She did a great job with it."

"You're good with her. She definitely seeks you out more than anyone else."

I tried to fight a smile but failed. It simply felt too good to hear that. "She's definitely . . . timid."

Ransom sighed. "Yeah, I wish we knew more about what was going on there so we could interact with her in a more informed way, but it is what it is, I guess."

"I'd definitely say she's a selective mute, and the way she reacts to certain people makes me think that's rooted in some kind of trauma."

He ran his hand through his hair. "Yeah, I thought it might be something like that too. Damn."

The last word sounded as if it had been pushed from him, as if the thought of something bad having happened to Cindy hurt him too. Not that I didn't feel that way, but it seemed to be deeper with Ransom. He always seemed to *care* so much about everyone else. It made me feel self-absorbed in comparison.

"Hey, it's late. Did you have plans for dinner?" he asked, the quick change in topic nearly giving me whiplash.

"Um, not specifically. I was just going to make something at home."

"Wanna grab something? My treat."

The desire to accept was strong, which was exactly why I said, "Sorry, I'm kind of tired. I think it's best if I just go home."

He nodded as if he'd expected the answer, but he also looked disappointed. It almost made me reconsider.

"Stop by Harry's office with me first," he said. "And then I'll walk you out."

"Okay."

We gathered what we'd brought into the gym, and after returning everything to where it belonged, we went to Harry's office.

"Any problems?" he asked after we'd told him we were

done for the night.

"Cindy's mom was late again," Ransom said.

Harry sighed. "I'll call her tomorrow."

"It was only ten minutes," Ransom defended. "It's not a big deal."

"I know, but if we let that kind of thing slide, more parents will start being late. I told her last time she was going to start being fined, but I don't know. I hate to do that." He rubbed a hand over his face. "I'll think on it. See you guys tomorrow. Have a great night."

"You too," I said.

"Yeah, get the hell out of here at a decent hour tonight," Ransom added. "Tell the fam I said hi."

"Will do."

We made our way out of Safe Haven and out of the center.

"Where are you parked?" Ransom asked.

"Oh, I walked."

Ransom stopped dead in his tracks. "You what?"

"I walked," I said more slowly. "It's only a few miles. I got a good parking spot outside my apartment, and I didn't want to move my car."

"It's getting dark."

I rolled my eyes. *Not this again*. "Well, I wasn't expecting to be here almost an hour late, Dad. It would've been fine if we'd gotten done on time."

"I'll take you home," he said matter-of-factly as he began walking toward his truck.

"No thanks. I'll walk." I turned away and headed down the sidewalk.

Screw stupid boys and especially screw *this* stupid boy and his overprotectiveness that was actually superhot even though it was irritating too. And screw me for thinking the word *screw* in relation to Ransom because it made my whole body warm. Well, *warmer* because it was actually still kind of hot out even though the sun was going down. Global warming could suck it.

A hand closed around my bicep, and even though I knew who it was, I still whirled around like a maniac.

"Don't touch me," I gritted out.

Ransom held his hands up. "Shit, sorry."

I took a calming breath. "Go home, Ransom."

But when I began walking again, he fell into step beside me.

"No can do. Not until I know you're safe."

I turned my head to glare at him, only to see him smiling widely.

"See! Look how good I'm getting at following directions," he said. "You didn't want me following you without you knowing, so now I'm being upfront about it. Very mature of me, if I do say so myself. You're a good influence on me."

"I somehow doubt that."

"So you think you're a bad influence?"

I stopped and sighed loudly. "Why are you this way?"

He thought for a long moment, the delay actually making me begin to anticipate his answer. So when he said, "I don't know," I was annoyed with myself for expecting something serious. But I was also a little amused too.

"You want to smile," he said as he pointed at my face.

"I do not," I argued as I began walking again.

"You do. You totally do. I have effectively annoyed you into happiness."

"Oh my God, do you ever stop?"

He hesitated again, this time going so far as to tap his index finger on his chin.

But I wasn't falling for it again. "That was rhetorical."

"But what if I have an answer?"

"I don't want to hear it."

"Well, that's not very nice."

"Guess I'm not very nice."

"I think you're nice."

He was making me exasperated. "You just said I *wasn't* nice."

"No, I don't think I did."

"Ransom," I warned.

"Taylor," he repeated.

I breathed deeply. "What will make you go away?"

"Letting me buy you dinner and then giving you a ride home."

"I already told you no about dinner."

"Your words said no, but your growling stomach said ask again."

This guy was going to drive me insane. "I'm *still* a no on dinner."

"But a yes to a ride?"

"Jesus, fine, yes, I'll accept a ride."

"Sweet," he said simply before changing directions and walking us to his truck. It was black, with an extended cab and four doors. It looked to be a few years old, but it was well-maintained. He went to open the passenger door, but the blaring of his phone stopped him before he could open it. He pulled his phone out of his jean's pocket and looked at the display.

The look that crossed his face was a far cry from the goofy

guy he usually was. He stared at the phone as it continued to ring.

"You wanna get that?" I asked him.

He glanced up at me. "Not really." Refocusing on the display again, he added. "I probably should, though. One sec." He took a breath and then answered. "Hello?" He turned so his back was to me, and there was little else for me to do but stare at his back through his tight T-shirt, letting me see the high set of his shoulder and the way his muscles seemed to be bunched together.

Whoever was on the other end, Ransom didn't seem to want to speak to them.

"Yeah, it's me. Fine. Yeah. That's good." He listened to whoever was on the line for a minute or so before turning a bit so he was leaning against the back door. He was looking at the ground as I studied his profile: all square lines and smooth skin.

"No, I don't . . . I don't think I'm ready to see you. We have a lot to work through before that happens. *If* it happens."

The person on the other end began speaking again, and I wondered who he was speaking to. I'd made a lot of assumptions about Ransom since I'd met him, and while I wasn't convinced some of them were unfounded—hello, black eye—I also didn't want to jump to conclusions. Mostly because the rigid set to his body and the words he was saying instantly made me think it was an ex-girlfriend, and that thought made me decidedly irritated. Not that I had any right to feel that way, but since when were emotions logical?

"Yeah, you can call again. I just— Never mind. I'll talk to you soon. Okay." He hung up without saying goodbye and pushed his phone back into his pocket. He looked over at me and flashed me a smile that didn't reach his eyes. "Sorry about that."

"No worries. You okay?"

He bit his bottom lip as he considered my question. "Honestly. I'm not sure."

Don't ask who it was. Don't ask who it was. "Who was it?" *Fuck it all to hell.* "Sorry, that was rude," I rushed to add. "It's not my business." *Please make it my business.* "You don't have to tell me." *For the love of God, tell me already.*

Though, maybe I didn't want to know. If he was going to say it was the love of his life calling to get back together with him, well, I could do without that information, thanks very much. Though maybe having a girlfriend would be a blessing. It would make him less . . . available, and I could get over this ridiculous crush I had on him.

Wait . . . Crush? No, not a crush. He was nice and attractive, so of course I was drawn to him. As a person. Not anything . . . more.

Clearly oblivious to my inner freak-out, he turned fully toward me. "It was my mom. Well, my bio mom. It's a long story. I mean, it's not a secret, but you probably don't want to hear it."

He pulled my door open, but I didn't get in right away. Instead, I studied him for a moment, trying to figure out what he wanted? Did he *want* someone to talk to? Did I want to be that someone?

Staring at him was awkward, so I slid into my seat, and he closed my door. As he walked around the truck, I wondered what the best thing to do was. Learning more about Ransom, opening us up to knowing each other better, was a bad idea for so many reasons. It was better to keep the wall between us that

I'd erected. We were acquaintances. Tangential friends. We didn't need to be anything more.

He climbed in behind the wheel and started his truck.

I chanced a look at him.

He gripped the wheel tightly, his jaw hard-set.

"Maybe you could tell me about it over dinner?" *Why do I even have an inner monologue if I'm never going to listen to it?*

His eyes flew to mine, and he looked . . . surprised. Surprised but also pleased.

"Yeah. That would be great."

Great was definitely one word for it.

Chapter Twelve

RANSOM

"How do you feel about diner food?" I asked Taylor.

Neither of us had spoken in the few minutes that had passed since she'd agreed to go to dinner. I was almost afraid to speak—worried I'd say something stupid to remind her why she'd declined in the first place. But prolonged silence made me antsy, and no matter how many times I told myself to stay chill, I always rushed to fill it.

I saw her glance over at me in my periphery. "I don't really feel anything about it one way or the other. Isn't that kind of the point of diner food? To be . . . inconspicuous?"

I wrinkled my brow as I processed her words. "That seems like a bad marketing strategy."

"How much marketing do you see for diners? No TV ads, no billboards. They're just . . . there. Like crabs without the anxiety."

I couldn't resist facing her in my horror. "Was your goal to ruin diners for me?"

She shrugged. "I wouldn't say a goal as much as a pleasant byproduct."

"You're a monster."

"Eh, I've been called worse."

I turned into a parking lot, pulled into an empty spot, and killed the engine. "Well, your punishment is to eat at the Greasy Spoon."

She bent her head so she could look up at the brick building with faded canopies over the windows. "Oh God, that's the name and not just a description." She turned toward me. "I'm going to get food poisoning and die, aren't I?"

I nodded solemnly. "After the crabs comment, this is just the way it has to be."

She sighed heavily before throwing her door open. "That's fair."

We walked up the stone steps side by side and our hands brushed, causing her to mutter a "sorry."

I wished, not for the first time, we'd met at a different time under different circumstances. Circumstances that could've led to me gripping her hand and twining her fingers in mine.

When we got inside, I stepped ahead of her to approach the hostess station.

"Hi. Just two?" the young girl at the station asked.

"Yes."

"Right this way," she said before grabbing menus the size of a poster and leading us toward a table. As we sat, she handed us the menus and said, "Helen will be right with you."

Taylor looked around before turning her eyes on me. "This wallpaper and I are fighting a duel to the death. Either it goes or I do."

I spun my head around quickly to take in the wallpaper. It was a floral pattern that had yellowed with age and was peeling in places, but it didn't seem *that* offensive. "That's... an odd comment."

She laughed. "Those were Oscar Wilde's last words. Seemed appropriate."

"And you just happen to know his last words because . . ."

She shifted a bit in her seat, and if I didn't know her better, I'd say she was embarrassed. "I have a bit of an obsession with people's last words." A blush creeped up her neck and highlighted her cheeks.

Definitely embarrassed. And because I was who I was, I couldn't resist poking fun at her. "Kinda morbid, don't ya think?"

Her eyes flashed, and it was as if I were watching her don her armor as she prepared for battle. Her shoulders straightened, her jaw hardened, and all motion ceased. It was incredible. Taylor, my little warrior. Well, not *mine*, unfortunately, but whatever.

"You're awfully judgmental sometimes," she accused.

My brow furrowed. "Me? You and Sophia were literally ranking men by their taste in footwear a couple weeks ago."

She rolled her eyes at me. "So? We didn't *know* them. And they couldn't hear us. It was harmless."

I cocked my head. "So knowing someone makes a difference?"

"Yes. Because when you know someone, you're making a judgment based on what you've learned. The attack is personal, not objective."

"Hmm, interesting. Okay, so tell me this . . ."

She looked at me expectantly.

I smiled. "What if I was just giving you shit and don't really think it's morbid? Is it still personal?"

"No, then it's just really freaking annoying."

"Ah, good. Glad that's settled, then." I leaned back into my seat and opened my menu. I didn't even know why I bothered to look. I always got the same thing at diners.

After setting my menu back down, I looked up to see an older woman—probably in her sixties—approaching. She had white hair that was haphazardly bundled on top of her head with a pencil sticking through it, a collared pink dress that was so shapeless it should be a crime, and a black apron tied around her waist with straws hanging out of it. She'd be the picture of a stereotypical diner server except for the fact that she also wore a pair of black sunglasses with lenses so dark, I couldn't even tell if she had eyes.

She came to a stop at our table, but she didn't fully face us. Instead, she stood slightly catty-corner to us. "Evening. I'm Helen. Can I get ya drinks?"

I ventured a look at Taylor, whose eyes had gone a little wide. "Uh, just a water for me," she said.

"Same," I added.

"Great. Be right back."

I watched Helen leave. She moved around tables easily, but there was also a stiffness to her.

"Oh my God, is she blind?" Taylor asked once Helen was out of earshot.

"No, she can't be." *Could she?*

"We're in a place called the Greasy Spoon. Anything's possible," Taylor retorted.

"This place isn't that bad," I said, sounding defensive.

"Whatever. Leave me to pick out my final meal in peace." Taylor pulled her menu up so it blocked my view of her face.

I reached across and pushed it down to be irritating. "What do you want your last words to be?"

Her lips twitched as if she wanted to smile but refused to

allow it. "I'll probably be throwing up and unable to talk."

I laughed. "Why would you be doing that?"

"Because there's no way my death will be anything other than mortifying."

"All the more reason to tell me what you want them to be. I'll lie and say you said them."

"How sweet," she said dryly.

"I know. You don't deserve me."

"For fuck's sake," she muttered and turned her attention back to her menu.

Which I was having none of. I pushed her menu down again. "You gotta tell me."

She slapped her menu down on the table and glared at me. "They'll be 'I murdered Ransom, and I'm not sorry.'"

My smile grew. Who knew getting on someone's nerves could be such a thrill? "You may have to write those down."

"Why?"

"Because if I'm dead too, I can't tell anyone you said them."

She shot me an exasperated look, so I decided to take mercy on her. "Okay, tell me your favorite last words, and I'll leave you alone."

"Alone, like forever, or . . . ?"

I pretended to think about it. "At least ten minutes."

She sighed. "Beggars can't be choosers. Fine, my favorite words were from Voltaire. On his deathbed, a priest asked him if he wanted to denounce Satan. And Voltaire replied, 'Now is not the time for making new enemies.'"

I laughed. "You are so dark."

"Shut up. You promised me ten minutes."

I paused for a beat, letting her sink into a false sense of

security before leaning over the table slightly. "You wanna know what my final words are gonna be?"

"No," she said simply.

"They're gonna be, 'I'm sorry I lied about leaving Taylor alone for ten minutes.'"

She sat back in her seat and looked at the ceiling. "Was I a serial killer in a past life or something? Is that why I'm being punished?"

I laughed a little too loudly, but I couldn't help it. I'd been wound tight after my short conversation with my mom, but annoying Taylor made me feel so . . . light. Carefree in a way I rarely felt. Maybe it was because she fought back with such well-placed snark. Or maybe because it was fun to have her attention. Whatever it was, I was quickly becoming addicted to it.

Helen reappeared with two waters on a black tray. Instead of putting them on our table, she held them out, not really toward either of us, but rather in the general direction of our table. I took the first, put it in front of Taylor, and then took mine.

"You ready to order?"

"I think so," I answered. "You ready?" I asked Taylor.

"Yeah. Can I get the turkey club?"

"Mayonnaise okay?" Helen asked as she stood there, not writing anything down.

"Yeah, that's fine."

Helen turned in my general direction, which I took to mean it was my turn to order.

"Can I get the hot open-faced turkey with mashed potatoes and corn?"

"That comes with a soup or salad," Helen informed me.

"I'll have a salad. Do you have a raspberry vinaigrette?"

"Sure do. I'll take your menus." She stuck her hand out, and I hurried to pick up our menus and put them in her outstretched fingers. "Be right back with your salad and some bread for the table."

"Thank you," we both replied in unison.

We both watched her walk toward the kitchen and disappear behind a swinging door that another server had to grab so it didn't smack Helen in the face.

Taylor turned to me. "Is there a hidden camera around here somewhere?"

"I'd like to say no, but the way our lives are going, anything is possible."

Taylor took a sip of her water and played with the straw. "Speaking of our lives . . ."

I took a deep breath. I'd almost allowed myself to forget the reason she'd agreed to come with me. "I, uh, I'm not sure where to start."

"Wherever you're comfortable starting. But, and this honestly pains me to say because I *really* want to know, if you don't want to talk about it, I'll understand. It's not really any of my business."

I want it to be your business. The thought popped unbidden into my mind, but I couldn't debate the veracity of it. "My birth mom was . . . not a good mom. Or person, really. She was an addict and couldn't be bothered with me most of the time. Child welfare took me away the first time after my mom had taken me to the hospital for a burn. She'd left the stove on to try to heat up the shithole apartment we were living in, and I'd touched it. I was four." I'd let the words flow quickly, wanting to get them out before I could stumble over how embarrassed they made me.

"Not to sound . . . callous, but I'm surprised you were taken away for that. It seems more like an accident than neglect."

"She let the burn go for almost a week. It got infected, and they almost had to amputate my hand."

"Oh," she said sheepishly. "Sorry."

Shaking my head, I tried to not let my brain remember what it had been like in the hospital. I'd been young, but I could still recall snippets of that day.

"Honestly, they probably wouldn't have taken me away for just that. But I was also borderline malnourished, and I told them she routinely left me alone in the apartment. I didn't understand why they were asking me those questions, so I didn't know to be anything other than honest."

"If you could go back, would you have lied? I mean, if she wasn't treating you well, wasn't it better to be honest and get out of that situation?"

I almost smiled at how naïve Taylor was. And I didn't mean that in a negative way. Part of me was glad she didn't have firsthand knowledge to know that entering foster care came with a whole new set of challenges. It made me want to temper how I described my experiences in the system. "Foster care can be . . . difficult. At least with my mom, I knew what to expect. But I got bounced around a lot, and one family was so different from the next. It was unsettling to say the least." Traumatizing would be more accurate. "But that first time, she actually made a solid attempt to get me back. Cleaned herself up, got a job, things were looking up. A judge let me go home, and things were okay for a while. They just didn't stay that way."

I was momentarily interrupted by Helen dropping silverware rolled in napkins on our table. It was hard to tell if she'd misjudged how high above the table the silverware had been when she'd dropped it or if she just didn't give a fuck. Or the third option: she was blind.

When she left, I continued. "I don't want to get into too much detail. Suffice it to say, I bounced back and forth from my mom to foster care. Things got a little better when my sister, Hudson, was born, but my mom just couldn't handle being responsible for other people. When Blink was two, she went to live with my mom's sister—"

"Wait . . . Blink?"

"Oh, that's my nickname for her. That's a story for another day." *At least that one's funny.*

"Sorry, I shouldn't have interrupted you. Continue."

"So Hudson—Blink—went to my aunt's, and I went back into foster care—for good that time."

"Why didn't your aunt take you too?"

As I picked apart a piece of bread, I thought of how best to answer. Finally, I decided to be honest and hope for the best. "I was a difficult kid. I had . . . *have* . . . ADHD, and I'm dyslexic. I got in trouble at school a lot, and my aunt didn't want the hassle."

"What a bitch," Taylor said, though it was clear she hadn't meant to blurt it out, because her eyes widened comically. "Oh my God, I'm so sorry. I didn't mean to say that out loud."

A smile split across my face. It felt good to have someone sound so outraged on my behalf. "It's an accurate description. She's horrible. I feel bad Hudson had to grow up with her."

"Well, I feel bad you went into foster care again."

"To be honest, I'm not. I had my fair share of rough placements over the years, but when I was taken that last time, I ended up with the Holts."

I watched realization dawn on her, probably as she processed that I'd taken their last name at some point. "While I was staying with my mom, I'd started escaping to an after-school program every day."

She smiled. "Like Safe Haven?"

"Similar in some ways. Though they didn't have a Harry Gillette. They had a Melissa Holt. When I stopped showing up because my caseworker had put me back into foster care, Melissa supposedly moved heaven and earth to find me. She and her husband became foster parents so they could take me in, and the rest is history. I lived with them until I turned eighteen and went away to college."

There was more to that story, but I could only be flayed open so wide. Telling Taylor about Emily would have to wait for another day.

Taylor looked at me intently. Her eyes glistened slightly, and I wondered if it was the light or if she'd been moved by my story in some way. The last thing I wanted was anyone's pity, but the idea of someone having compassion about what I had gone through was unexpectedly moving.

"I'm glad you had them," she said after a moment, her voice sounding a bit raspy.

"Me too."

"Do you see them often?"

"Not as much as I should. They're down in Georgia, and I moved north for school and don't make my way back home too much." As much as I loved them, there was a lot of pain split between us. Staying away was better for all of us, no matter how much I wished it wasn't true.

"How long has it been since you last saw your mom?"

I rubbed a hand over the back of my neck. "I'm honestly

not sure. I'm sure I saw her at some court dates, but I have no memories of it. So as far as I'm concerned, I haven't seen her since the last time I was taken away from her."

"How old were you?"

"Nine."

"*Nine?*" Taylor's eyes nearly bulged out of her head again. "You haven't talked to her since you were nine, and then she called you out of the blue today?"

"She called for a couple birthdays here and there, but I haven't heard from her in, God, since high school. Melissa told me she was trying to get in touch with me, though, so the call wasn't a total surprise."

"Jesus. I'm . . . I don't even know what to say that won't sound like an empty platitude, but I'm so sorry you went through all that."

"It is what it is. It made me who I am, and I like who I am, so there's that," I said, offering her a small smile.

Taylor opened her mouth to speak, but we were interrupted by a young guy—probably early twenties—bringing out our food.

"Turkey club?"

"That's mine," Taylor said.

The guy placed it in front of her and then put my dinner in front of me.

"Can I get you anything else?"

"I don't think—" I started but was interrupted by a yell from the kitchen.

"Damn it, Rudy, what did I tell you about taking over my tables? Trying to steal my tips is what you're doing. I'm onto you. What, do you think I'm blind?"

The guy—Rudy—closed his eyes and took a deep breath.

"No, Grandma, I don't think you're blind," he said without turning around. "I know it," he added under his breath. When he opened his eyes again, he looked between Taylor and me. "Sorry. I have to take her food out or else her customers will be wearing it. You all good here?"

Taylor opened her mouth, and a giggle escaped. She cleared her throat and said, "Yeah, we're good."

"Great."

"Rudy!"

"Give me strength. Coming, Grandma." And then he turned on his heel and hurried toward the kitchen.

Taylor and I looked at each other for a second before dissolving in laughter.

"I swear, I'm coming here every week," she said.

"I told you you'd love it. Never doubt my taste in diners. And you better not come without me."

"Wouldn't dream of it," she replied, her tone more serious than it had been.

I gave her another small smile. "Good."

We fell into companionable silence as we started eating our meals. But after we'd taken a couple of bites, she spoke again.

"Ransom?"

I looked up at her and waited for her to continue.

"I like who you are too."

As we sat in the Greasy Spoon with a blind grandmother named Helen reaming out her grandson Rudy amid the aging I and heart-clogging portions, Taylor and I had a moment. And it was utterly perfect in its imperfection.

"I'm glad to hear it."

Chapter Thirteen

RANSOM

"What kind of tuxes do you think would be best?"

The question came from Brody, who looked deep in thought as he held his beer between both hands and rolled it back and forth slowly. Drew and I exchanged glances across the pool table. We were used to Brody saying random shit, but this question had come out of the blue even for him.

I raised an eyebrow. "Are you . . . like . . . taking someone to prom? Did I miss something?"

Brody jolted out of whatever trance he'd been in and jerked his head back. "Gross, man. I'm in my mid-twenties. I'm not taking someone to a high school dance."

"Well, what the fuck are we talking about, then?" Drew asked.

"The wedding," Brody replied as if the question were a stupid one. "*Your* wedding . . . to my sister."

Drew and Sophia never really talked about being engaged, so I almost forgot about it.

"I don't know what tux would be best," Drew said. "We

just started talking about dates. I think Sophia has a few places she wants to check out, but beyond that, we haven't given it a whole lot of thought. We've got time."

Drew appeared completely relaxed about the planning, while Brody seemed flustered.

"That's what you think," he said as he ran an anxious hand through his hair. "One second you're buying a ring and proposing, but before you know it, you're promising to spend your entire life with one woman in front of everyone you love."

I wasn't sure what exactly this was about, but I had a feeling it didn't have much to do with Drew and Sophia's engagement.

Drew laughed and shook his head before refilling his glass from the pitcher that was sitting on a nearby high top. "And you're an expert on this because you let your mom plan a fake wedding for you and someone you barely knew?"

Brody smirked. "Yes. And you don't know the stress involved in having your parents think you're married when you're not, and then planning a wedding to the person they think you married, all so they don't have to tell your extended family you eloped, which you didn't even do."

Drew stared blankly at him. "Yeah, I'm thinking I'm not gonna take your advice on this one." Then he turned back to the pool table, lined up his shot, and missed the cue ball entirely. "That's your fault," Drew joked, pointing his stick at Brody. "Now you have me distracted, like I should be doing something more than just looking at pictures of places Sophia finds and saying whether I like them or not. You think I should start a wedding board on Pinterest?"

I couldn't tell whether he was serious, but either way, his comment had me laughing. "Make sure you don't pin any black tuxes. Dark colors make Brody look paler than he already is."

"Asshole," Brody said with a smirk. "But yeah, a light gray would be good. I mean, if you want."

Drew went up to the bar a few minutes later to get our pitcher refilled, and I couldn't help but ask. "What's with all the wedding questions?"

Brody shrugged but didn't say anything.

"This isn't about *Drew's* wedding, is it?" I'd had a hunch something was up, but I couldn't put my finger on it until I remembered Aamee was coming home this weekend.

"Of course it is. Who else is getting married?"

"You?"

Brody did his best to look surprised, like my comment was completely unwarranted, but he was shit at acting, despite the fact that he was always getting into situations that required him to do so.

"Uh, *not* me," he said.

"You get her a ring yet?"

Brody's sigh told me he'd given up his attempt at pretending this wasn't about him. "No. I'm not sure whether I want to, but I just miss her so damn much." His mouth twisted a bit after he said it, like hearing the words come out surprised even him. "God, that's so embarrassing."

"It's not."

"Uh, it definitely *is* embarrassing. I'm just feeling the distance, I guess. We both are. But that doesn't mean we're ready to get married. We're still so young, and we don't even have real careers. I'm helping run a part of a bar until we're ready to move on to something bigger, and Aamee's working with her mom, who I know she hates even though she won't admit it."

"Why do those things matter? You're talking about love, not opening up a 403B."

"Yeah, but marriage is forever." He looked up at me. "Or it's supposed to be. Sorry, man, but I'm sure you know better than anyone that marriage isn't as easy as everyone says it is."

"Do people say it's easy?" I tried to keep my words lighthearted when my chest felt like it was being stripped of all oxygen. Nothing about that time in my life was easy.

He seemed to ponder my question for longer than necessary before finally saying, "No, I guess they don't. So what's the story with you and your . . . ?"

"Emily."

"Your Emily," Brody said.

I knew his question was an innocent one, mainly to make conversation more than to probe me for details that would help him figure out his own shit. Which was good because nothing in my past could help anyone. All it could do was hurt.

"Not much of a story there," I said, trying my best to sound casual. "We were best friends who got married young."

I hoped that was enough to explain it and was relieved when I saw Drew approach with another pitcher of beer.

"Sorry it took so long. I miss anything?"

Brody held out his glass for Drew to fill. "Ransom was just about to tell us about his ex. They were like fourteen when they got married."

"That's like some Romeo and Juliet shit right there. Weren't they around that age too?" Drew asked.

"We weren't fourteen," I said, even though I figured Drew had enough sense to know that couldn't possibly be true.

"Okay, then how young is young?"

"Nineteen," I answered, already regretting sharing

anything at all about the situation.

"Fourteen? Nineteen? What's the difference?" Brody joked.

"Five years."

Brody laughed as he brought his glass up to his mouth, and I wondered how long I was going to have to figure out how to avoid talking about a subject I tried not to even think about.

"Well, maybe the marriage didn't work out," he said, gripping my shoulder and giving it a squeeze. "But at least both of you didn't end up dying."

"Right," I managed to squeak out. *Not both of us.*

TAYLOR

I exited the Treehouse feeling like I was finally starting to get ahead. Now that I was able to handle more tables on my own, I'd been getting pretty good tips, even on weeknights, which was great because I usually didn't get scheduled for both weekend nights. That, combined with the money I made from Safe Haven, meant hopefully soon I could stop feeling like I was squatting in some abandoned apartment.

Over the last month or so, I'd been slowly outfitting the place, but I still needed some of the more expensive stuff. It might be a while until I could invest in furniture, but at least the steady money meant I could pay off some of my credit card. I'd put more than I would've liked to on there for essentials once my dad had stopped paying for anything other than my classes.

I was just getting ready to get into my car when my phone rang. I smiled when I saw Ransom's name on the screen.

"Hey," I said, pulling my car door open and tossing my bag onto my passenger's seat.

"Hey."

"What's up?"

"Nothing, really."

I waited for a few seconds before I said, "Um, you called *me*."

"Right, yeah, sorry. I was just out with Brody and Drew, but I got tired of beating them in pool, so I left."

"Sounds like a rough night."

"What are you doing right now?" he asked.

"Well, right now I'm sitting in my car in the Treehouse parking lot talking to you."

I heard him laugh softly. "Fair enough. What are you *about* to do?"

"I have big plans that involve returning my mom's three calls from earlier today, at least four episodes of *Schitt's Creek*, and my pajamas. Though not necessarily in that order. I live an exciting life."

"Well, is there any chance you want some company living your exciting life? Because clearly mine's so exciting that I'm begging someone who's just waited tables for most of the day and will most likely fall asleep watching a show I've never seen to entertain me."

It was amazing how well Ransom knew me. There was a chance I wouldn't even make it more than one episode. "First of all, we need to rectify the never seen *Schitt's Creek* problem."

"Is it really a problem?" he asked before I got a chance to bring up my second point.

"Yes. A big one. I've seen all six seasons twice and a few of my favorite episodes more than that. It gets funnier every time."

"It actually sounds like you're the one with the problem."

"Shut up," I said, laughing. "And second of all, it didn't sound like you were 'begging' for me to hang out with you, so I feel like I'm missing out. What does a begging Ransom Holt sound like?"

"I'm not even sure *I* know what he sounds like."

"Well, then I guess it'll just be me and the Roses tonight." I sighed dramatically.

"Am I supposed to know what that means?"

"It means I'll be watching Netflix alone in a pair of teal pajamas with cats all over them unless you beg me to do otherwise." He didn't say anything, and I wondered whether he was rethinking his decision to be my friend. "Also, the cats have these creepy eyes that almost seem like they're following you when you look at—"

"Taylor Peterson, please let me binge-watch some comedy with you because I need a good laugh, and if that doesn't do it, I'm sure your cat outfit will." He said it in one breath, and I tried my hardest not to laugh.

"It's not a cat *outfit*," I said, trying to sound disgruntled but likely failing miserably because I was too excited at the prospect of seeing Ransom. *Damn it.*

Chapter Fourteen

TAYLOR

It felt weird to have Ransom on his way over because even though we hung out as a group and worked together, we hadn't really spent any time with just each other. It made me wonder if this was a good idea, especially considering the fact that I'd been trying to shake Brad for months and had obviously failed. Getting involved with someone else would only complicate things.

But then there was the small problem of how much I liked Ransom. I couldn't shake that either. I'd tried. And it wasn't just that his body looked like it'd been sculpted by Michelangelo—chiseled and large and hard—*God, I need to stop thinking about how gorgeous he is.*

Except he was so much more than his looks. He'd been through hell but still held a sense of optimism that was inspiring.

I looked forward to going to Safe Haven for more than just the chance to make a difference in the kids' lives. It was a chance to see Ransom, a chance to *talk* to Ransom. And he'd opened up to me about his past, which had been more than unexpected—not only what he'd been through but also that he'd been comfortable enough to share it with me.

And now he was on his way over to see me in my cat jammies and watch episodes of a show he had no idea if he'd like. *What did I get myself into?* At least I had a few minutes before he arrived since he'd said he was going to head home to change into comfortable clothes too before he came over.

I was just stepping out of the shower when I heard my phone ring. Expecting it to be Ransom, I ran over to the mattress that was my bed, where I'd tossed my phone before heading into the bathroom.

"Hey," I said, pressing the phone between my shoulder and ear.

"Hey, TayTay." The high-pitched voice was definitely *not* Ransom. I was so thrown off, it took me a second to realize it was my mom. Like when you picked a glass up off the counter expecting it to be full, but it wasn't so your arm flew up into the air. If Ransom was chocolate milk, my mom was sour lemonade—an acquired taste that, well, I hadn't quite acquired yet.

"Oh, hey, Mom," I said, trying my best to sound more excited than I felt. I loved my mom and I knew she loved me, so I felt bad that I had no real desire to speak to her most of the time.

"Are you having trouble with your phone?"

"No."

She was probably asking because I never answered and often silenced her calls, causing it to go to voicemail after only a ring or two.

"Huh." She didn't sound convinced. "Because I can get

you a new one or pay for unlimited data if that's the problem. I completely sympathize with your situation, having to pay for your own food and housing. At your age, that must be practically unbearable."

"I'm getting by." I looked around at my bedroom, which still only consisted of a foam mattress and a side table I'd gotten from IKEA. I'd barely even managed to put the thing together.

"Well," she scoffed, "I don't like the idea of my daughter 'getting by.' You should have money to go out with your friends or treat yourself to a mani-pedi from time to time."

"It's honestly okay," I told her. "I'm adjusting to all of it." I put my mom on speaker so I could look through the piles of folded clothes I'd put on a bedsheet on my floor. It wasn't quite a dresser, but it would do for my T-shirts, workout clothing, and pajamas since my closet was only big enough to fit my work essentials and other pieces that would get wrinkled easily.

"But you're young. You should be going on adventures and enjoying life. Speaking of, did I tell you I'm riding a kangaroo in a few days?"

"You did not tell me that, no." I pulled on some underwear and the teal cat tank top that I was just realizing was more worn than I remembered. Ransom would be here any minute, and I didn't want to disappoint him by wearing something other than my PJs with creepy cats all over them. So I found the matching pants and put those on too.

"Are you sure? Because I feel like I mentioned it."

"Nope. I'd definitely remember you telling me about your impending death."

She laughed like *I* was the one who sounded ridiculous. "Oh, stop. This is a once-in-a-lifetime opportunity."

"Right," I said dryly. "Because you're going to die, so you won't get to do it again."

"Nonsense. Joe told me about this wildlife sanctuary not too far from here. It's very expensive, but it's a whole experience. They let you pet the roos before you ride one."

Did she just say roos? "Aren't kangaroos known for being aggressive?"

"Well, I'm sure they're heavily sedated, honey. There's no way they'd let you on otherwise."

"Sounds like quite a sanctuary they have there." I headed to the bathroom to run a brush through my hair and brush my teeth.

"It is!" she said, missing my sarcasm. "They have their own restaurant. They make their own wine and even have kangaroo on the menu."

"So you ride it . . . ? And then you eat it . . . ?" I wasn't sure why I was even engaging in this conversation, but I found it too ridiculous not to.

"Well, not the same one. That'd be cruel."

"Right." *Because they love being sedated and forced to carry around middle-aged women who have nothing else to do with their husbands' money.*

"Anyway," she said, "that's not why I called. I sent you something that should be there tomorrow, so I just wanted you to be aware. Also I looked on Street View on Google Maps and saw a man relieving himself into a recycling bin. Honestly, Taylor, I'm happy your new community is doing its part to preserve the environment, but I'm more than a little worried about the types of characters you might be encountering. It seems a bit dangerous."

"No offense, but it's hard for me to take any of your safety concerns seriously when you're paying to drink and ride a wild animal. Does Australia have DUIs?"

"I'm not drinking *before* the ride." She let out an exasperated sigh. "But seriously, Tay, I wanted to get you something, and I didn't wanna risk having it left outside your apartment, so you'll have to sign for it. It should be there sometime in the morning. Will you be around?"

"Should be. I'll let you know when it gets here. You really didn't have to send anything," I told her.

"Of course I did. I should've sent you something sooner."

"Well, thank you," I said, and I meant it. I didn't want to be my mom's and Joe's charity case, but I wouldn't turn down a little housewarming gift. "I'll text you tomorrow when it gets here because you'll probably be asleep."

"Okay, love you. Have a good night."

"Love you too. You have a good night too. Or . . . morning? Day? What time is it there?"

I laughed, and she did too. "It doesn't matter. I'll talk to you tomorrow."

That was one of the strangest phone calls I'd had with my mother in recent memory, and our conversations were usually a little odd, mainly on my mom's end. After straightening up the kitchen a bit, I heard a knock.

I waited a few seconds to answer so I didn't look like I'd been sitting by the door anticipating his arrival. I'd expected to hear the buzzer first, but obviously someone must've let him into the building. Why someone would allow a nearly six-and-a-half-foot male they didn't recognize into the apartment made me realize how right my mom had probably been about it being a little dangerous.

Pulling open the door, I straightened the cat tank top as

if it might make me look more presentable. It didn't, since my decision not to put on a bra—which I realized only after opening the door—was really weird. Or maybe it was weirder to put one on. No one wore bras under their pajamas.

"Hey," he said, a lopsided grin on his face that revealed one of his dimples.

In a white fitted T-shirt that hit just below the waistband of his navy workout shorts, he was more dressed down than I usually saw him but no less beautiful to look at. The muscles stretched the fabric on his chest and biceps, and his quads bulged below the hem of his shorts. It made me want to see other bulges that might be in there.

Not many guys looked good in shorts above their knees, but Ransom was definitely in that minority. The short distance between us made him seem even taller, and I was suddenly aware that my head had probably been moving up and down the length of his body as I ogled him.

"You okay?" he asked, reminding me that I hadn't said anything in response to his greeting.

"Hi," I said, but it came out as more of a breathy sound than an actual word with any sort of meaning. "And yes, yes, I'm fine. I just... I don't think my contact's in." I reached up to my eye to make it more believable.

"I didn't know you wore contacts."

"I don't... anymore," I explained. "I used to wear them, but I recently switched to glasses, and now I keep thinking a contact fell out even though I never put them in at all." I hoped he didn't comment on the fact that I wasn't wearing glasses either.

He nodded slowly, but I wasn't sure if it was because what I said actually made sense or if he just wanted to make me stop talking. "So . . . can I come in?"

I moved out of the way and gestured for him to enter. "Of course. Sorry. Yes. Come in."

He almost laughed. "Thanks. I was hoping you weren't rethinking hanging out tonight."

"Nope. The only thing I'm rethinking is my outfit choice."

This time he did laugh. "I'd offer to get puppy ones to coordinate, but I wouldn't look very good in that tank top."

You look good in pretty much everything.

"*Pretty* much?"

"Oh my God, I said that out loud?"

"Yup. But I guess I should return the compliment since it's true. Not many people could look good covered in feline faces, but somehow you make it work."

I didn't know what to say to that, so I was glad when he held up the bag he had in his hand and said, "I brought three flavors of ice cream. Why don't you start up that Shit Show or whatever it's called and point me toward the spoons?"

RANSOM

Even though Taylor didn't have much furniture, she somehow managed to make the place feel comfortable. She'd propped some large pillows at the head of her bed—or mattress—against the wall so we would have a place to relax while we watched the show. She still only had two bar stools and an oversized chair in her living room. And though it looked comfortable as hell, it probably wouldn't fit both of us without things feeling awkward.

And even though we found ourselves physically close by

most standards of intimacy, nothing about lying—or sitting—in a bed with Taylor felt strange. Maybe it was the chocolate marshmallow or the fuzzy gray blanket we had draped over us, but everything about this felt right.

I wondered if she felt the same.

"What do you think of the show?" she asked when the fourth episode ended.

"You couldn't tell by the way I was laughing? The mom's hysterical. She's so self-involved and not even really a good mother in the beginning, but somehow I can't help but like her."

"I know. It's actually amazing," she said, looking over at me. "My mom's been self-centered and materialistic for years, and I don't like her nearly as much."

As soon as the words left her mouth, I knew she wanted to take them back, even without her saying, "I'm so sorry. I didn't mean—"

"It's fine, really," I assured her. "People can have issues with their parents without them being complete fuckups. Even though Melissa was a fantastic mother to me, we definitely had our differences."

I watched her take a large breath, and when she let it out, she seemed slightly relieved. "Really?"

"Yeah, she was pretty overprotective. I always wondered if it was because I'd already been through so much that she wanted to do everything she could to make sure I didn't experience any more trauma."

She hit pause on her iPad, which was between us, causing the room to sound uncomfortably silent. "That's sweet, though."

"It didn't feel sweet when she told me I couldn't go to

my buddy's lake house with him and a few other guys from the team. She told me it was because she was worried about snakes and flesh-eating bacteria." I laughed because the memory was funny now, but at the time I'd wanted to just up and leave the Holts' house and go anyway.

I wasn't used to having rules or restrictions, and even though the rules at the Holts were probably for my own good, it felt suffocating then. "I don't even know what that means, but it freaked me out enough that I didn't put up a fight. I'm thinking she just didn't want me drinking and doing God knows what else with four other seventeen-year-old boys. It actually doesn't seem that strange thinking about it now."

Taylor seemed to be listening to every word, and when I finished, she raised an eyebrow and said, "My mom just paid an obscene amount of money to ride a kangaroo later this week."

We stared at each other for a moment, neither of us even cracking a smile even though it was clear we both wanted to erupt in laughter. The silence lasted a few more seconds before we couldn't hold it in any longer, and we fell into hysterics.

"She's really riding a kangaroo?"

Taylor nodded but didn't say anything because she was still laughing. When she finally calmed down, she said, "So I guess 'strange' is a relative term."

"Someone better take a video of that adventure so I can see it."

"Oh, don't worry. Adeline Daws never misses a photo op. A few weeks ago, she uploaded a TikTok dance. It actually wasn't too bad."

"I'll definitely have to see that eventually too. I'm trying to picture Melissa or Matt doing something like that." It occurred to me that years ago—in a time that seemed like another life entirely—they might have done something carefree and goofy like that, but now I wasn't so sure. They'd always tried to remain positive and enjoy life, but after . . .

"She's in booty shorts with the words *Perfect Peach* written on them."

"Okay, so that's probably a no to my parents doing something like that. I'm pretty sure Matt doesn't own any booty shorts." I was thankful that Taylor's comment had pulled me from my memories, because the present was pretty fuckin' good. I had to stop letting yesterday interfere with today. "Should we keep watching?" I was already reaching for the iPad but waited until she said yes before I pushed play.

Before long, we were back to the show, and as the night faded into early morning, I felt myself dozing off.

"I should probably get going." I went to turn toward the edge of the mattress, but Taylor's arm stopped me. Not physically, because I could've easily escaped if I'd wanted to. The problem was I didn't want to. It didn't matter that Taylor must've fallen asleep at some point and her movement could probably be attributed more to my shifting my weight than her desire for me to stay. But with her arm draped over me and her head on the pillow next to mine, I wasn't going anywhere.

I did my best not to disturb her as I slid down a little so I could lie flatter until she woke up and kicked me the hell out. But for now, she was snuggled against me, her head on my shoulder and her blond hair spilling over my chest. With my free arm, I moved the iPad to the side of the bed and pulled a thin throw blanket over both of us. I'd just stay like this until Taylor woke up or moved off me.

But when an hour passed without her doing either of those things, against my better judgment, I allowed myself to fall sound asleep too.

Chapter Fifteen

TAYLOR

Parts of my body felt so stiff they were almost sore. But I'd slept better than I ever had in this apartment. I must've been in one position all night, so my muscles needed to move, especially my arm and neck. I shifted my weight from my side to my back and reached above my head to stretch.

But before my hands made it more than a few inches, one of them made contact with something hard. I heard teeth crash together and then a pained groan followed by an "Aww, fuck."

It took me a moment to register the voice had come from someone in my bed, and I jolted before realizing it was Ransom.

"If you're mad I'm still here, you could've just told me. You didn't have to punch me in the face."

"Sorry. I'm not mad. I was stretching." I sat up so I could face Ransom, who was holding his nose. "Oh my God, you're bleeding. Hang on."

I jumped up, managing to hop over Ransom without hurting him but not without touching him completely. I did some kind of maneuver that looked like a poor combination of a burpee and an awkward roll like the ones they teach you in elementary school in case your clothes catch on fire.

I didn't land steadily on the ground, but I managed to right myself quickly and head to the bathroom. When I returned with a wet washcloth and some tissues, Ransom was already sitting up, pinching his nose. I was caught in some sort of mental purgatory, unsure of whether I should help clean him up because I was to blame for the bleeding or just hand him the stuff I'd brought and let him do it himself because . . . well, it was someone else's blood. Instead, I just stared for a little too long without doing anything.

"Can I have that?" Ransom reached out to take the washcloth from me so he could wipe his face. Then he took the tissues and pinched his nose before putting them in his nostrils.

I couldn't help but laugh at the sight.

And even though Ransom said, "Do you always laugh at the people you physically assault?" he was laughing too.

"Don't laugh. You'll make it bleed again," I said, but it only made both of us laugh harder. "You gonna tell people you got hit with a door again?" I teased.

"Nope. I'm gonna tell people you punched me in the face."

"I'm not sure who that looks worse for, you or me."

He seemed to consider my comment thoroughly. "Good point. I'll buy you a new washcloth too. And some new sheets," he added, looking at the spots of red that had peppered the gray-and-white-striped fabric.

"Thanks, but I was the one who punched *you*, so it's not really fair to have you buy all that. Four hundred thread-count organic Egyptian cotton sheet sets can be pricey."

"Organic sheets? It's not like you're eating them." Ransom's eyes looked like they were going to pop out of his head, and I tried to keep a straight face.

But eventually, after he rubbed his forehead and asked how much I thought it would be, I told him I was kidding. "Not about them being organic Egyptian cotton, but about you buying me a new set. I'll throw them in the wash. It's not like I'm hosting any social events anytime soon where I'll need to show off my bed."

"Will you be hosting events where you'll need to show off your bed at *some* point?"

I didn't know Ransom well enough to tell whether he was messing with me, so I needed to set him straight. "I don't need money so badly that I need to run a brothel out of my apartment, Ransom!"

"That's good to know," he said dryly, "because I definitely would've appreciated a heads-up on that before I fell asleep here."

The door buzzer sounded, and as I headed over toward the speaker, I said, "Must be one of the clients."

Ransom shivered dramatically before heading into the bathroom.

"Who is it?" I asked into the intercom.

"Delivery for Taylor Peterson."

I buzzed them in and then ran to my room to put a bra on. It was bad enough I was in these ridiculous pajamas. I couldn't answer the door with my nipples popping through my shirt.

But apparently I *could* have my boobs out in front of Ransom, because right as I was pulling off my shirt to put on my bra, he exited the bathroom.

"I guess I'm gonna get go— Oh, God. Sorry. I didn't realize."

I pulled on my bra as quickly as I could because Ransom was still standing there looking at me. He wasn't staring at them, exactly. It was more of a deer-caught-in-boob-headlights look. He seemed to be putting a lot of effort into focusing on my eyes, which only made the situation more awkward.

When I heard a knock at the door, I grabbed my shirt. "Can you get that? I'll be out in a sec."

Ransom exited my room robotically without saying anything and closed the door behind him.

I pulled my shirt on, and when I entered the living room, I found two delivery men in my apartment. They'd already put several large boxes on the floor and were standing with a clipboard.

"We just need you to sign this, and then we'll bring the rest up."

"The rest?" I asked, taking the pen from him.

"Yeah, there's a four-piece bedroom set, a couch, and a chair. Doesn't exactly fit in these boxes."

"Oh my God."

He looked quizzically at me. "Didn't you order this stuff?"

"No, actually . . ." I muttered slowly. "I didn't order any of it."

"I'm confused."

"Me too," Ransom chimed in.

"So are we getting the rest of the stuff or no?" the delivery guy asked me.

"Yes, sorry. You can get the rest. Thank you."

Once both of the guys had left the apartment, Ransom said, "I'm still confused."

"They're gifts from my mom," I said with a sigh. I knew I sounded unappreciative, but I was more embarrassed than anything else. "I'd told my mom I didn't want her help—or more specifically, Joe's help—but in typical Adeline style, she couldn't resist."

Ransom gave me a tight-lipped smile that made me think he was trying to hold back a laugh. "Sounds like a real asshole."

"Shut up," I said, smiling now too. I punched him in the arm, and he moved backward and began rubbing his arm and wincing.

"Well, I was gonna offer to put some of this together for you, but since you've now hit me twice this morning, I'm worried for my safety if I stay any longer."

"You were gonna put it together for me?" I couldn't hide my excitement because fuck if I wanted to try to assemble all this. I didn't even know if I *could* assemble all this.

"I was thinking about it."

The delivery guys came in and set the couch down in the middle of the living room.

"Then I was thinking about making you breakfast," I told him with a smile.

RANSOM

Apparently Taylor had been kidding about making breakfast.

She'd realized quickly that the only things she had to offer that could've counted as a breakfast food were two pieces of bread and some peanut butter, so she ran out to grab something to bring back for us. But that was over an hour ago.

This neighborhood wasn't known for its cafés, but it had a few good diners, which I figured she'd hit up for some breakfast sandwiches.

If she didn't make it home in the next half hour, I'd send out a search party for her. Or maybe I'd just call her. Whichever.

It hadn't taken me long to put together the dresser and nightstand, but the bed was another beast entirely. Lining up the holes in the rails that attached the headboard to the footboard so that I could drill the screws in while still holding everything at the right angle had proved virtually impossible for one person to accomplish. I decided to hold off until Taylor got home so she could help and went to the kitchen to make another cup of coffee while I waited.

A few minutes later, Taylor rushed into the apartment, the bags in her hands swinging around her like a tornado as she tried to shut the door.

"Did you go to France to get French toast? I was about to put your face on a milk carton."

She hefted the bags onto the counter. "When was the last time you saw milk in a carton?"

It was a good point. "When was the last time you saw milk in your fridge?"

She smiled widely and removed a half gallon of organic grass-fed whole milk. "Well, there'll be some now. Along with eggs, thick-cut bacon, fresh multigrain bread, and freshly squeezed orange juice." She'd already begun taking all the items out of the bags and getting out some pots and pans.

"Oh, okay, so you went to a farm to get these. *That's* why it took so long."

"I didn't go to a farm, smartass. I just made a few stops and had to drive around a little to get what I was looking for."

"You didn't have to do all that."

"I promised you I'd make you breakfast." She smiled

widely, her white teeth framed delicately by her pink lips.

"Well, thanks," I said. "I'm not used to people going to so much trouble for me." For some reason, it was hard for me to make eye contact with her when I said it, like I'd just revealed some deep dark secret and was scared to let my vulnerability show. Which was strange considering I'd told her so much about my past.

"I feel like putting together a bunch of furniture is way more trouble than picking up some groceries, but you're welcome."

"How about I help you make breakfast, and then you help me finish putting your bed together? Your mom sent sheets too, by the way."

"She's so extra," she said. "But totally appreciated. I called her while I was out before it got too late there, but I said I'd text her a picture when it's all put together."

Taylor got out two mixing bowls, one for an omelet she wanted to make and the other for French toast. Once all the ingredients and utensils were out, we went to work quickly, both of us moving in beside the other toward our common goal. She cooked some spinach and onions before adding the egg mixture, and I crisped up the bacon and then used the same pan to grill the French toast so the bacon flavored the slices of bread too.

When everything was finished, we put all of it on plates and set everything down on the counter, along with some fresh orange juice. We'd done such a good job, it almost looked too good to eat.

"We make a pretty good team," I said, smoothing my napkin over my lap.

She put the piece of French toast on her fork inside

her mouth and chewed slowly, her eyes closing in a way that looked too sexy for eating breakfast. "We do. So good."

"So are the eggs."

"I'm glad you like them. I'm a little worried that my bed-building skills won't quite come close to my cooking, though."

I smiled as I put another forkful of food into my mouth and washed it down with some juice. "You'll be fine. You don't have to chop down any trees to build the wood. You just have to hold the footboard in place while I drill the rails in."

"I think I can handle that much."

We finished eating, mostly in silence except for the occasional scraping of forks, and then headed into Taylor's bedroom. I positioned the footboard so that it lined up with the holes in the rails and asked her to hold it in place. I got one side screwed in, and a few minutes later, the bed frame was together. We maneuvered it against the wall, and after putting the new box spring and mattress on the frame, we opened the sheets and blankets Taylor's mom had sent.

"Uh-oh, these aren't organic," I said. "Are you sure they won't make you break out in a rash or something? Maybe you should send them back."

"Shut up," she said, clearly teasing me as I held the sheet away from me like it was some sort of venomous snake I wanted to keep at a distance. "Give me that." Then she snatched it from me with a smile. "Help me make my new bed."

"Um, I did help you make your new bed," I pointed out but was already pulling the fitted sheet over one corner of the mattress. "I actually made most of it."

We shook out the top sheet and the comforter in an act that felt oddly domestic and then positioned the decorative pillows on the bed. When we were finished, we both collapsed onto the mattress and stared up at the popcorn ceiling.

"This mattress is so much more comfortable," Taylor said.

"The comforter too. It's so thick and smooth. Feel it on your skin." I turned to face her so my cheek was against the fabric, and when she turned her head to face me, she couldn't hide her smile. "Can we forget I said that?"

"Not a chance. Tell me again how thick and smooth it feels on your face."

"It was a really poor choice of words."

"I think it was the perfect choice of words." She laughed quietly before turning the rest of her body toward me. Both of us were fully on our sides now, our faces only inches apart.

I wondered if she felt like I did—hyperaware of how close we were but still far away because I couldn't bring myself to close the distance completely . . . even though I was desperate to.

She breathed so slowly, so carefully, it seemed like she was worried any disruption to the moment might ruin it completely.

But with her eyes locked on mine, I doubted anything could ruin this. Everything about this felt right, natural, like we were meant to share this space together, and I was sure Taylor could feel it too. Or maybe I just hoped she did.

I'd never been shy about taking a chance with girls I was into, but this thing with Taylor felt different, like there was a flashing neon sign above her beautiful face with warnings like *Keep Out* and *Beware*. But a small spark of hope flickered deep inside me that maybe the warnings were more of a *Proceed with Caution* than a *No Trespassing*.

Or maybe all this shit was just in my mind. Maybe for once being rejected by a girl scared the hell out of me because this girl wasn't just *any* girl. I felt safe with her. I felt wanted, even if I wasn't sure she wanted me the way I hoped she did. *If I fuck this up now, I might fuck it up forever.* Taylor felt like glass in a storm that could shatter with a strong wind sometimes.

But then other times—times like right now—it felt like every single thing from our breathing to our heartbeats was in sync, and if I didn't take this opportunity, I might never get another one.

And *choosing* not to kiss Taylor would be worse than not kissing her any fucking day of the week. Even if she shoved me off the bed I'd just built, which was a distinct possibility.

So I made a promise to myself that I'd stop overthinking every little thing in my life, especially Taylor, and I'd just kiss the hell out of her.

Well, maybe not at first. I drifted my lips toward hers until they couldn't get any closer without touching. And that was where I hovered for a moment. Not because I was scared to go any further, but because I wanted to savor this moment before both our eyes closed and our lips pressed together in a way I'd imagined so many times in the privacy of my own bed.

When our lips finally touched, all of it felt so much softer, tasted so much sweeter, than I'd fantasized about. Every sensation felt like it journeyed through my entire body before making its way to my core and finally settling in my pants.

I couldn't remember the last time I'd been this turned on from just kissing a girl, but fuck if this wasn't better than what I'd been waiting for.

We went slow at first, but a gentle kiss slipped into something so much deeper, hungrier, and soon both of us had more than just our mouths on each other. Our hands entered into the action, sliding under shirts and down the back of pants.

I groaned when Taylor's nails grabbed a hold of my ass, and I instinctually pressed my hips toward her in response. Even the slight friction over my shorts was dangerous.

"God," I said in between nibbles on her neck, "this is . . ."

"I can't do this," she blurted out as if her brain and her hands belonged to two different people.

What the . . .

"We don't have to do anything you're not comfortable with. I'm sorry, I didn't mean to . . . I thought you were into it."

I wasn't even aware of when we'd gotten up, but both of us were on different sides of the bed now, staring at each other.

"I am. I mean, I was," she corrected herself, like the semantics affected the meaning.

"Did I do something wrong?" God, I wished I wasn't still hard while I was having this conversation. "We can take things slow. I just, I really like you, Taylor, and now I feel like I fucked everything up." The fact that my initial fear might've come true wasn't lost on me.

"It's okay," she told me, but we both knew it wasn't. "I think it's probably best if you just go."

"Are you sure? We can talk about it if you—"

"Please," she said, and her eyes held a sadness that almost looked regretful. Whether the regret came from asking me to leave or making out with me, I might never know.

And I knew then I'd been wrong. Choosing not to kiss Taylor would've been the better option.

Chapter Sixteen

TAYLOR

"No, wait, I think a few of the girls missed the first part," Aamee said. "Tell it again."

"Please don't," Sophia pleaded, already plopping her chin into her hand. Her other hand held prosecco that she was drinking out of a gigantic glass with the words *Look Like a Beauty, Drink Like a Beast* written on it.

When I'd been invited to Sophia's surprise bachelorette party being thrown by her sorority sisters, I wasn't sure how I'd fit in. I knew the dinner would be fine, but the girls had rented a suite at a local hotel to continue the party, and I figured they'd all be having fun talking about the past few years at Lazarus while I had to make myself look busy on my phone so I didn't feel awkward.

But the opposite was true. They'd practically surrounded me, begging to hear embarrassing childhood stories about her. I was like some sort of celebrity unicorn.

"It was our teacher's son who she asked to dance. He was tall for a fourth grader." I looked over at Sophia and tried not to laugh. "I'll give you that. But there was no way Mrs. Kersey was gonna let her little boy put his arms around a thirteen-year-old girl who was already a B cup. Besides, he said no anyway."

Aamee, Gina, Macy, and a few of the other girls laughed even more hysterically the second time I told it, probably because I hadn't mentioned he'd declined her invitation the first time.

"I thought he was from another school," Sophia said. "What was he even doing at that dance?"

"How would I know? It's not like I have some sort of insight into Baby Boy Kersey's Friday night plans almost a decade ago."

Aamee'd been standing to the side, leaning on the arm of the leather couch with her glass of champagne. I hadn't even noticed her on her phone, but suddenly she was thrusting it in our faces.

"Well, Baby Boy Kersey is a snack now," she said, drawing out the last two words in a way that was a tad cringe.

Most of us tried to catch a glimpse of him, but Aamee spun the phone around before we even had a chance to properly gauge the caliber of his looks.

"Bryce Kersey, it's a good thing I'm not thirsty, because I might have to—"

"How did you even find him that fast?" Sophia asked.

Aamee scoffed as if the question were ridiculous. "Googled Mrs. Kersey and Brighton Elementary. I know the name of the school because Brody went there too obviously." She was speaking so quickly, I could barely keep up. "I got her first name—Bridget," she said with a smile and something that resembled a slight bow. "So then I checked Insta for a Bridget

Kersey, but they were obviously all way too young to be her. That's when I remembered Boomers don't have Instas, so I hopped on my Fakebook account and typed in her full name and the town you guys grew up in."

"Did you say your 'Fakebook' account?" Gina asked.

"Yeah. It's the Facebook profile I made for moments just like this. I use it to do stalking mostly, and on the rare occasion to enter a contest. You're making me lose focus. Anyway, I found her easily, clicked on her friends list, but teachers are super private. So I had to go to one of her profile photos because they're public and find one that had a lot of comments."

All our mouths were open as we listened, even though none of what she said actually had any importance.

"So I found someone with the last name Kersey who'd commented, went to *his* profile, and then searched his friends list for people with that last name. I found a few and scrolled through their pictures until I found a family picture that included Bridget, her husband, and their son and daughter. Someone had commented what a beautiful picture it was of them and how grown up Bryce and Ava looked. From there I went to Snap and Insta and found Baby Bryce in like six seconds. Simple."

"You are, like, way beyond creepy," I told her. "But as a Criminal Justice major, I'm actually quite impressed with your abilities."

"Thank you," Aamee said, sounding genuinely surprised at my compliment before going back to the phone. "Oh my God, he's a baseball player!"

"In little league?" Sophia asked. "Is he even legal yet?"

"Yes, he's legal. He has some graduation pictures up from last year."

"He could still be seventeen."

"Not when his birthday was in June. He went with some of his friends to Mexico. Currently, he's playing baseball for Willistown University, which, as you all know, is like twenty minutes away and a D1 school, so if any of you ladies are interested, you might wanna check out a game this spring, because Bryce will be starting. As a *freshman*. Molly, how about you? You're a sophomore, and if I recall correctly, the only men you had any contact with last year were the ones in tweed blazers who assigned your grades."

Before Molly had a chance to answer, Sophia said, "Can we talk about guys who *aren't* related to my old teachers and barely old enough to drive?"

"Sure. It's *your* party. Or one of them anyway," I said. "I obviously plan to throw one for you too with everyone back home and your family." I'd assumed I'd be Sophia's maid of honor, though she hadn't technically asked me. She had no sisters, and I was her closest and oldest friend.

Aamee smiled widely, seeming way too excited to say, "I'll be at that one too."

"Can't wait," I said, my tone high with sarcasm. "But seriously, let's talk about that fiancé of yours since this is technically a celebration of the two of you."

"Is it though?" Gina asked. "It's more of a celebration of her single life. Or the end of it, I guess. But since she doesn't even know when she's getting married, it's mainly just a reason for all of us to hang out and get drunk."

Macy raised an eyebrow. "We need a reason?" She was coming back from the small kitchen with a tray of JELL-O shots. Two for each of us it turned out.

Once we'd all slurped down the strawberry jiggly

deliciousness, Macy's eyes widened with excitement. "So tell us what he's like in bed. Did the accident affect his ability to get an erection, or like do you have to be super careful when you're on top?"

I looked to Sophia, knowing she was probably heating up from the inside out. I bit my bottom lip to keep from laughing. Her face was getting close to the color of the shots we'd just had.

"His . . . *erections*"—she said like the word caused her physical discomfort when it left her mouth—"are fine. No complaints in that department."

"That's good," Aamee said, refilling her glass before moving to some of the other girls to top them off. "People don't realize how important an active sex life is in a marriage."

"Thank you, Doctor," Sophia said.

"Seriously. I know I don't know much from my own experience. Well, sexually speaking I do, because Brody—"

"Ew, stop!"

"Anyway, my parents have been married for like"—she looked to the ceiling like she was trying to come up with an answer to a calculus problem—"I don't know, a million years or something. They always gave me two pieces of marital advice. My mom always said marry a man who ruins your lipstick, not your mascara."

"Oooh, I like that one," I said. "What was your dad's?"

"Never waste a piece of cake or a hard-on."

The room filled with sounds of horrified disgust, along with a few fits of laughter.

"It's not as bad as it sounds," Aamee said. "You have to know my dad. It's more like his vulgar way of saying that if you love the person and they turn you on, don't let moments slip away." At our silence, she added, "Okay, maybe it is as bad as it sounds. But it's sweet if it didn't come from my dad."

"It is kinda sweet," I admitted. "To have that much passion after so many years." I wondered if one day I would have that. I saw how happy Sophia was with Drew, and as far as I could tell, Mr. and Mrs. Mason seemed pretty happy. Not that I knew for sure. But I was definitely familiar with dysfunctional relationships. My own parents had divorced when I was young, and though my mom loved the *life* she was living, I wasn't sure she felt the same about the man giving it to her.

It didn't make her a bad person. Mainly because I wasn't sure she knew what it felt like to really love someone. Or to *be* loved, for that matter. And I couldn't help but wonder if I was destined to follow in her footsteps.

I'd been lost in my own thoughts as the girls shared advice their moms had given them, everything from *don't sweat the small stuff because it's all small stuff* to more sentimental advice for the future like *everything your child says is important.*

"What about you, Tay?" Sophia asked. "What advice do you think your mom would give me before I marry Drew?"

I thought back to the random shit my mom had told me over the years, but I couldn't really remember her giving me much actual advice when it came to relationships. At least she knew her wheelhouse.

"The only thing I remember her ever saying about marriage was *never marry a man you wouldn't divorce.*"

All of us burst out laughing, myself included.

"Only your mom," Sophia said, shaking her head. "I guess it makes sense, though."

"It makes zero sense," I told her.

"It does. Like there are so many combative relationships

out there between exes, and that affects the kids. But if you think about how your future husband would act during a situation like that, it can say a lot about who they are as a person."

"Huh." I hadn't thought about it like that because I'd never actually given much thought to it to begin with.

"So would you divorce Drew?" Aamee asked.

"Yeah," Sophia said. "I think I would. I mean, I hope we don't, but Drew's a good guy. What about Brody?"

"I'd divorce his ass no problem." She took a sip of her drink as everyone stared at her. "In the context we're discussing, of course."

I thought about Brad and what a piece of shit he was. We hadn't even been together long, and our "breakup" had resulted in something that caused me to move. Definitely not someone I'd want to marry, let alone divorce.

But then my mind drifted to Ransom—the guy who loved working with kids, offered to help someone he barely knew move apartments and then put their furniture together. The guy who worked for everything he'd gotten in life and was appreciative of the little that was given to him. He and Brad weren't the same person. Not even a little bit. How did I *not* take a chance on a guy like that?

But before I could really formulate any solid thoughts about the situation, Aamee turned up the music that had been playing softly on the TV in the background, drowning out any more images of Ransom or us together. And maybe that was for the best right now.

"Okay, now enough serious talk," Aamee said. "Let's have some fun!"

RANSOM

I rarely had a gig booked with another guy, but tonight I'd be teaming up with Darius. He'd been stripping for longer than I had and had taught me the entire *Magic Mike* routine one afternoon with the promise that it would make me some extra cash, especially with the thirty-something crowd.

He was about that age himself and, to my knowledge, had no plans of settling down anytime soon. Never hiding the fact that he was a stripper pretty much ensured he only hooked up with women who wanted something casual too. It was actually a genius idea. Too bad I didn't have the same goal.

"So what'da you know about this crew?" Darius asked. He fixed his vest in the elevator mirror and rubbed a hand over his short beard.

"Not any more than you do."

"Well," he said with a slap to my shoulder, "hopefully it's a bunch of drunk college girls and not a group of middle-aged moms, right? That eye all healed up?" He lowered his sunglasses so he could inspect my face.

"Funny. And having the party be college girls doesn't exactly guarantee our safety, you know."

"It's not *my* safety I'm worried about. Been doin' this for a decade and haven't gotten a scratch."

The elevator stopped at the eighth floor, and an elderly couple boarded.

"Good evening, gentlemen," the man said, and his wife smiled sweetly at us.

"Don't you both look handsome," she said, referring to our suits.

"Thank you," we both said back with a nod like we were Will Smith and Tommy Lee Jones getting ready to fight some aliens.

It occurred to me that I should've pointed out that we were going up, not down, but it was too late for them to exit, and I felt like an asshole pointing it out now. Maybe they'd meant to go up.

"Were you just at the wedding downstairs?" the woman asked.

"Oh." Feeling guilty about what I had to say next caused my throat to feel clogged, so I cleared my throat before fully answering. "Yes. A friend of ours was the groom."

"Isn't that nice."

Thankfully, the elevator stopped at the eleventh floor, which was where we'd be getting off. "Well, you know what they say," Darius said as we stepped off. "Always a groomsman, never a groom."

"If only that were true," the man grumbled.

The woman swatted her palm at him, and I couldn't help but be impressed with how little he flinched. Then right before the doors closed completely, I heard her say, "Oh, shit. We're going up."

"You just broke up a marriage for something no one even says," I joked.

"I do. I basically live by that saying."

"That doesn't mean it actually *is* a saying."

He ignored me and instead asked, "What's the room number?"

"1144."

"Allow me," he said when we arrived, his body helping to frame the door as he leaned against it. "Def college chicks. I hear the music."

A few seconds later, a tall brunette wearing a gold halter top with sequins answered the door.

"Woohoo! Well, damn," she said, dragging out the second word into two syllables. "Come on in."

I followed Darius into the hotel room until I heard a squeal that I recognized immediately.

"You hired strippers!" The voice had come from my left, almost behind me, but I didn't have to turn around to know who it was.

Sophia. Shit, shit, shit.

"I might have to leave," I whispered to Darius.

"What? Why? You can't leave."

"I know some of these girls."

"Nice. They're hot!" He'd already begun taking his jacket off and tossing it to the couch.

I felt like my stomach was going to come out through my mouth. I hated that some of my friends might find out I was a stripper, especially like this. I wondered if Aamee was here because I knew she was home and said she'd had some sorority thing to go to tonight.

"Stop being weird, dude. These girls want it."

With a sigh, I began dancing too, trying my best to imagine I wasn't where I was and doing what I was doing in front of who I was doing it in front of.

And there's Aamee.

She looked absolutely thrilled after locking eyes with me for a moment, and then she immediately began texting. My guess was that it was Brody she was contacting. It was like one of those nightmares where you were in a crowded room and you recognized some of the people in it, and then you looked down and you were completely naked.

Though I wasn't *completely* naked... yet. I tried my best not to look at Sophia or Aamee as I removed my white shirt, leaving just the bow tie around my neck and my tear-away pants. Darius was already grinding on the girl who'd opened the door for us, which I hoped didn't mean I'd have to give Sophia a lap dance because that shit definitely wasn't happening. I couldn't think of anything worse.

Until my eyes locked with Taylor's. I had no idea when she'd sat down at the kitchen counter. I hadn't noticed her until now, but now that I had, I couldn't stop looking at her.

"Don't let *my* presence stop you."

Her comment made me realize I'd completely stopped moving. Unfortunately, I wasn't participating in some sort of freeze dance game. Apparently the game was more like some sort of fucked-up version of Jumanji I couldn't figure out how to escape.

"No. Seriously. Don't stop. I'm enjoying the show." Her legs were crossed, and she gestured toward me with her hand. "Please. Continue."

Was she serious? The other day she'd pulled away during a kiss that would be burned in my memory like it'd been done with a flamethrower. And now she was leaning on the counter of a hotel room during what looked like Sophia's bachelorette party, telling me to continue stripping like it didn't fucking bother her?

Her raised eyebrows told me that, yes, that was exactly what she was saying.

The next ten minutes or so were a blur, like I'd somehow been a victim of PTSD that was causing temporary amnesia. I had vague memories of some of the girls screaming, and of Darius giving Sophia a lap dance, but I didn't dare look at Taylor again because nothing good could come from her knowing this was my job.

Or *one* of them.

How did someone reconcile a person who helped kids out and stripped on the side? I knew it made no sense, and no matter how I explained it, it wouldn't make any sense to her either. Not to mention I'd kept it from her. Lied to her, technically.

So I gathered my clothes, thinking I'd put them on in the hallway because this hotel suite was an escape room I needed to get the hell out of. Against his pleading, I told Darius I was leaving and went toward the door as quickly as possible.

I barely made it to the elevator when I heard Taylor call my name.

I'd at least gotten my pants on, though they weren't completely snapped on the side yet. My shirt was draped over my shoulder, and my back was still turned toward her as I pushed the button for the elevator.

Thankfully, the doors opened soon, and I climbed on as soon as the occupants exited.

"Wait. Ransom!" she called. "You're just gonna leave like that?"

She hadn't gotten on the elevator, but was waiting in the hall, staring at me as the doors began to close.

I maintained eye contact with her as long as I could until both of us looked too sad for me to continue. And as I let my head drop, the doors began to close. *Don't be a pussy.* Against my instincts, I brought my hand out to catch the door. Taylor was right. I couldn't just leave like this.

"I'm a stripper," I forced out like a fucking moron.

"Yeah, I pretty much caught on to that part." She stepped closer to me but didn't enter the elevator, which I was thankful for because the idea of being in a confined space with her right now seemed like more of a risk than I was willing to take. "Why?"

The question sounded intimate somehow, quiet in a way I hadn't expected.

"I need the money," I said with a small shrug.

"Again, I figured as much. But why didn't you tell me?"

"I don't know. It's not like I won a Nobel Peace Prize or something. Taking your clothes off for a couple bucks isn't exactly something you brag about to everyone."

She was quiet for a moment, a few shallow breaths filling her lungs before she stepped onto the elevator with me. The proximity felt too close in a way that somehow made me both uncomfortable and calm as the doors slid closed and she pushed a button.

"No," she said. "Why didn't you tell *me*?"

Her voice was low, and I wanted to take the sadness out of it. Sighing heavily, I tried to think of the best way to explain why I hadn't told her, but the truth was I had no idea. I'd convinced myself early on that people wouldn't accept it—that *Taylor* wouldn't accept it. And if she didn't accept that part of me, she'd never be able to accept more of me, let alone all.

But none of that was true. I'd revealed so much more to her. Parts of my childhood even people who knew me for years didn't know. She'd accepted all that with zero judgment, so why would she judge something so insignificant as this?

"I honestly have no idea," I conceded. And because I couldn't help breaking the tension with a joke, even if it was a poor one, I said, "Maybe I was worried you'd ask me to take my clothes off all the time or something. I don't know." I waved my hand at her like the thought was ridiculous.

Surprisingly, her lips curled up into the beginning of a smile. I wished I could savor that moment forever—that exact instant when we could both feel the air in the room thin enough for each of us to breathe comfortably again.

"Well, it certainly wouldn't make sense for me to pay you to keep them *on*."

I wanted to ask if she liked what she saw and what happened the other night. I didn't, though. I couldn't. So I stayed silent, hoping she would speak before I had to. I was scared to say the wrong thing as much as I was scared not to say anything.

And as the atmosphere around us seemed to heat up, I had to resist the urge to tell her everything I wanted to say: that I was sorry I didn't tell her the truth, sorry I'd *lied* to her all this time about something that in hindsight didn't matter. I had to resist the urge to tell her how beautiful she looked tonight, the soft curls of her blond hair falling perfectly around her face. And I wanted to tell her how I missed the feel of her skin—that it was all I could think about since I'd touched her.

But still I let the silence stand between us until I knew she could feel it too.

Matt once told me to listen more than I spoke because sometimes saying too much meant you really said nothing at all. Some moments, he said, were meant to exist in the in-between.

Besides, if you let the silence continue long enough, usually the other person felt the need to fill it because you knew something they didn't. There was a reason there was music between verses or a timeout after the two-minute warning when your team was down by four.

The in-betweens were where the real action happened. And sometimes all you needed to do was hold on and wait for it.

Or not, I thought as the elevator descended quietly. I stepped off when the doors opened to the lobby, giving Taylor a slight nod goodbye.

And as I walked off, I heard it.

"Don't go."

"I can't go back up there," I told her before turning around to meet her gaze.

"It's your job. I'll leave."

"I'm not gonna show back up in front of Sophia and Aamee. It was bad enough they saw me earlier."

Rubbing her eyes, she seemed to be thinking hard about what to say next. Like she was weighing her words before they left her mouth.

"This is all so complicated," she said, looking at me again.

"Darius will still give me my half if that's what you're worried about."

"That's not . . . what I'm worried about. I mean, I'm glad you'll get paid. That's not what I meant. I just meant . . . God, I don't know *what* I meant."

"Why don't you take a minute to think about it?"

"I have. I've taken like a million minutes, and I can't make sense of any of it."

"Make sense of what?" I tried to think about what she could be talking about because we'd already discussed the whole stripper thing.

"The other night. My feelings for you. I can't . . . There's a reason I couldn't . . ."

Watching her stumble over her words made me want to close the small space between us and wrap her up in a hug, but I knew better than to touch her without knowing how she'd feel about it.

"It's okay."

"It's not." She shook her head. "Nothing about me is okay right now. And I can't let my problems become someone else's. I'm sure you think I'm crazy." She almost laughed, but the sadness that seemed to be stuck in her throat prevented it from fully forming.

"I don't think you're crazy," I promised her.

"Really?" She seemed genuinely surprised.

"I'm standing in a hotel lobby wearing nothing but rip-off pants, so I don't really think I have room to judge anyone's sanity."

This time she laughed, and I never thought such a small sound could make me so fucking happy.

"You don't need to explain yourself to me. Now or ever. Not if you don't want to."

Her eyes closed, and I could sense the relief in them somehow. Like she'd been holding this weight since the night we'd kissed, and I'd finally allowed her to put it down.

"Thank you," she said quietly. "For not getting pissed. Some guys would've . . . Well, I don't wanna think about what some guys would've done."

"Then don't," I told her. We stared at each other for a few more moments before I spoke again. "I'm gonna go. You go back to Sophia's party and enjoy Darius and a few more drinks."

I wasn't sure what made me tell her to "enjoy" Darius, and it was clear she wasn't sure either. But both of us knew better than to bring it up. We weren't anything.

Or really we just weren't anything together.

Chapter Seventeen

TAYLOR

I closed my eyes as I sat in the empty coffee shop near my apartment and tried to visualize myself doing something—*anything*—fun.

Well, maybe that wasn't fair. Forensic psychology was probably a lot of fun for the students who were meeting with the professor in the classroom. But it definitely lost some of its luster online. Without the ability to discuss and debate case studies in real time, the topic simply wasn't as fascinating as I'd thought it would be when I signed up for it.

Oh well. There was nothing to do but get through it at this point. And it wasn't like I wasn't learning anything. I just wasn't learning it as dynamically as I wished I were.

I sighed, reprimanding myself mentally for being negative. I'd woken up in a funk that I hadn't been able to shake all day. I'd thought getting out of my apartment and doing some of my work at the coffee shop would be a nice change of pace, but instead, I found myself being distracted by every noise around me. And then I got irritated that the place was so distracting, even though it was my fault for having the attention span of a gnat.

Taking a deep breath, I refocused on my laptop. I had to be at Safe Haven in two hours, and I was damn well going to be productive for at least half of that time. I scrolled through the online textbook, taking notes on the notebook beside me as I went. The text was interactive and allowed for note taking on the screen, but I always remembered things better when I wrote them down.

I'd made it at least five minutes before my phone dinged with a text alert. *Goddammit!* Clearly the universe was against me.

"I'm not going to look at it. Just gonna keep on working," I muttered to myself like I was one of the psychopaths I was learning about.

My intentions were good. I *wanted* to ignore it. But then I started to obsess about who it could be, and that made focusing even more impossible.

"Fine, I'll just look who it's from," I whispered to myself as I unlocked my phone so I could view the message. "Then I'll get back to work."

But when I looked down at my screen, I knew there was no way I'd be getting any more work done. It was from another unknown number—probably because I'd blocked the other—but there was no doubt who'd sent it. Because filling my screen was a selfie of Brad, smiling widely, with the caption *Guess who's in town? Can't wait to see you.*

What. The. Fuck? Goose bumps spread across my skin, and I shivered.

This couldn't be happening. I clicked on the picture to enlarge it, and I nearly threw up.

Brad hadn't just sent me a random selfie. He'd sent me one from the Treehouse. He seemed to even be at the table Sophia and the gang had sat in when they'd come in. I could even see Gail in the background.

My heart was hammering in my chest as my breaths started to come out in short, harsh pants. I stood up quickly, making the chair I'd been sitting in clatter to the ground behind me. I didn't even waste time to right it. Instead, I grabbed my stuff and hauled ass out of there.

I made it to the end of the block before I had to lean against the brick wall of some apartment building. I forced breaths in and out.

This wasn't the first panic attack I'd had over the past year, but it felt like the worst. Doubling over, I tried to focus on my breathing. *Deep breath in. Hold. Let it out slowly.*

I felt my body starting to relax slightly, but then it occurred to me that I wasn't paying any attention to my surroundings. What if he was watching? What if he was following me back to my apartment? What if he was already at my apartment?

Fuck, fuck, fuck.

I needed to get control, but my brain was spiraling. Without even consciously thinking about it, I tried to focus on my phone, which I'd had in a death grip since leaving the shop. Calling Sophia would be the smart thing to do. She already knew what was going on and would come if I needed her.

But as if my fingers had a life of their own, they stopped on another name. I pressed Call without contemplating what I was doing.

"Hey," Ransom said, his voice soft and welcoming. "I'm glad to hear from you."

"I—I need, I can't . . ." My brain was whirring so frantically it was difficult to find the words I needed.

"Taylor," he said, all softness gone from his voice. "Where are you?"

I was so thankful he'd asked a direct question with a simple answer, I nearly wept. Though I was pretty sure I was already crying. That or I was sweating profusely. Or I guess both were possible.

"My apartment." Not entirely accurate, but I was close. I could be there in under five minutes.

"I'm on my way. Just sit tight and try to breathe. I'll be there as soon as I can."

"'Kay," I managed to force out.

"Do you want me to stay on the phone with you?"

God, did I ever. But I also knew he had to drive, and I'd likely freaked him out. I didn't want him to get into an accident on the way because of me.

I took a deep breath and tried to sound calm. "No, it's okay. I'm okay. I . . . I'll see you when you get here."

"Fifteen minutes, Tay. I'll be there in fifteen minutes."

"'Kay. Good. See you soon."

"Absolutely."

I disconnected the call because I knew he wouldn't. It was okay. Ransom was coming. Forcing myself to stand up straight, I then squared my shoulders as if I was heading into battle.

I was strong. I could handle this. It would all be all right.

I forced one foot in front of the other and made it to my building soon after. I briefly contemplated waiting for Ransom outside, but I felt too vulnerable out there. Instead, I put in the code to disengage the front door and headed inside. Thankfully, I didn't encounter anyone on my way to my apartment. Once I keyed myself inside, I closed and locked the door, then leaned back against it before sliding to the floor.

Resting my forearms on my knees, I dropped my head so that I was coiled in a ball. God, I really wanted to be over this. Brad had never actually hurt me. I wasn't sure why I reacted this viscerally to his presence in town. What was the worst that could happen?

And that was when my whole body shuddered. Because even though he'd never hurt me, there was something menacing in his demeanor. Something that warned me that he *could* do something. That his behavior had been slowly escalating before I left for summer break, and there was no telling what he was capable of.

And for those reasons, I needed to cut myself some slack. I was my own worst enemy at the best of times, and this situation had left my brain making me turn myself into a punching bag—beating myself up over the what-ifs... What if I'd never gone out with him? What if I hadn't overlooked the possessive behavior he'd exhibited from the beginning? What if I hadn't stayed with him for three months before breaking it off? That was a fact I still hadn't been honest with Sophia about. What if I'd faced the demon instead of running? It wasn't helping me. I couldn't change what had happened.

The question was, where did I go from here?

My intercom buzzing kept me from finding an answer.

I leaped up and pushed the button. "Hello?"

"It's Ransom." He sounded slightly out of breath, but still, nothing had ever sounded better.

"Come on up," I replied as I hit the button to open the front door of the building.

I quickly swiped my hands down the front of my jeans

and burgundy T-shirt as if that would erase the fact I'd been sitting on my floor for the past five minutes. My hair was probably a horror show, but whatever. I had bigger things to worry about, even though the fact that Ransom would see it did make me want to fix it real quick. My priorities were a total shitshow.

A heavy knock came on my door, and nothing mattered after that other than getting the damn thing open. Once I flung it back, I slammed into Ransom, throwing my arms around him. I didn't have it in me to care about how clingy I was being. He was so big and solid and *nice*, and I needed all those things desperately.

His arms circled around me, and he pulled me tighter to him. "It's okay, Tay. I'm here. I got you." He kept up his litany of soothing words as he gently moved us inside my apartment so we weren't embracing in the hallway. With the way my face was buried in his broad chest, I heard more than saw him close the door and flip the lock, all while keeping one arm firmly around me.

He held me for a while before he said, "Do you want to sit down?"

I nodded against his chest but didn't move, and neither did he. But after a few more moments, I took a deep breath and pulled away. Making my way to the couch, I tried to regain my composure.

We both took a seat, instinctively turning toward each other.

"Can you tell me what happened?" he asked, his voice soft and reassuring.

I took in his face: the concern evident in the furrow of his brow, the tightness of his lips. But it was his eyes that set me at ease. They were intense and focused. And I knew right then—though I could admit I probably knew it long before now—that this man would move heaven and earth to help me. I just had to open my mouth and ask for it.

So I did.

RANSOM

Getting a panicked phone call from Taylor was enough to permanently raise my blood pressure. I'd been sitting in class when my phone had rung, but seeing as how Taylor never called me—even *before* I'd shown up to Sophia's bachelorette party to strip—I jumped up to take the call in the hall.

There'd been no question that I'd leave class to go to her. I'd explain to my professor later. He'd either understand or he wouldn't. Being here for Taylor was all that mattered.

I could tell by the way she was wringing her hands that what she had to say was hard on her. But I hoped she found it within herself to confide in me. I wanted her trust as much as she seemed to need someone *to* trust.

"I met Brad at a frat party at the beginning of last year," she began. "He was . . . handsome. Charismatic. Attentive. And unfortunately, crazy. Though I didn't know that then."

She cleared her throat before continuing. "I told Sophia that we only went on a few dates. I'm not sure why I lied to her about it." She paused. "That's not really true. It was because I didn't want her to know how long I let it go on. That I willingly let this guy infiltrate my life until he'd practically taken it over.

"He was okay at first. Sweet, thoughtful. But after date three or four, I started to notice that he was getting a little . . .

controlling. Wanting to know where I was going, who I'd be with. When I told him he was suffocating me, he said it was just because he cared so much. And I fell for that for almost four months."

Taylor looked down as if ashamed, and I wanted to reach over and lift her chin so she knew she didn't have to hide from me. But at that moment, I wanted to hunt this Brad fucker down, punch through his sternum, and rip his heart from his body—and I wasn't sure how well I was concealing that rage. So it was probably for the best if she didn't look at me for a few seconds.

"I was so stupid," she whispered.

"Hey, none of that," I said softly. "This is all on him. None of this is your fault."

She took a shuddering breath, and when she looked up, her eyes were full of tears. "I never told Sophia about him."

"What? But you said she knew?"

"No, I mean while I was dating him. I never told her because I knew she'd hate him. I just . . . knew it. So I didn't tell her. I came to visit her in the fall and everything, but I never breathed a word about him."

"That doesn't make you responsible for his fucked-up actions."

"But the writing was on the wall. And I saw it, Ransom. I saw it and ignored it. Even after I got back from seeing her and found him waiting for me outside my apartment, yelling at me that I was thoughtless and inconsiderate because I hadn't checked in with him enough, I still didn't stand up to him."

She laughed, but it was a humorless, awful sound that I never wanted to hear from her again.

"I even apologized to him. Said it wouldn't happen again.

It wasn't until I went home for winter break and got some distance that I got clarity. I broke up with him through text an hour before I was supposed to get on a train to spend New Year's with him. I didn't take his calls anymore after that."

"I'm guessing he didn't stop trying, though?" I knew the answer. She wouldn't be telling me this story after calling me in hysterics if he'd left her alone after that. But I wanted to help her along in this story as best I could—provide the transition between plot events.

"I refused to see him after that. I wouldn't answer my door when he came to see me when school started up again, wouldn't respond to his texts or emails. Nothing. But then he started showing up places I was. He'd come up to me and my friends and strike up a conversation as if everything was fine. But he'd inevitably always try to get me alone, and it was exhausting trying to dodge him."

"Didn't your friends have your back?"

"They would've. If I'd told them the full story. But I was embarrassed. So I said we broke up and that he wanted to get back together but I wasn't interested. A few of them thought I was being too hard on him, and he used that as a way to get to me. It ended up distancing me from my friends, which in retrospect, was probably exactly what he wanted.

"Last semester was horrible. I couldn't wait to pack my shit and get out of there. I drove straight to Sophia and tried to forget all about him. But then the texts started."

She told me about the things he'd said, and when she got to the picture he'd sent earlier that day, she broke down again.

I pulled her close to me, wrapping my arms around her and hoping that she'd know she could lean on me. That I wouldn't let that fucker hurt her.

After a while, she pulled away and rubbed her hands over her face. “God, I’m sorry. This is way more than you should have to deal with. I can call Sophia if you want. I just… I was panicked, and my first thought was to call you, but you barely even know me, and this is way, *way* too much. So it’s okay if—”

“Taylor,” I interrupted, waiting until she actually made eye contact with me. “Breathe.”

“Yeah, okay. Breathing is good.”

I let her regain her composure for a minute before continuing. “I’m glad you called me. I wasn’t sure… with how we left things.”

“Ransom?”

“Yeah?” I responded, lifting my head and forcing myself to lock eyes with her.

“I didn’t tell my family or almost all my closest friends that I’ve had a stalker for the majority of last year. You being a stripper is really pretty tame in comparison.”

She smiled at me, and I chuckled in return.

“I still should’ve said something.”

“Maybe, but…” She shrugged. “You would’ve told me eventually.”

The surety with which she said it warmed me from the inside out. “Yes. I would’ve.”

We stared at each other for a moment, and I wondered if she was as lost in me as I was in her. Probably not, especially with everything she had going on. But maybe one day she could get there.

But even if she didn’t, it didn’t change the fact that I was going to have her back.

“Okay, show me the text he sent today, and then we can come up with a plan.”

She handed her phone to me with a small, sweet smile on her lips that I was absolutely not reading into. We were friends, and maybe we could be more one day or maybe we wouldn't, but I was damn sure going to see to it that we'd always at least be that.

And *no one* fucked with my friends.

Chapter Eighteen

TAYLOR

Over the next hour, I filled Ransom in on everything I knew about Brad. I even showed him Brad's social media. I slunk back into my couch and let my eyes stray across the room.

"Shit!" I exclaimed, jolting to sit upright. "We're late for our shift."

Ransom patted my knee like I was a wayward Cocker Spaniel. I was surprised by how much I liked it.

"I texted Harry a while ago. Told him there was an emergency and we wouldn't be in for our normal shift, but that I'd come in to work the after-hours program. He said it was no problem. He'll cover for us."

I groaned, both in frustration and relief. "I've never just not shown up to work before." But I also didn't feel like I was in the right mindset to be around kids.

"You didn't. I texted."

"At the last minute."

"Harry knows we wouldn't call out if it wasn't important. He's a good guy. It'll be fine."

Ransom cleared his throat and shifted, which made me feel like I wasn't going to like whatever he said next.

"So, what did your dad say about all of this?"

Ugh. "Well... he didn't say anything. Because I never told him."

Ransom raised his eyebrows almost to his hairline. He opened his mouth to say something, but I cut him off.

"I'm thirsty. You want something to drink?" I practically threw myself off the couch and headed for the kitchen.

"Taylor," Ransom said from behind me.

Rounding the corner into my kitchen, I flicked on the light and scurried over to the fridge and looked inside.

"I have water and Sprite and these V8 juice things. They're supposed to give you energy."

"Taylor," he said again, this time from the entryway to the kitchen.

"I could also make some coffee," I said as I closed the fridge and began riffling through a cabinet. "Or tea! I think I have some tea in here somewhere."

"Do I look like I drink tea?"

I side-eyed him. "I wasn't aware someone had to look a certain way to like tea."

"I feel like I have a solid Red Bull look."

I wrinkled my face in disgust. "Do you also wear shirts with skulls on them and drive a monster truck?"

"Wouldn't a monster truck owner drink Monster?"

I thought for a second before shaking my head. "Why are we having the dumbest conversation in history?"

"Because you don't want to tell me why you haven't told your dad about Brad."

I really didn't like Brad's name coming from Ransom.

It was like dousing my wholesome superhero in radioactive sludge. I also really didn't want to explain myself so I said, "You know, I think monster truck drivers *would* drink Monster."

Ransom turned to bonk his head on the wall and muttered something I couldn't hear.

"Did I break you?" I asked. I was teasing, but part of me was also genuinely concerned. My drama was a lot to dump on anyone, let alone someone I'd known only a few months.

He straightened and faced me. "Nah. It would take way more than this to break me."

We held gazes for a pregnant moment before I felt the need to look away. A small wave of what I could only describe as panic flared up. Not the horror show kind like Brad inspired, but the oh-my-God-I-want-to-climb-you-like-a-tree-in-my-kitchen-and-that's-totally-inappropriate kind.

It was reckless at best to try to get involved with Ransom romantically while I had a whackjob following me around. He deserved more than a basket case who couldn't stop looking over her shoulder. Dealing with all that might very well break him, and I liked Ransom just the way he was.

"So . . . your dad," he said again.

Groaning, I flopped down dramatically, splaying my arms onto the counter and dropping my head on top of them.

"And the Oscar goes too . . ." he teased, the jerk.

I turned my head toward him but didn't lift it. "In my defense, I tried to tell my dad almost two months ago."

"Tried to?"

"Yeah. He called me a boy-crazed follower, so I left and moved into this place in a fit of petulant rage. We haven't spoken since."

"That's . . . extreme."

"It felt incredibly justified at the time."

"And now?" he asked, looking genuinely curious.

"And now I think I probably should've thrown it in his face. Would've been much more gratifying to leave him wondering if I'd be abducted on my way home."

Ransom scowled at me.

"Too soon?" I asked.

"It'll always be too soon for that."

"Sorry. I'm making inappropriate jokes to hide my discomfort." And my fear, but I didn't want to admit to that much. Not that he hadn't already figured that out. I'd called him in the midst of a panic attack after all. The guy wasn't just a pretty face.

He shook his head but didn't comment on what I'd said. Instead, he gave me a look that made me feel like a schoolgirl who'd asked her teacher about the functionality of the rhythm method.

"You have to tell him, Taylor."

"Honestly, I'd rather race the Iditarod with a sled pulled by Chihuahuas than have that conversation at this point."

His lips twitched at the corners, but he schooled his features as he took two steps toward me and rested his forearms on the counter so he was more in line with where I was still draped.

"I'll do whatever I can to help you, but I can't be the only one who knows. If something happened . . ." He trailed off as he took a deep breath. The emotion on his face was almost jarring.

Ransom was scared for me. It was clear as day on his face, and I felt wholly unworthy of his concern but was thankful to have it nonetheless.

He cleared his throat before speaking again. "If something

happened, your dad would probably be able to get things in motion a lot faster than some dudebro who works as a stripper. Please. You have to tell him."

Letting a sharp yet brief exhale leave me, I stared at the way light stubble dotted his otherwise smooth skin, the intensity of his blue eyes, the hard set to his angular jaw. It was a lot to put on his shoulders, even if they looked strong enough to handle it. But more than that, I didn't want to let him down. He was basically pleading with me to do what I knew was the right thing. Only an asshole would discount that. Not that I could say all that.

"You're not a dudebro."

"You thought I was. At first at least."

I shook my head, which was difficult since it was still pillowed on my arms. "Never."

He gave me a small smile, and I almost got lost in it.

Then he ruined it by saying, "Call him, Taylor."

I jerked to a stand. "What? Now?"

"No time like the present," he said as he stood and made his way out of the kitchen.

I followed like an ornery duckling. "I'll do it when you leave. What kind of host would I be if I abandoned you while I took a call?"

He scooped my phone off the coffee table and held it out to me. "I can leave."

"No!" I yelled with a little more alarm than I would've conveyed if I could've had a do-over. "I mean, no," I repeated at a more acceptable volume. "I don't want you to go."

He wiggled the phone that was still in his hand, causing me to take it from him with the same degree of enthusiasm one might have if they'd been handed a rattlesnake. Then he plopped down on the couch, grabbed the remote, and settled back as he turned on the TV. By all accounts, he was making himself at home.

"Then I'll wait," he said as he rested one ankle across the opposite knee.

"At least one of us is comfortable," I muttered.

He dropped his leg and leaned forward. "I'm not trying to make you uncomfortable. But I'm also worried that if I let you put it off, you won't call him. And I can't . . . It's your safety we're talking about here. I can't take that chance."

I stared at him for a second before breaking. "Ugh, fine. God, I wished I'd known you were some kind of guilt-trip expert."

"If there was one thing my mom taught me, it was how to be an exemplary manipulator." He kicked back again, a tad smug with having gotten his way.

"I'll have to thank her with a postcard laced with anthrax," I said drolly.

"With as much gin as she's consumed in her lifetime, bacteria doesn't stand a chance."

"Guess I'll have to get more creative, then."

"Guess so." He watched me earnestly for a minute before waving me toward the bedroom. "Hurry up. I'm hungry."

"We can always eat first—"

"Taylor," he warned.

"Okay, okay, I'm going."

I approached my bedroom as a nun might approach the second circle of hell. Once inside, I wasted some time observing the room as if I'd never been in it before. Then I plopped down on my bed and stared at my phone for an emo-filled moment before acknowledging that I was going to make the call—if for no other reason than I didn't want to disappoint Ransom—and that putting it off was only making my anxiety higher.

Taking a deep breath, I found my dad's contact info and tapped Call.

Part of me worried he wouldn't answer. That I'd pissed him off enough that he'd send me straight to voicemail. In the split second between connecting the call and the first ring, I'd almost convinced myself of this scenario, so when he picked up after the second ring, I fumbled the phone in surprise and nearly dropped it.

"Taylor?"

"Dad. Hi. How are you?" *Lame.* I rolled my eyes at myself at how formal I sounded.

"Oh, I'm okay. Better now that I've heard from you."

"Phone works both ways," I said before I could censor it. Being acrimonious wasn't the way to kick this off, but my words were the truth.

"Yes, well, I thought you needed a . . . cooling-off period."

He thinks I've come to my senses. That I'm calling to apologize. And maybe, in a way, I was, but not how he thought, and my feathers ruffled at the implication that I was the only one in the wrong.

Ransom was right. I should've been more honest about my reasons for leaving school, but my dad wasn't free from blame. He had been an epic twat the night I tried to talk to him, and I couldn't let it go. Not completely.

"I think we both did," I said even though I actually wanted to tell him I'd like him to cool down in the Arctic Ocean with an anchor strapped to his ankle.

He hesitated. "Yes, maybe you're right."

It was a small concession, but one I clung to like a life

preserver. I didn't want to fight with him, but I didn't want to do all the fence-mending either.

"I have something I need to tell you," I said. "It's what I was trying to tell you that night before everything went to hell. And I need you to just listen to me so I can get all of this out."

I was a little curious about what was running through his mind: torrid love affair that led to an unwanted pregnancy, drug-muling for a cartel, an accidental murder of a hitchhiker on a stormy night. But I didn't ask.

Instead, I told him the story of Brad. And he honored my wishes to not interrupt until I got to the part about him showing up and confronting me at various places around campus last spring.

Then, the man I always knew him to be, erupted in a fit of parental rage.

"What's this asshole's last name? I'm calling the school. He'll be expelled before the night's over. We'll have you safely back in classes by the end of the week. We can get a restraining order for good measure."

I blinked back tears. *This* was the exact reaction I was counting on when I went home to dinner that night almost two months ago. My protector, my dad, ready to draw his sword and fight for me.

But that wasn't what I got, and something about getting it now seemed hollow. I had no doubts my dad was already looking up the number for the dean. He could and would fix it for me, which was exactly what I'd wanted.

It just wasn't what I wanted anymore. Or at least not the whole of what I wanted. I didn't want him to simply fix it. I wanted him to understand. To ask how I felt about going back to school instead of assuming it was a foregone conclusion that

I'd want what he wanted for me. That we could wipe the slate clean and go back to life as it had been a year ago.

Unfortunately, there was no wiping Brad clean. I had a feeling his imprint would remain on my psyche, like a fly smudged by windshield wipers leaving streaks of what was left behind.

There was more to my story, but I decided not to finish it.

When I'd gotten Brad's text, my first instinct had been to go to Ransom, not my dad. And Ransom had come immediately. Maybe with that kind of backup, I could face this. I wouldn't ask anyone to fight my battles for me, but there was definitely something appealing about knowing people had my back if things went to shit. And really, what did I actually have to fear? Brad had never been violent. I could handle him.

So I attempted to assuage my dad by lying. "Brad already graduated. The campus just holds . . . bad memories. I'd feel better if I could just be done with it."

"I don't want him to get away with how he treated you though, Taylor."

"I appreciate that. But I honestly think it would do more harm than good to have to dredge all that up again. I just want to move on."

"Well . . . all right . . . I guess." He sounded like it was very much *not* all right, but I was glad he wasn't going to fight me on it.

"Thanks, Dad."

"Do you need anything else? Money? You can come home and stay if you want."

Maybe it was petty, but I didn't want anything from him.

"No, I'm fine. Really."

"Okay, if you're sure . . ."

"I am."

"Maybe we can go to dinner sometime soon? Just the two of us."

It was an olive branch, and I wasn't going to punish us both by refusing it. I didn't want to have a bad relationship with my dad. He and I had never fought like that before, and being upset with him was draining.

"Sure. I'd like that."

"Great. I'm away on business next week, but I'll call you when I get back to set something up."

"Looking forward to it."

He paused for a second before speaking again. "I love you, Taylor."

I'd never doubted it. "I love you too, Dad."

We hung up, and I gave myself a moment to get my head together. The talk with my dad hammered home for me how much I still needed to grow up—learn to fight my own battles. I couldn't rely on other people to swoop in and save me. While I trusted my friends to be there for me when I needed them, I didn't want to need them for this. Brad was a sickness, and I desperately wanted to stop the spread.

With at least a few things decided, I stood and took a steadying breath before leaving my room and rejoining Ransom in the living room. I threw myself beside him and concentrated on the TV.

"All done. My dad's going to take care of it."

"That's a relief, right?"

I shot him a quick glance before refocusing on the television. "Absolutely."

Chapter Nineteen

RANSOM

I walked into Safe Haven later that night so I could be there for the after-care program like I'd promised Harry. He'd said he could stay, but the guy worked pretty damn hard already. I didn't want to add to his plate.

I swung by his office, popping only my head inside. "Hey, Harry. Just wanted to let you know I was here. The kids already in the gym?"

He jerked his head up and looked at me with red-rimmed eyes and a sallow expression as he frantically pushed papers around his desk and threw a few things into his satchel.

"Oh, Ransom, hi. Thanks."

He went back to his task, his movements jerky and harried. He looked about two steps away from a panic attack. And man, I'd had my fill of those for a few days at least.

Despite that, I still felt torn about what to do. Though Harry and I were friendly, we weren't actual friends. His problems were none of my business. But he was a good guy, and I wanted to help him if I could.

"Hey, uh. Harry? You okay, man?"

He looked up at me again before pulling off his glasses, tossing them on the mound of papers on his desk, and rubbing his eyes.

"Sorry, uh, I just got off the phone with Justin. His dad had a heart attack. His mom isn't sure . . . It looks bad. We're heading up there as soon as I get home."

"Oh, shit. Harry, I'm so sorry." I knew from conversations over the past year that Harry was close with his in-laws. "What can I do?"

"I don't . . . God, this is such a mess. I'm going to have to be out for a while. I've already contacted Stacey. She'll step in in the interim, but could you help her out? It's been a while since she filled in over here."

Stacey was one of the community center directors. She spent most of her time dealing with funding and program implementation for high school kids and adults during the school year, but she worked closely with Harry for the summer camps. They often covered for one another when necessary.

"Yeah, sure. No problem," I assured him.

"Great, thanks." He grabbed his jacket from the back of his chair and gave his office one more cursory glance before heading for the door.

I stepped back to let him through, but he stopped suddenly in the doorway as his phone started ringing.

He answered it immediately. "Hi, babe. I'm on my way. Oh. Shit," he hissed, grimacing so hard I thought he'd hurt himself somehow. "It's okay, we'll figure it out. Did Paul have any recommendations for other dog sitters?"

Justin said something on the other line I couldn't hear, but whatever it was made Harry's lips thin into a line.

"Maybe you should go on ahead until we can find someone else for the dogs."

That suggestion was *not* well-received if the loud voice emanating from the phone was anything to go by.

"I know you need me and the kids with you. I'm just not sure what else to do," Harry said in a voice that sounded close to breaking.

I waved my hand in front of Harry to get his attention.

"Hang on a second, Justin." Harry looked at me expectantly.

"I'm great with dogs."

"Huh?" Harry said, his brain clearly a bit sluggish with all he had going on.

"I'm assuming your dog sitter isn't available. I can watch your dogs."

Harry bit his lower lip for a second, and then Justin said something to him. "What? Oh, yeah. Well... Ransom just offered to watch the dogs." He waited a beat for Justin to respond before continuing. "Yeah, he is. Definitely. I'm sure. Okay. Be there soon." Harry disconnected the calls and put the phone in his pocket before looking at me. "Are you sure you don't mind?"

"Not a bit." Which was a bit of a lie. Cramming dog sitting into my schedule would be a nightmare, but Harry was great, and if I could ease his burden a bit, I would.

"I... I really appreciate it, Ransom. We'll pay you, of course."

Shaking my head, I said, "No, you absolutely will not."

"Ransom," he warned.

"Harry," I said, mimicking his tone.

He sighed. "We'll hash it out when I get back. Is there any

way you can follow me to my place so I can introduce you to the dogs and show you where everything is? Then I'll give you a key so you can go grab your stuff and come back."

My stuff? "Oh, you want me to stay at your place."

He rubbed his jaw. "It would be easier. We have three dogs, one of which is a new rescue, not even a year old. He chews everything in his path, so it would be better if someone could be there for more than just to walk and feed them. Is that okay?"

"Sure," I replied, because I'd already offered so I wasn't going to split hairs at that point. Harry and Justin both worked, so I was sure the dogs would be able to spend enough time on their own for me to do the same.

Harry looked relieved. "Great. Ready to go?"

"Don't you need me to stay for the after-care kids?"

He waved me off before starting to walk out of Safe Haven. "I asked Roddie if he could stay in case you ended up not being able to come in after all. Speaking of that, is everything okay with you and Taylor?"

"Yeah, we're good. She just needed some help with something."

He nodded. "Well, if either of you ever need anything, don't hesitate to come to me."

I smiled. *Such a nice guy.* "We won't."

Once we were in the parking lot, I climbed into my truck and followed Harry the twenty or so minutes to his house. It was in a nice neighborhood where everyone had well-maintained lawns and lived-in homes. Harry pulled in the driveway of a blue split-level house while I parked on the street out front. There was a basketball net at the top of the driveway and some scattered toys littered across the lawn. It looked like a happy place, and I briefly wondered what it would've been like to grow up in a place like this.

Harry hustled to the front door, and I jogged to catch up to him. He threw open the front door, and we walked into pandemonium. There were bags scattered around the base of the staircase, toys strewn everywhere, dogs running toward us with kids following close behind.

"Papa, Daddy was crying!" an adorable little girl yelled as she crashed into Harry and hid her face in his stomach.

Harry bent to drop a kiss on her head. "It's okay, baby. He's just sad. It'll be all right."

Two young boys crowded around, and Harry drew them into quick hugs when he managed to untangle his daughter from his body.

"Ransom, this is Benjamin, Oliver, and Grace. Kids, this is Ransom. He's going to watch the dogs."

I smiled as I waved hello. They were all cute as hell. Oliver looked to be the youngest at probably about five. Grace was maybe seven and Benjamin a couple of years older than her.

"Now for the rest of the brood. That one"—Harry pointed at a black-and-white dog—"is Jetson. He's half border collie, half hound as far as the vet can figure. Don't throw a ball around him unless you're prepared to throw it for hours." He pointed to a yellow Lab and said, "That's Bamm-Bamm. Anything on level with his tail will be knocked over, so be wary. And that," he said, his tone growing harder, "unholy creature is Taz. He's a mutt, but we think there's some boxer in there. Maybe a little shepherd. All I know is he's totally insane, and I never should've let my family talk me into rescuing another puppy, but here we are."

As Harry spoke, Taz began running in circles by my feet as

if he could lure me in by creating some kind of cyclone.

"I assume you were into cartoons when you were younger?" With names like Jetson, Bamm-Bamm, and Taz, what else could be the case?

Harry chuckled. "Justin was."

"Justin was what?" a voice asked from down the hall.

I looked up to see a tall, thin guy with shaggy blond hair walking toward us. Harry opened his arms, and the man, who I felt safe in assuming was Justin, walked into them and buried his face in Harry's neck. The kids all joined in the hug, and while it was a beautiful thing to witness, I felt like I was intruding. Crouching down, I began playing with the dogs to give them a moment.

"Sorry," Justin said, and I looked up to see that he'd pulled back but stayed close enough for Harry to keep an arm around him.

"You have nothing to apologize for," Harry said before pressing a soft kiss to Justin's temple.

I stared at the adorable family unit in front of me and felt a pang of want. Even with Melissa and Matt, I'd never felt as part of something as everyone in Harry's family clearly did. They were like intricate puzzle pieces that snapped together perfectly. I'd always felt a bit jagged, like I didn't fit in cleanly anywhere.

Justin didn't look how I'd expected. He almost had a surfer vibe about him, with his shaggy blond hair, tan skin, and slender build. But the connection was there in the way Justin leaned into Harry, knowing Harry would keep him on his feet.

I stood and extended a hand. "I'm Ransom. It's great to meet you."

Justin smiled, though it was a bit brittle. It reminded me

of origami—like it could be easily twisted into something else.

"Justin. I've heard a lot about you."

"All good things, I hope."

"Good enough to leave my precious babies with you. Thanks so much for doing this. It means so much to us."

"I'm happy to help."

Justin turned toward Harry. "I packed our bags, but do you want to run up and see if I missed anything while I show Ransom where everything is?"

"Sounds good," Harry said before pressing another soft kiss to Justin's temple. "I'll be right down."

Justin watched him go for a moment, his smile small but intimate. Then he turned to me and said, "Ready to watch the Unholy Trinity?"

"As ready as I'll ever be."

Chapter Twenty

RANSOM

"Why are you out of breath?" Taylor asked as I struggled to hold my phone to my ear.

"Because I'm walking Harry's dogs."

There was a pause on the line before she asked, "And why are you doing that?"

"Harry's father-in-law had a heart attack yesterday. They needed someone to watch the dogs while they went to see him."

"And you became that someone how?"

"You ask a lot of questions," I groused, struggling to hold the leashes as the dogs pulled me down the street. Well, really only Taz pulled. The other two simply kept pace with him.

I knew Harry had said he was a boxer mix, but I was fairly certain he was part hellhound too. Since Harry had left, the dog had chewed the laces of my left sneaker, stolen my bagel, and was well on his way to dislocating my arm. In short, Taz was a total asshole.

"I have an inquisitive mind," she replied nonchalantly.

"Is that a nice way of saying you're nosy?"

"Yes. So?"

I had to think back to what she'd asked me for a second. "Oh, I had just gotten to Safe Haven when Harry told me what happened. His husband called while we were standing there and said their normal dog sitter wasn't available, so I offered. It's no big deal."

"Ransom, Ransom, Ransom."

"What?" I asked, my tone a little defensive.

"That heart of yours is too damn big for your own good."

I snorted. "Only you could make a big heart sound like a syphilis diagnosis."

"Have experience with those, have you?" she teased. "Don't you have class today? Can you leave the dogs?"

"Justin said if I took them for a long walk in the morning, they should be good for most of the day. I'll just have to pop home to let them out again before I head to Safe Haven."

"Okay, well, if you need me to let them out, I can. The benefit of online classes is I can do them from anywhere that has Wi-Fi."

A slight flutter resonated in my chest at her offer. Even though I'd met a lot of great people in my life, I'd also met a lot of shitty ones. And being around some of the worst humanity had to offer made me appreciate when someone offered to help me, no strings attached. It made me feel . . . special, important. The prospect of being special to Taylor made my body light up.

I cleared my throat so I didn't sound like the sappy fool I was. "I think I'll be okay, but if something comes up, you'll be my first call."

"'Kay."

'Kay was a pretty standard conversation ender, but I didn't want to hang up with her yet. I was pathetic and not nearly as

ashamed of that fact as I should've been.

"Working at the Peter Pan trafficking ring later?" It was Friday, so I assumed she was.

A surprised laugh erupted from her. "What?"

I smiled. "That weird place that looks like where Peter Pan took all those kidnapped boys."

"Neverland?"

"Is that what it's called?"

"It's what Peter Pan's island is called. The bar is called the Treehouse."

"It's a weird concept for a bar."

"Why?" She seemed amused, which gave me the confidence to keep going down this strange, and in some ways dark, line of thinking.

"Because it looks like a place kids would hang out."

"Maybe that's its appeal. People can revisit their childhood while partaking in the perks of adulthood."

"Sounds . . . Freudian."

A laugh burst out of her. "In what way?"

"Wasn't he all about regressing to being a kid again when things happen that we don't like?"

"Not sure. I'm not up on my Freud."

"What kind of criminologist are you going to be if you don't know about Freud?" I asked in mock outrage.

She laughed. "A bad one, I guess. Especially since I plan to be a lawyer."

Bantering with her was my favorite thing. I felt as though I could live off it. That said, I didn't want her to think I hadn't been paying attention.

"I knew that."

"I know you did." Her tone was soft and affectionate, and

God, I wanted to kiss her again. If I could've crawled through the phone, I would've.

Instead, I let the moment drop like the punk bitch I was. "I'm almost back to Harry's. I need to get these monsters settled and get to class. But I'll see you later, right?"

"Yup. You won't be able to miss me. I'll be the one surrounded by little girls and arts and crafts materials."

A laugh burst out of me at the image I could picture perfectly. The girls had definitely adopted Taylor as their craft buddy. She was a good sport about it too, often sitting there for hours making whatever the hell and talking about boys, unreasonable parents, demanding teachers, and whatever mean girl had flown into their orbit that day.

"See you then," I said.

"See ya," Taylor replied before ending the call.

I stuck my phone back into my pocket and moved their leashes to my free hand, though a sudden jerk from Taz had me almost lose my grip on it.

"Taz, my man, pardon my language, but what the fuck? There's nothing even over there," I said as I cast a glance in the direction he was pulling. "I think your dads need to look into getting you on some CBD."

He barked, which I took as wholehearted support for my idea. And to punctuate his point, he gave another hard tug.

I looked down at Jetson and Bamm-Bamm. "You guys just let him get away with this?" They had to trot like stallions just to keep up with their unruly brother. It was no way to enjoy a walk.

"When we get home, they're getting two treats and you're only getting one," I told Taz.

He turned to look at me, and I could've sworn I saw a

challenge in his eyes.

Harry's house came into view, and I nearly wept with relief. I was a sweaty mess. Thank God I'd been smart enough to take the dogs out *before* my shower. I'd get the boys a snack before getting them set up in the sun-room so I could get ready and get to school.

Justin had explained that Jetson and Bamm-Bamm could be trusted to roam the house while no one was home, but Taz definitely could not. Since they—and by they, I was pretty sure he meant everyone except Harry—didn't want to crate one dog while the others were free, they'd transformed their sun-room into a doggy oasis, with comfy beds and hardy toys. The room even had a Dutch door so the dogs could be contained when necessary but not cut off from the goings-on in the rest of the house.

As we approached Harry's house, Taz started to whine and pull harder—a feat I didn't think was possible. I figured he was just happy to be home, but then I noticed a car in the driveway.

Who could that be?

Maybe the dog sitter had made time for them after all. We crossed the lawn, and that was when I saw an adult and a child standing on the porch.

"Can I help you?" I asked.

The woman whirled around and looked at me quizzically. "Ransom?"

It took me a second to place her because I'd never seen her outside Safe Haven, and the change in geography took me a moment to overcome.

"Taryn, hi." Then I looked down beside her. "And Cinnabon! What are you guys doing here?"

Taryn smiled. "I was wondering the same about you."

I held up my hands holding the dog leashes. "Helping out Harry with the dogs."

"Oh." Her brow furrowed. "And where is Uncle Harry?"

Uncle?

"Justin's dad had a heart attack. They all drove upstate to be with him."

Her hand flew to her chest. "Oh no, how horrible. I'll have to call him and check in."

I watched as Cindy slid her hand into her mother's, and Taryn jolted as if she'd forgotten the young girl was there.

Taryn gave her daughter a small smile. "Guess we're out of luck, baby girl."

Cindy didn't smile back.

"Did you need something?" I asked.

"No, no, it's no big deal. I was just going to ask Uncle Harry if he could watch Cindy for the weekend. A job opportunity came up, and I can't really afford not to take it. But it's okay, Cindy can stay with her grandmom."

The way Cindy whined and pulled on her mom's hand told me that plan might not be okay with Cindy.

"I don't have any other choice," Taryn told her.

Cindy's eyes welled with tears.

"We'll talk about it in the car, okay?" Taryn said to Cindy before turning back to me. "Good luck with the dogs. I'm sure I'll see you next week when I pick up Cindy."

"I'll be there."

Taryn gave me a quick smile that seemed forced before leading a sad-looking Cindy off the porch.

This whole situation was weird. Who just showed up randomly to see if an uncle could watch their kid? Wasn't that a call-first kind of scenario? And what kind of job did Taryn do? And who was Cindy's grandmother? Miss Hannigan from *Annie*?

Those questions, combined with the gloomy way Cindy was walking to the car, were the only excuses I had for what came out of my mouth next.

"Is there anything I can do to help?"

Chapter Twenty-One

TAYLOR

I jogged from my bedroom to the living room, where I'd left my phone after talking to Ransom a while ago. I grabbed it off the table and looked down at it, a little worried at who I'd see was calling. But it was Ransom again.

"Hey."

"Hey. Remember when you asked me if I needed help, and I said no?"

"Yes."

"I've changed my mind. Or rather, my circumstances have drastically changed, resulting in me now needing help. Like a lot of help. And possibly an intervention, because seriously, who even winds up babysitting a pack of dogs and a little girl within the same twenty-four hours? A helping junkie, that's who."

I tried to let Ransom's words percolate in my mind for a second to see if they'd wind up making sense, but no dice.

"You're harder to follow than IKEA directions right now. Start at the beginning. What little girl? And what the hell's a helping junkie?"

"I came home from walking the dogs and found Taryn and Cindy on Harry's doorstep. Turns out Harry is Taryn's uncle, but he never told anyone because he pulled a lot of strings to get Cindy in the program and didn't want anyone to accuse him of nepotism or whatever it is when it's your niece. Anyway, she wanted Harry to watch Cindy so she could go work a blackjack table in Atlantic City this weekend. Guess there's some convention and she's a pretty good dealer—of cards, not drugs—and she could make a ton of money. She wanted Harry to watch Cindy, so she showed up on his doorstep, but I was there and it was me or the wicked grandmother, and God, Taylor, what am I gonna do all weekend with a seven-year-old?"

He was breathing heavily after his word vomit, and I wasn't sure if it was because he hadn't taken a breath, was having a panic attack, or both.

"Okay, you made sense for a good part of that, but you started to lose me at the end. How did it go from Taryn wanting Harry to watch Cindy to you doing it?"

"Because I offered."

"Why would you do that?"

"Because I'm stupid," he hissed, his voice low, making me wonder if Cindy had walked in the room.

"You're not stupid. Well, not for this."

"Shut up."

I laughed before continuing. "Where is Cindy now?"

"Taryn took her to school."

I scrunched up my face. "Why wasn't she in school to begin with?" I'd talked to Ransom a little after nine the first time. Cindy definitely should've already been at school by the time Taryn showed up on Harry's doorstep.

"I don't know. I kinda think she thought it would be harder for Harry to say no if Cindy was there."

"That's . . . very manipulative."

"I know. I don't know whether to be impressed or concerned."

Considering Taryn was going to leave her kid with a virtual stranger, I thought concerned was more apt but kept that thought to myself.

"Okay, so you're taking her home after Safe Haven?" I asked.

"Yeah."

"What do you need from me?" My question was sincere. Ransom had been there when I'd needed him. I was more than happy to return the favor, even though the circumstances of this were bizarre as hell.

He groaned. "I don't know. I offered without thinking it through. Or thinking Taryn would take me up on it. I mean, Cindy is super skittish around guys. The grandmother she was going to have to stay with must be a close personal friend of Hannibal Lecter for Taryn to choose to leave her with me instead of sending her there."

"So tell me more about this grandmother." Who left a child with a guy named Ransom when there were other options?

"Yeah, but Cindy looked really distraught about the possibility of staying there. It broke me."

I sighed, but the sound was affectionate. Sweet, silly, selfless Ransom.

"I can come hang out with you guys for the weekend. I'm supposed to work tonight and tomorrow, but I could see if someone could take my shifts."

"No, don't call out of work. I don't want to interfere with

your job. But maybe you could hang out with us for, like, every other second of the weekend?"

I laughed at the undisguised hope in his voice. "I can do that. I'll pack a bag for the weekend. I'm only working until midnight tonight, so I shouldn't be totally useless tomorrow. And I'm a closing cocktail server Saturday, so I don't have to go in until nine."

"Perfect," he practically yelled, making me wince. "You're the best. Seriously."

"I know." I huffed a laugh when he clucked his tongue at me. "But, Ransom?"

"Yeah?"

"We're going to have to tell Harry about this. Taryn shouldn't have left Cindy with you like that. I get that you work at Safe Haven, but it was still irresponsible of her. I mean, *I* know you can be trusted, but..." I let the end of my sentence hang there, not exactly sure how much I should drag Taryn to the guy she'd entrusted with Cindy.

"You're right. But I'd like to wait until they get home at least. They have so much on their plate right now."

"That's fine," I quickly assured him. I wasn't trying to stress anyone out. "Did she drop off everything Cindy needs?" I asked to change the subject.

"Yeah, she had it in the car, so it's all at Harry's. I didn't have a chance to look through what she packed, though. I had to leave for school."

"Are you there now?"

"Yeah, I just pulled in. My class starts in ten minutes."

"I'll let you go, then. I'll see you at work later."

"Can't wait." His voice was husky, as if the words had escaped around a closing voice box.

Warmth flooded me, and I couldn't resist returning the sentiment. "Me neither."

We hung up, but I stared at the screen for a bit longer. Ransom had somehow crawled under the defenses I'd built, and I wasn't sure how I felt about it.

Well, that was a bit of a lie. I felt happy about it. But I wasn't sure that was how I *should* feel about it.

Ransom wasn't Brad. There was absolutely no question about that. But I still had a lot going on, and I wasn't sure getting involved with someone was the best idea. Not that I even knew that Ransom wanted to be involved with me. It seemed like he did, but he also could've decided I was much more hassle than I was worth. It'd be hard to blame him.

I forced myself up and went back into my room to finish getting ready. Even though I didn't have to leave my apartment for class, I always got dressed anyway. It made me feel more productive. I also had a live session to attend today, and while a lot of my classmates showed up in ratty clothes they'd probably slept in, that wasn't me. My dad had always taught me that impressions were important, and I wanted to make sure a professor I might need a recommendation from down the road had a good one of me.

The day passed surprisingly quickly. I managed to focus on my classes and assignments, despite all that had gone down yesterday. When it came time for me to head to Safe Haven, I only had a small thrum of anxiety when I left my apartment building. The unbidden thought that Brad could be out there watching me was definitely in my head, but it didn't stop me from holding my head high as I casually made my way to my car and hopped in. And if I breathed a small sigh of relief when I locked the doors around me, so what?

When I pulled up in front of Safe Haven and parked in the small lot across the street, I was actually excited. Ransom needed my help, and it made me giddy to think that he'd decided he could rely on me. Even if I was the most logical choice because I knew Cindy. Semantics be damned. I was gonna rock the shit out of being Ransom Helper.

Maybe I need to work on that name.

When I got inside, I swept my gaze over the room in search of Ransom. His truck was in the lot, so I knew he was here, but I didn't see him anywhere. I felt a brief surge of disappointment that I quickly told myself was ridiculous. Since when did I need to see Ransom so badly?

Get a grip.

The kids weren't due to show up for another half hour, so after saying hello to everyone, I set about helping Marty get snacks ready. Once we were done divvying up trail mix into small plastic cups, I moved to the sink to fill the water pitcher. With my back to the room, I was startled by a loud bang and a muffled curse behind me.

Twisting around suddenly, I sloshed water all over the floor. "Damn," I muttered before looking up to see what had caused the racket.

Ransom and Roddie were struggling to bring a gigantic couch into the room—a feat the narrow doorway was making difficult.

"Bro, I told you we shoulda come in the other way," Roddie said as he wiped his forehead with the back of his hand.

"That would've meant going through the entire center. Stacey would've caught us."

I dropped a few paper towels on the mess and then made my way over to them. "Why are you bringing a ratty couch in here?"

Roddie pressed a hand to his chest as if he'd been an insulted maiden. "This baby's in near perfect condition."

He and I clearly had very different concepts of what constituted "near perfect." There were tears in the upholstery and a dark mark at the base. And that was just what I could see with it wedged in the door.

"Where'd you get it?" I asked.

Roddie sniffed. "Next to a dumpster down the street."

"Hmm. And you thought you should trash pick it and bring it here because . . . ?"

"Because I figured it would be awesome to sit on while we play video games."

I couldn't suppress an eye roll. Safe Haven had a good-sized TV that was hooked up to a PlayStation. It was supposed to be a privilege for kids who completed their homework when they first arrived, but Roddie often set up tournaments that he said nullified that rule because it was a special circumstance. And even though this special circumstance happened damn near every week, causing Harry to make a number of hollow threats about disconnecting everything, Roddie remained resolute in his assertion that he was providing a valuable service by educating kids in the fine art of gaming.

"We don't even know what that thing is crawling with," I said. "You can't let the kids sit on it."

"I know, Mother," Roddie said, sounding more like a preteen than a college student. "I plan to deep clean it and get a slipcover. But it's supposed to storm tonight, so I can't leave it outside while I do that. I'll just put caution tape on it or something until it's clean."

"Where are you going to get caution tape?"

"From Edith. She has everything."

He was probably right. Harry's secretary was like a Mary Poppins of office supplies. Though I thought caution tape might be beyond her scope.

"Hey, guys," Ransom called from where he stood outside with the other end of the couch. "This is a fascinating argument, but can we finish it *after* we clear the doorway of this thing? The kids are gonna be here soon."

"Oh yeah. Sorry, man," Roddie said as he crouched down to grab the couch. "Give it a solid push on the count of three."

I looked around at the array of toys and puzzles behind Roddie. "I don't think this is gonna work."

"One," Roddie started. "Two."

"Guys—"

"Three!" Roddie yelled, tugging his hardest as Ransom pushed.

I was relieved when the couch didn't budge. I'd had mental images of Roddie falling over the objects behind him as a couch drove him into the floor.

"Roddie," Ransom called. "Back up. I'm gonna get a running start and push it through."

"I don't think—"

"Hell yeah! Use those football muscles, brother," Roddie yelled.

"Ransom, maybe you should try a different way."

"Never give up, never surrender," he yelled back at me.

"I don't think that applies here."

"Stand back," he yelled, sounding farther away than before. I wondered with concern at how long this running start was going to be.

Roddie and I moved a good ways back just as the sound of sneakers hitting blacktop reached us.

"Oh God," I whispered.

A second later, Ransom made contact with the couch. It felt as if the entire room shook, which ordinarily would be an exaggeration, but I could've sworn Ransom's hit on the couch jolted the entire center. The couch inched forward with his momentum behind it, but Ransom didn't stop pushing. After a second, there was a sharp crack, and the sofa tumbled forward, hurtling into the room like someone had flung it from a slingshot. The wooden feet groaned across the linoleum flooring before it crashed into the games and toys I'd been worried Roddie was going to be tossed into earlier.

An "oof" came as a heavy thud sounded from the doorway. I turned to see Ransom lying on the ground like Superman, all his limbs spread wide.

The doorjamb was ripped open, the wood exposed after the couch had ripped part of it away. Splintered wood lay all over the floor. It looked like the sloppiest breaking-and-entering job ever performed.

I took the few steps I needed to get to Ransom and knelt beside him. "Are you okay?"

He rolled to his back, groaning with the movement. As he gazed up at me, I couldn't help but let my eyes track over his body, looking for injuries. When I brought my eyes back to his face, he had a dopey grin stretching across it.

"I saw that going very differently."

A soft laugh escaped me. This guy was really something else. And I was totally gone for him.

"I'd certainly hope so."

He looked up at the doorway, examining the mess he'd made of the door. "Think Harry's going to be mad?"

I also looked up to survey the damage. "Without question."

"Damn."

I laughed again. I grabbed on to his arm as I stood, trying to pull him with me. A wasted action since he outweighed me by probably almost a hundred pounds, but he did move to sit.

"Come on," I said as I tugged on him again. "We can call Bill to come take a look at it."

Bill was the head of the maintenance crew at the center. I was sure he'd be simply thrilled to deal with a destroyed door this late on a Friday.

"Oh God, do we have to?" Ransom asked. "Maybe I can fix it."

Bill was gruff and grumpy on a good day. And this would certainly not be a good day in his book.

"I think you've done enough," I said.

"Dude, that was *epic*," Roddie enthused from behind us.

"Oh, it was epic all right," I said, staring meaningfully at Ransom.

"Epically stupid?" he asked.

I tapped my nose twice to indicate he was right on the money.

"Come on, get up," I told him. "The kids are gonna be here in"—I checked my watch—"ten minutes."

He sighed heavily. "I'll never find my pride by then."

I barked out a laugh as I helped Ransom to his feet. Roddie moved the couch against a wall and set about cleaning the mess the couch had made as Ransom and I walked out to where Edith sat.

"Edith, love of my life," Ransom said, laying it on a little thick, even for him.

"No," she said without even looking up from the paperwork she had spread across her desk.

"You don't even know what I was going to say," he objected. "Maybe I just came to declare my undying devotion to you."

She eyed him over her glasses without moving her head. "Did you?"

"Well, no, but—"

"Then my answer is no."

Ransom dropped to his knees beside her desk and put his elbows on top so he could clasp his hands in prayer. "Please, Edith. I'll never ask for another favor as long as I live."

She eyed him doubtfully until he added, "Or until I *really* need something else."

The sigh that fell from her lips would've made my eternally agitated grandmother proud. "What is it this time?"

"I need you to call Bill, and—"

"No, absolutely not."

"But . . . think of the children, Edith!" Ransom's wail was plaintive and dramatic.

"I prefer to think of myself, thank you."

Ransom stood then. "I don't understand why they let such an evil creature work around children," he groused at her.

"It brings balance to Harry's eternal piety."

"This selfish act will come back to haunt you one day, Edith. Karma is an unyielding force."

Edith looked unmoved. "Bill should be in his office about now for his afternoon snack."

Finally losing my battle with the laughter bubbling inside me, an amused snort escaped me.

Ransom glared at me. "Et tu, Brute?"

Unable to hold back anymore, I began laughing. It actually bordered on hysteria. All I could do was throw my hands up in an exaggerated shrug, causing him to storm off in the direction of Bill's office. At which I only laughed harder.

God, I loved this job.

Chapter Twenty-Two

RANSOM

Bill wasn't thrilled to see me. Especially since, as Edith had predicted, he was eating his afternoon snack. To his credit, he kept his grumbling to a minimum as he followed me down to Safe Haven and set about sanding down the jagged pieces so we didn't have to worry about the kids being impaled as they came in.

But I'd evidently done irreparable damage, because he had to board it closed after the last bus had arrived because a new door would need to be installed. Thankfully we had a door at the other end that opened to the courtyard out back as well as a doorway that led to the main center, so it was able to be boarded closed without being a fire code violation.

Of course, the order for a new door prompted a visit from Stacey, for whom we had to recount the whole tale. She looked at the couch dubiously, and I was filled with a growing sense of dread that she was going to force me and Roddie to take it back out. God only knew the damage we'd do if that happened.

Thankfully, Roddie jumped in and convinced her to give

the couch a chance—his exact words. He promised to have it cleaned and presentable by early the following week, at which point she'd come back and determine whether it could stay or not.

With all the drama, Taylor and I hadn't gotten to work out much about the weekend other than she'd be over the next morning. I only had to survive one night alone with Cindy. How bad could it be?

I'd worried that I'd have issues leaving Safe Haven with Cindy. I didn't really want to put Harry and Taryn's business out there, so I was thankful when Marty took me up on my offer to let him leave a half hour early. Parents usually came earlier on Fridays to pick up their kids, so when only two brothers and Cindy remained, Marty told me to have a good weekend and hightailed it out of here.

The brothers were picked up ten minutes later, and it was just Cindy and me.

"Ready to go?" I asked her, trying to infuse cheer into my voice.

She shrugged, not looking overly impressed with the situation she was in.

Ditto, kid.

"Okay, let's head out."

I grabbed her schoolbag and carried it while she followed me silently. When we got to my truck, I opened the back door and then hesitated.

"Uh, I don't have a car seat. Do you need one of those?"

Shooting me another blank look, she shrugged again.

I ran a hand through my hair. "We'll have to make do without one. Don't tell on me, okay?" I said the last part with a smile, hoping conspiring with her would endear me to her a little.

It didn't. She climbed in, buckled her seat belt, and sat ramrod straight in the seat, facing forward. I suddenly had a flashback to a movie I watched as a kid. *The Bad Seed* I thought it was called. A cute little blond girl with pigtails went on a killing spree. I cast a quick look at Cindy's feet. Thankfully she was wearing sneakers and not tap shoes like the ones the girl in the movie used to bash people's heads in.

I gave my head a slight shake to clear my thoughts. Jesus, I was getting dark. Who knew being a philanthropist made a person morbid as fuck?

As I got us on the road, I struggled to get my nerves under control. I was way out of my depth with this. There were so many things I hadn't thought of.

What if she needed help getting a bath or getting changed? There was no way I could help her do those things. I wasn't built for prison. I mean, I was maybe built for it physically, but mentally, I'd collapse like a Jenga tower. But, no, she was in second grade. Surely she could handle those things.

But then my worries became more practical. What if she got sick or hurt and I had to take her to the hospital? What if she sleepwalked and ran off into the night, never to be heard from again? The possibilities were endless. How did parents function with all these what-ifs rattling around in their brains?

"Do you like pizza, Cinnabon?" I asked to keep my thoughts from deteriorating further.

Crickets.

Why did people say *crickets* anyway? Weren't crickets loud? Though I guess Cindy was loud in her own way: the silence emanating from her was damn near deafening.

"Why don't we play a game? I'll ask a question, and if it's a no, you kick my seat once, and if it's a yes, kick it twice. Sound good?"

I waited for a long moment before I felt two kicks on the back of my seat.

Jackpot.

"Great. Do you like pizza?"

Two kicks.

"Awesome." *Get a grip on the superlatives.* "Pizza is one of my favorite foods. I like lots of toppings. Do you like toppings?"

One kick.

"Ah, a plain cheese kinda gal, huh?" *What the fuck is the matter with me?* "Guess we'll each have to get our own pies for dinner, then. Can you eat a whole pizza?" I was teasing, knowing she couldn't but I sure as hell could.

Still, I reveled in her reply of a single kick.

"That's okay. The best thing about pizza is having leftovers."

That was about as far as I could take that conversation, so I let silence reign for the rest of the drive to Harry's. I ushered Cindy inside and handed her schoolbag to her.

"Your stuff is over there. Do you wanna see what your mom packed?"

Cindy hesitated a second but then gave a small nod. *Progress!* As she moved toward her things, I hustled to the back so I could let the dogs out. When I entered the sun-room, they all went a little crazy, probably anxious to be let outside. I slid open the deck door and let them bound out into Harry's fenced-in backyard.

As the dogs did their business, I leaned against the wall and tried to get my head in the game. I watched Jetson and Bamm-Bamm chase each other around the yard. They were so funny, dipping their front legs and trying to juke each other out as the other gave chase. I was so absorbed by their fun, I forgot about Taz.

I quickly stood up straight and scanned the yard.

Where the hell is he?

After a few seconds, I caught sight of a wriggling butt. And that was all I saw because the rest of Taz's body was wedged under their synthetic fence as he tried to dig under.

"Taz. No! Here, boy. Come here." I ran toward the fence, but just as I got close enough to make a grab for him, he inched the rest of the way free and took off down the alley behind the house.

I could just barely see over the top of the fence and quickly lost sight of the dog. "Shit. Taz! Come back."

I turned and glared accusingly at the other two dogs. "You were his diversion, weren't you?"

They looked at me guiltily. Or maybe I was reading into it. It didn't really matter at this point.

Scrubbing my hands over my face, I groaned. "Fuck my life." Taking a deep breath, I got myself together and then took off into the house. I grabbed a leash and started toward the front door, stopping in my tracks when my eyes caught on Cindy's tiny figure in the living room.

"Uh, so, I... uh..." I pointed over my shoulder like a moron. "I lost one of the dogs. Well, *I* didn't lose him. He escaped. While I was watching him. So I guess basically, I lost him."

Cindy's eyes were wide as if she didn't know what to make of my rambling.

Join the club, kid.

I wasn't sure what to do. I had to go after the dog, but I couldn't leave Cindy in the house alone. Which I guess left only one option. "You up for a recovery mission?"

She looked alarmed.

"We need to go find Taz. Can you come help me? He probably likes you better than me, so he may come back if you're with me." I held out my hand to her without waiting for a response because no wasn't really an option. She had to come. I just hoped I'd sold it well enough that I didn't have to drag her kicking and screaming.

She eyed my hand like it held a tarantula, but she took a few steps forward and slid her tiny hand into mine.

I gave her a squeeze and opened the door. "Off on the Great Taz Adventure!" When I looked down, I thought I saw the ghost of a smile on her face but didn't have time to inspect it more closely. That, and bending down to examine her face so I could see my first Cindy smile, while tempting, would probably ensure I never saw another one.

Rushing as fast as I could with Cindy in tow, I made my way down the street, my head swiveling all around.

"Taz," I whisper-yelled repeatedly as we walked.

There was no sign of the mutt, and after fifteen minutes of searching, I was starting to contemplate what I was going to tell Harry. "*Hey, sorry, Harry, while you were visiting your dying father-in-law, your dog pulled a Houdini and is likely lost forever. My bad.*"

Though I didn't know his father-in-law was dying. Harry had texted earlier to check in but hadn't given me any details, and I hadn't asked. If the guy actually passed away, I was going to feel guilty for throwing that thought into the cosmos.

I didn't realize I began muttering under my breath until Cindy pulled on my hand.

I looked down at her. "Sorry, Cinnabon."

When I made to move farther down the street, Cindy didn't budge.

"What's wrong?" I asked her.

She pointed toward a playground.

I squatted down so I was on her level and smiled. "It's a little late to go to the playground now, but we can come tomorrow."

She shook her head at me, her eyes drifting closed like she was dealing with a dolt. Her hand lifted again to point at the playground.

"Cindy, we can't..." I finally looked where she was pointing and saw that wild beast Taz curled up under a slide. Thank goodness there were lights around the area, or I never would've seen him. Or Cindy wouldn't have. I was pretty sure I wouldn't have seen him even if a UFO had been beaming light onto him.

I approached Taz like one might approach an alligator. If he took off again, I'd have to let him go. I couldn't keep dragging Cindy around the neighborhood.

"Okay, Taz, easy does it. Just stay right there and let me get my hands around your neck."

Cindy, whose approach had been a slow creep beside me, stopped and looked at me.

"I didn't mean that how it sounded," I promised.

She seemed to take my words at face value, which was good because I hadn't meant them. Finally, we reached the slide, and I crouched in front of it, which caused Taz to scoot back farther. He looked ready to bolt, the bastard.

I looked at Cindy. "Maybe you should try calling him."

Cindy tilted her head as if considering my suggestion. Then she knelt down, no doubt getting the knees of her jeans filthy, and patted her lap.

"Come here, Tazzy," she said in a voice so soft I wouldn't

have heard if I hadn't been so close. Her words took me aback a bit, having only heard a seldom singular word here and there over the months I'd known her. Her voice was as sweet as a second grader's should be.

Taz inched forward. Cindy patted her thighs again. "It's okay, Tazzy. It's time to go home."

At the mention of the word *home,* Taz stood up and pushed himself onto her lap, licking her face affectionately while I secured the leash on him.

"What did I tell you?" I said to her. "I knew he'd go to you. I never would have caught him without you."

She smiled and readily accepted my hand when I held it out to her. We walked Taz home and then I quickly fed the dogs and took them into the backyard again—on leashes this time—with Cindy hovering behind me. When we came back in, Cindy went over to settle on the couch as I tidied up a bit. After a couple minutes, I lifted my head to ask if she needed anything, and I saw tears streaming silently down her face.

"Hey, hey, what's wrong?" I asked as I sat beside her on the couch.

She didn't answer. There was no sound escaping her, but tears were steadily streaming down her face, and she was clutching a stuffed armadillo. I wasn't sure how an armadillo was comforting, but the way Cindy held it tightly against her said it was.

"Do you feel okay?" I asked.

No answer. I reached over and gently pulled her hand to rest on the back of mine.

"Can you tap once for no and twice for yes?"

Thankfully, she gave me two taps.

"Are you hurt?"

One tap.

"Sad?"

Two taps.

"You miss your mom?"

Two taps.

I sighed, unsure of how to fix that. Taryn had said she'd try to call Cindy when she had a break, but other than a text an hour ago asking if everything was okay, there'd been nothing. Taryn had said she would be on the casino floor and would be unable to check her phone, so us calling her would be pointless.

Then I had an idea. "You want to record a message for her, and I'll text it so she can watch it when she gets a break?"

One tap.

Shit. "How about I order our pizza and we can watch a movie? Your pick."

Two taps.

"Great." Feeling relieved to have a plan, no matter how flimsy, I pulled my phone out of my pocket and searched for local pizza places. Only one came up that delivered within a ten mile radius. How did Harry and Justin survive under such conditions?

When the call connected, I asked for delivery.

"Our driver had to go home sick. We got another guy coming in, but we're not taking any more delivery orders until he gets here."

Okay, not ideal, but we could roll with it. "Okay, I'll come pick it up."

"Wait's over an hour. It's been a helluva night."

Fuck this whole night sideways.

"Okay, thanks anyway, man." I hung up and looked at Cindy. "Like anything else besides pizza?"

And when the tears started again . . . I panicked.

TAYLOR

Fridays were usually busy at the Treehouse, but tonight we'd been slammed. I'd walked in for my shift to see the servers and bartenders all running their asses off and so many people that we had to be over our max capacity.

I hadn't stopped moving since I'd clocked in. But as it approached ten, things started to calm down. Friday exhaustion had finally caught up to the after-work crowd, and they settled their tabs and headed home. It was still crowded, but it was no longer quite so manic.

I was taking a sip of water and catching my breath at the server's station when Gail walked over.

"You have a table."

I looked at her, my brow wrinkling. "I just got one. Isn't it Jessie or Lana's turn?"

"You were requested."

"Oh." No one had told me they were stopping in, but it wasn't uncommon for it to happen. "Okay, I'll go right over."

"I'd hurry. They look . . . desperate. It's a look I know well."

Smirking, I set down my water and asked, "You know it because you wear it a lot or because you cause it in others?"

She thought for a second. "Both."

I laughed at that. "Thanks, Gail. What's the table number?"

"They're sitting in the tree house."

That stilled me. "But there's no table in there." Against one wall, there was a small wooden structure that resembled a tree house, but it was just a model. It wasn't a place people could actually sit.

"The guy kind of begged. And since I love it when men do that, I caved," she said.

I was sure my eyes widened in alarm as I took off in the direction of the house. When I got close enough to peek inside the doorway, all I could see was a large body crammed into what amounted to a wooden box. And there was a blond head just barely visible through the window.

Bending down, I poked my head in the doorway. "Ransom?"

The man looked utterly ridiculous jammed into the tiny house. His long, bulky limbs were folded in ways that seemed to defy human physiology. It was like a LeBron James hanging out in a kid's playhouse.

Next to him sat a wide-eyed Cindy. She was looking at her surroundings in wonder, looking happier than I'd ever seen her.

"Taylor. Hey," Ransom said.

"Hi, Cindy," I said.

The little girl gave me a small wave before returning her attention to the walls of the tree house. I'd never looked in there, but the walls were painted with everything someone might find in an actual tree house.

"What's going on?" I asked Ransom.

"I think bad parenting is a genetic trait," he said.

"What?"

"So far this evening, I've lost a dog, failed to feed a seven-year-old in a timely manner, and had a panic attack at the first sign of emotional distress. I think my mom passed her crappy parenting ability down to me. As if it's not bad enough I have her eyes and hair."

"You're great with kids. I see it every day." I'd seen Ransom's insecurities peek through from time to time, and it always made a fierce surge of protectiveness well up inside me. He was amazing, and I hated when he doubted that.

"I'm great at *playing* with kids. Maybe because I'm just a big kid myself. But actually caring for them . . ." He finished his thought by shaking his head.

Movement out of the corner of my eye stole my attention for a second. Cindy stood as best she could and looked at Ransom for a few seconds before stepping closer to him and wrapping her little arms around his neck.

He stilled for a moment, shock clear on his face, before he wrapped his large arms around her tiny frame and returned the hug.

I smiled as I watched the tender moment unfold in front of me. "I think you're doing just fine."

After a moment, Cindy pulled away and Ransom let her go immediately. She settled back on the floor and let her hands roam over the walls as if nothing extraordinary had happened.

Ransom still looked a bit stunned.

In order to snap him out of it, I cleared my throat. "So you haven't had dinner? What can I get you guys? Cindy, we have nuggets, macaroni and cheese, and grilled cheese. Any of that sound good?"

She looked at me blankly. Ransom held out his hand toward her. "Do you want nuggets and fries?"

She stretched her fingers toward him and tapped his hand once.

"Grilled cheese?"

Two taps.

"With fries?"

Two taps.

He looked at me. "She'll have grilled cheese and fries. And can I get a bacon burger? And two waters?"

Answering him was a struggle because my heart was fluttering wildly in my chest. How could this man ever think he wasn't good at taking care of kids? He'd found such a simple way to give Cindy a voice. It was amazing.

"Absolutely. Coming right up."

I was thankful our kitchen didn't stop our regular menu until eleven, so I wouldn't have to beg one of the cooks to rustle up a grilled cheese. I did ask if they could hurry the order, which they graciously agreed to do. I returned to them with their waters before checking in with my other tables.

Their food was done quickly, and I took it to them, wishing I could crawl in the house and hang out with them while they ate. But I made the rounds instead, refreshing drinks, delivering food, and dropping off checks.

It was shocking I managed to avoid making any mistakes, because my mind was firmly inside the tree house for the entire time Ransom and Cindy were there. Making a decision, I walked over to where Jessie was waiting for drinks from the bar.

"Hey, I was wondering if you'd want my cocktail shift tomorrow?" Saturday was our best money-making night, but even though I'd just been given both weekend nights recently, I knew my time was better spent with Ransom and Cindy. I also knew Jessie was working to pay for school, so odds were good she'd take it.

"Sure," she replied. "Thanks."

"Thank you. I'll let Jerry know. And if you want me to take

a shift for you sometime, let me know."

She smiled. "Will do."

I tracked down Jerry in his office and let him know of the change. As long as *someone* would be there to cover the shift, he didn't care who it was, so the conversation was brief.

When I made my way back to Ransom, they had finished their food and Cindy was looking tired.

"Can we get the check?" he asked. "I want to get her to bed."

"It's on me. I'll see you guys bright and early tomorrow morning."

"No, I can't let you do that," he argued.

"You can't *let* me?" I asked, my eyebrows raised in challenge.

Ransom raised his hands. "Never mind. Poor choice of words. Thank you for dinner."

"My pleasure."

Watching Ransom extricate himself from the tree house was a comedy act worthy of being taken on the road. He didn't so much walk out of it as fall through the doorway. It was spectacular to witness, and I was sad we weren't allowed to have our phones out on the floor while we worked, because it was really something that should've been immortalized via iCloud.

Once he was upright, I said, "I'm glad you guys came in. Though I'm a little surprised you brought her to . . . what did you call it again? A Peter Pan kidnapping ring?"

"Trafficking ring," he corrected. "And I told you, I'm predisposed to making bad parenting choices."

The joke was clear in his voice, so this time I laughed at the reference to him being bad at anything. "I think it worked out okay."

He glanced down at Cindy before returning his gaze to me. "Yeah, I guess it did. So . . . we'll see you tomorrow?"

"Bright and early."

"Can't wait. Come on, Cindy."

And as I watched them leave, I couldn't resist whispering a response. "Me neither."

Chapter Twenty-Three

TAYLOR

I'd set my alarm for seven the next morning so I'd make it to Harry's by eight. When I got there, Ransom had burned two batches of pancakes and looked close to donning a straitjacket. I removed the spatula from his hand, told him to grab a shower, and cooked Cindy breakfast.

After that, we spent the day roughhousing with the dogs, hanging at the playground, and playing every board game we could find—which was a ridiculous amount. Harry and his husband could probably start some kind of store with the collection they'd amassed.

Ransom and I made a good team, and we managed to keep Cindy content for the whole day. By the time bedtime rolled around, we were all exhausted, and Cindy drifted off without any fuss after we got through the two books she'd wanted me to read to her. She'd turned a sweet look on me that I was powerless to refuse.

When I finally got back downstairs, Ransom had straightened up the living room and was kicked back on the couch with the remote in his hand.

"Wanna watch a movie on Netflix?" he asked.

"Sure," I replied as I settled beside him.

"Genre preference?"

"Something lighthearted and funny."

Ransom scanned through the choices, stopping on *Twilight*.

I looked over at him. "Let me guess. Team Jacob?"

He turned his head toward me quickly, looking surprised, as if he'd forgotten I was there.

"Huh?"

"In the teenybopper gang war that was Team Edward versus Team Jacob, I put you firmly on Team Jacob."

He smiled slightly. "Nah, I was Team Volturi. I wanted them to wipe out everyone so I didn't have to endure any more of those horrible movies."

I laughed. "Who made you watch them?"

His smile grew wider but somehow shier. "Emily."

Astutely ignoring the stab of irrational jealousy that shot through my chest, I kept my tone light. "Oh yeah? Who's that?"

It shouldn't have mattered who this Emily was. He'd never mentioned her before, that I remembered, so even if she'd been someone to him at some point, she clearly wasn't anything to him anymore. Maybe she was an elderly neighbor he spent time with. Or a foster sibling he'd had once. So there was no reason for me to worry about this Emily person.

"She was my wife."

"She was what?" I had to have misheard. Maybe I needed to see an ENT or something. My hearing had to be truly fucked, because it had sounded like he'd just said she was—

"My wife. We got married right after high school."

"Oh," I said dumbly because my brain had completely short-circuited. "When did you divorce?"

He looked at me confused, which quite frankly, made my feathers ruffle a bit. *He* was the one being confusing. Not me.

"We didn't."

I stood abruptly, banging my knee on the coffee table. "Ow, shit, fucking . . . wood . . . thing."

"Are you okay?"

"Peachy," I practically growled at him.

What was wrong with me? I'd played house with the man for a day, and all of a sudden I was acting possessive and insane.

I plopped back down, rubbing my throbbing knee. "So you're married?"

"No." And again with the confused look.

"Why do you look like I should know this already?" I asked.

"I didn't. I just . . . figured you thought better of me. I wouldn't hang out with you while I had a wife somewhere."

Okay, well, when he said it like that, I felt like an asshole. "I'm sorry. I *do* think well of you. My brain just . . . fried a little at the mention of a wife."

He smiled. "I can understand that." When he didn't attempt to say any more, I stared at him disbelievingly.

"Ransom," I said firmly. "If you're not married and you're not divorced, what are you?"

"Widowed."

My whole body locked in place. There had been many times in my life where I would've characterized myself as having frozen in place, but I'd never had a complete, all-systems shutdown like this one before. I was pretty sure even my heart had ceased to beat.

After coming back online, my lips moved a few times without any sound coming out. Finally I was able to push a few through my mouth. "Oh my God. Ransom, I'm—I'm so sorry."

Am I? I mean, of course I *was*. Dying was obviously horrible, and I'd imagine losing a spouse at a young age was devastating, but part of me was legitimately relieved. I'd never worried about my soul burning in hell before, but I was most definitely concerned now.

He sighed and settled back into the couch. "It's a complicated story. Emily was Melissa and Matt's daughter. When they took me in, Emily and I immediately became inseparable. It was only ever platonic, but I loved her. No one had ever had my back like Emily."

As he spoke, I could see the pain etched in the furrow of his brow and the downturn of his mouth. His adoration of her was almost palpable, and it hurt me to see him so hurt. But I didn't move, because he seemed to have gone to another place in order to tell me this story, and I didn't want to break him out of it.

"She'd been diagnosed with leukemia when she was eleven. Before I met her. She'd gone into remission a couple times, but ultimately, it always came back. When she was seventeen, the doctors told her she had three to six months. I was heartbroken. But Emily . . ." He laughed, the sound jarring in the midst of such a heartrending story. "All she cared about was she'd never fall in love and get married like stupid-ass Bella and Edward. I mean, their love story isn't even a good one."

He sobered. "But I think there was something to it for her. How Bella came back stronger after dying. How Edward gave her that strength." He rubbed his hands over his face. "I dunno.

I'm overthinking it. Anyway, one night she was making me watch those terrible movies and complaining about how she'd never get to wear a wedding dress, and I just . . . proposed. Said we should get married so she could have all that."

He laughed again before he looked at me, his smile at war with the glistening in his eyes. "She told me I was crazy. But I didn't see what the big deal was. Granted, I'd never love her in the same way Edward loved Bella—we'd never had those kinds of feelings for each other—but I loved her with the same fierceness, ya know? It wasn't romantic, but it was still powerful.

"So we got married. Matt and Melissa were a little hesitant at first, but they knew how much it meant to her. Understood why we wanted to do it. We were married in a small wedding in their backyard. Emily got to wear the dress of her dreams and have a first dance and all the bells and whistles." He paused and sighed heavily. "She died five weeks later. I left two weeks after that. It was . . . too much. For all of us. I love Melissa and Matt, and I know they love me, but the grief . . . It's always there, but it's damn near suffocating when I'm with them. Emily made us all promise we'd keep living our lives, but she was their only daughter—their only real child. They lost the light of their life and were left with a son-in-law they never asked for."

"That's not fair," I interjected. "They fostered you. You were more than just some random guy they picked up off the street."

Ransom smiled and patted my leg. "Easy, Tiger. They're not bad people. Melissa still calls to check up on me. But the relationship is . . . different now. Yeah, they took me in, but our bond was only strong because of Em. With her gone, the relationship was bound to suffer."

“Well, I think that’s shitty.”

He shrugged. “Some things are the way they are. I don’t want to waste time worrying or being angry about things I can’t change. I just want to keep living my life the best I can, like Emily told me to. It feels like the best way I can honor her.”

“You’re . . .” I shook my head, not sure of how to adequately describe what I was feeling. “You’re amazing, Ransom. Truly. You’ve gone through so much, and you’re still just . . . you. Funny, sweet, dependable Ransom. I feel like I’m a better person just by being in your orbit.”

“I think you’re putting me on too high of a pedestal,” he said before smirking. “I’m into it.”

I laughed, the sound deep and husky. A combination of feeling a little raw and being a tad overwhelmed by the emotions swirling around inside me. Suddenly, I felt like if I didn’t kiss Ransom, I might die. And even though that was a truly poor choice in thoughts in light of what we’d just discussed, I couldn’t help it. This was a man who gave so freely of himself, and I didn’t know how else to express my sincere gratitude for the fact that I got to spend time with him.

Ransom licked his lips, and his eyes became hooded, as if he could sense the direction my thoughts had gone. But he stayed still, evidently waiting for me to make it clear.

“I really want to kiss you right now, but I’m not sure I should.” The sentiment was blunt, but at least it was honest.

“Why not?”

“Because we were just talking about your wife? Because my life is a dumpster fire with Brad as the gasoline? Because we both have a lot going on with school and work? I’m not sure I’m in a good place to start anything? Take your pick.”

“Excuses will always be there for anything we do.”

"But they're good excuses," I argued.

"It's never a good excuse if it keeps you from going after what you want."

I wasn't sure I agreed. There was a good chance I'd cross a line tonight that I'd think better of tomorrow for one or all the reasons I'd listed.

But he was looking at me with that sweet smile and those hopeful eyes, and I couldn't resist. I'd worry about later... later.

I closed the distance between us, pressing my mouth to his. The contact made me gasp, causing my lips to part.

Ransom took full advantage of the opening, pushing his tongue into my mouth and tangling his with mine.

This wasn't our first kiss, but it somehow felt that way. Everything was out in the open now. We both knew exactly who we were kissing, messy baggage and all. And as we devoured each other, I wanted to get closer. Needed to. So I pushed up and threw a leg over his lap so I was straddling him.

I felt his hard length pushing into me as I sat on him, and lust burned through me. I wove my hands into his hair and held on as he moved his down my back until they slipped beneath the hem of my shirt.

Moaning at the way he kneaded my skin, I broke the kiss so I could get a breath. Ransom trailed openmouthed kisses down my neck as I ground down onto him. He moved one of his hands around to fondle my breast over my shirt, and my eyes rolled heavenward.

When I dropped my gaze back to Ransom, I registered where we were. Not that I'd forgotten necessarily, but there was nothing quite like my eyes catching on a family portrait of my boss hanging on the wall.

"Ransom," I whispered.

He hummed at me but didn't stop his exploration of my body.

"We can't do this here."

All I got was another hum, so I gripped his hair and pulled.

When his face was tilted toward mine, he looked dazed. It was a great feeling to know I made him look that way.

"We're in the middle of Harry's living room with Cindy asleep upstairs."

It took a minute for reality to set back in, but I saw the moment when what I said registered. But that look was quickly replaced with one of determination. He stood, me in his arms, and began walking toward the stairs.

I wrapped my arms around his neck. "Where are we going?"

"Master bedroom."

I gasped, scandalized. "We can't do anything . . . *sexual*"—I hissed the word—"in Harry's room."

"I'll clean the sheets first thing in the morning."

"That's not—"

Ransom stopped halfway up the stairs and turned so I was pressed against the wall. He ground himself into me and kissed me deeply. Then he pulled back just far enough to look in my eyes as his forehead rested against mine.

"If you really want to stop, I will. But if you're just searching for excuses . . ." He let his sentence hang there, waiting for me to decide what I wanted.

I stared at him for a moment before drawing him into another kiss. He took that for the answer I'd intended it to be, because he resumed our trek to the bedroom.

When we got there, he walked to the bed and gently put

me down on it before going back to lock the door.

"What do you want?" he asked as he made his way back to me.

"You."

He crawled onto the mattress, causing me to lie back as he settled above me. "You have me. But I want to be clear about how far we want things to go."

I stared up at his earnest face, knowing that if I said I just wanted to cuddle, he would. The future might come between us in any number of ways, but tonight we'd pushed everything else aside. And I wanted all of him in case I never had the opportunity again.

"I want everything."

He smiled before pressing a chaste kiss to my lips and getting up from the bed.

I darted forward, sitting upright. Had he somehow misconstrued "everything"?

He reached into his jeans and withdrew his wallet, pulling a condom from it and tossing it onto the bed. Then he began removing his clothes, slowly, but not in the overexaggerated way he'd done when I'd seen him at Sophia's bachelorette party. This was only for me, and I couldn't tear my eyes from him as more and more skin became exposed.

His tight abs and corded muscles were covered with taut, golden skin that was smooth and perfect. When he was in only his boxers, he moved closer to the bed, reaching down and unbuttoning my jeans. I lay back, allowing him to disrobe me as he wanted.

He pulled my jeans down my legs before putting a knee on the bed so he could get close enough to pull off my shirt. Left in only my thong and bra, the cool air of the room caused goose bumps to pop up, but the searing way Ransom looked at me quickly warmed me.

He seemed unsure about where to go from here, as if he was worried he was moving too quickly. I arched my back so I could slip my arms around and unclasp my bra. Throwing it somewhere off the bed, I settled back and let Ransom look his fill.

His reached out to tweak a nipple before drifting his hands down to my underwear, pausing for a second as he looked at me with a question in his eyes.

I nodded, and he pulled the flimsy fabric down my legs, letting it fall to the floor. He quickly shed his own boxers before settling back on top of me.

Having his weight press me into the mattress was likely as close as I could get to experiencing heaven on earth. We let our hands roam as we kissed and ground against each other.

And when he finally put on the condom and pressed inside, all I felt was relief. It was like we'd been building toward this moment since we'd met, and finally getting there made me feel more content than I had in a long time.

Neither of us lasted as long as we probably wanted to. We were too desperate for it. When we finally crested, we did so together. Pleasure washed over me, pulling all my muscles tight before relaxing them to the point of bonelessness.

Our heavy pants filled the air as we stayed close, soaking up each other's warmth, trying to keep reality from intruding on our perfect moment.

RANSOM

The next morning, I woke early, the sun just barely lighting the sky outside—which I could see past the curtains we forgot to close. I hoped we didn't give a free show to any of the neighbors. Taylor was next to me, her blond hair fanned over the pillow, her breaths still deep and even.

Last night had been incredible. While I'd be lying to say I hadn't been wanting to sleep with her for a while, it was so much more than that. There was something about her that drew me in, and I hoped to hell she felt it too. I didn't think last night would be a one-off, but I'd been wrong before. The only thing I could do was hope she wanted more.

I slipped out of bed, dressed, made a stop in the bathroom to take care of business and freshen up a bit, and then eased Cindy's door open enough so I could poke my head in. She was still sleeping soundly, and I found myself standing there watching her.

I'd never imagined this for myself—being a caregiver to a child. I loved working with kids, but part of that was my need to make a difference, to pay the kindness Melissa and Matt had shown me forward. Fatherhood... I'd never thought that was for me.

I was a good guy. I wasn't delusional about that. But it was so fucking easy to screw a kid up. It was a responsibility I didn't want. Or *hadn't* wanted. Now I wasn't so sure.

Cindy's mom was clearly not perfect, but Cindy loved her anyway. My mom was as far from perfect as a human could get, but—and this pained me to admit to myself—I loved her anyway. And I hadn't done a terrible job of watching Cindy.

Granted, I hadn't fed her dinner until after ten on Friday, but Taylor and I had found a groove with her yesterday.

And that was likely the difference. Taryn and my mom had been doing it on their own. And Taryn was managing that a helluva lot better than my mom ever had, but I hadn't given enough credit to single parents before. I'd screwed up in a variety of ways Friday night, but I'd done my best. And sure, people's best varied. Taryn's best was better than my mom's, and someone else's best might outshine them both.

But maybe it was only fair to give credit where credit was due.

Life with my mom hadn't been all bad. There had been beach trips, carnival visits, home-cooked meals, and surprise gifts during the good times, when she'd managed to keep her demons at bay. Maybe we could have some of those times again. Maybe she didn't have to be all good or all bad. Maybe I could learn to be okay with her being both.

I closed Cindy's door before hurrying downstairs and grabbing my phone from where I'd left it on the coffee table last night. Thankfully it still had half a charge, so I was able to type out a text.

Are you awake?

My mom had always been an early riser. Even high out of her mind, she'd still managed to get up before me most days. Or maybe she'd just never gone to sleep.

The reply came almost instantly.

Yes. Are you okay?

It was such a motherly thing to ask, and my eyes burned as I realized I wanted that. Melissa had been a great mother to me, but I wanted the woman who gave birth to me to give a shit too. She couldn't do that consistently when I'd been a kid, but perhaps she could do it now. Or maybe I was setting myself up for a crushing disappointment.

But I'd told Taylor not to let excuses get in the way of going for what she wanted. I could follow my own advice. I clicked on my mom's name and held the phone up to my ear.

"Ransom? Is everything all right?"

"Hi, yeah, everything's fine. I just . . . I want to try. To know you again. If you're sober," I added hastily because I wasn't an idiot. I already knew who Kari was on drugs, and I had no interest in rekindling a relationship with that version of her.

"I'm"—I heard her take a sharp breath—"I'm so happy to hear that. And yes, I'm sober. I'll even take a drug test if you want."

"No, it's . . . that's okay. If you say you are, then I believe you."

"Thank you. I know that's more than I deserve."

It probably was, but I didn't think agreeing with her would move us forward in the way I was hoping.

"So we can talk. Get to know each other again."

"I'd love that."

"Okay, good."

"Good."

I could hear the smile in her voice, even on a single word, and it filled something inside me.

I was sure most people whose parents were addicts wondered at one point or another why their parents chose drugs over them. And logically I knew it was much more complex than that, but my inner eight-year-old would always wonder why I wasn't enough for her. So hearing her sound so happy at the prospect of getting to know me was . . . warming. And comforting. Like being wrapped in a favorite blanket fresh out of the dryer.

"I know this is probably too much too fast," she said, and I instantly steeled myself against whatever she was going to say next. "But my mom's family is having a reunion in two weeks. It would give you a chance to see some family you haven't seen in years. God, you probably don't even remember them. You couldn't have been more than four the last time you saw any of them. But they know all about you, of course. And they'd love to see you. We all would. Sorry, I'm rambling. I just wanted you to know you are more than welcome, but no pressure."

"Thanks. That's probably . . . too much. At least right now. But I appreciate the invite."

"Okay, well, the offer stands if you change your mind. But you're right. It's a lot to ask."

"Let's start with you and me talking for a while, and then we can build up to . . . meeting up and stuff."

"That works for me."

I heard a creak on the stairs and whirled around to see Cindy and Taylor hand-in-hand at the bottom of the stairs looking at me. Cindy still looked half asleep, but Taylor looked vaguely concerned. Probably because I was on the phone at seven a.m. on a Sunday.

"Hey, Mom, I gotta go. But I'll call you this week. Okay?"

"Can't wait."

"Great. Talk soon. Bye."

"Bye, Ransom."

I disconnected the call and pushed the phone into my

pocket. "That was my mom. Kari."

Taylor tilted her head slightly, as if prompting me to go on.

"We're going to talk more."

"Because *you* want to?"

I smiled. "Yeah."

She returned it. "Good."

We stared at each other for a few more seconds, getting lost in a moment that was charged with so many emotions I couldn't even discern them all. There were so many things I wanted to ask, but I was afraid of the answers. In a split second, I made the decision to let my heart guide me. It would be on her to tell me to back off.

Though it probably wasn't the best time for my heart to guide me in that exact moment, because Cindy was looking back and forth between us like she was trying to solve a Rubik's cube.

"Who's hungry?" I asked to break the moment so I didn't go over and maul Taylor while Cindy was with us.

Cindy raised her hand, causing Taylor to chuckle and follow suit.

"Then let's get to it."

I took the dogs out while Taylor pulled out the ingredients for what she called eggs in a basket. Fifteen minutes later, I learned that meant cutting a hole in a perfectly good piece of toast and cooking an egg in the hole.

Cindy and I looked at each other warily before taking a bite. It was definitely better than it looked.

"Told you," Taylor said before digging into her own breakfast.

None of us had taken more than two bites when the door flew open and a harried Harry appeared with three kids trailing in behind him.

I stood quickly. "Hey. Did I miss a text?" I asked, pulling out my phone to look at it. "I thought you said in your last text you'd be a couple more days."

"I was. But then . . ." Harry's gaze landed on Cindy. "Taryn called me. She has an opportunity to stay on for a couple more days, so Cindy's going to stay for a few more days."

That struck me dumb for a second. Had Taryn really called Harry while he was visiting his sick father-in-law because she needed a babysitter? *Jesus.* I looked from Cindy to Taylor back to Harry.

"But . . . Justin's dad. Is he . . . ?"

"Doing better. Justin wants to stay up there a bit longer until he gets released, so he can help him get settled back in at home, but we thought it was important the kids get back to their routine since he's out of the woods."

"Oh. Okay. Um, can I talk to you in the other room for a second?"

Taylor stood. "Do you guys like eggs in a basket?"

"What's that?" Oliver asked.

"Can you eat it?" Grace said.

"You sure can." She started moving around the kitchen as the kids took seats at the table.

Harry followed me into the living room.

"I'm so sorry I didn't tell you about Cindy," I said. "I didn't want to add to your stress."

Harry blew out a long breath. "I do wish you'd told me, but that responsibility falls more on Taryn's shoulders than yours. When she called me last night . . ." He rubbed a hand over his face. "It's not that I didn't know she was safe with you, but Cindy's a particular kid. Justin and I had already discussed me coming back today, but I may have panicked a bit and left earlier than anticipated after a fairly sleepless night. Taryn should've been more responsible." He hesitated as he cast a look back at the kitchen. "I think it's time we sat down as a family and faced some hard truths and do what's best for Cindy."

"You'll let me know if there's anything I can do?"

He turned to me and laughed. "I think you've done more than enough." His words didn't come across as sarcastic. More disbelieving that I'd offer to do *more* to help him. "But I'll keep the offer in mind."

I nodded, unsure of what else to say.

"Let's go get some of those weird egg things Taylor was making," Harry said.

"They're not too bad."

"Huh. That... surprises me," he said. Taylor's lackluster snack preparations clearly preceded her.

"I know, right?"

We finished breakfast, and then Taylor and I excused ourselves to gather our things. When it was time to leave, the whole family saw us off.

I knelt down in front of Cindy. "See you soon, Cinnabon. Thanks for hanging out with me this weekend."

She didn't respond, which I expected. But when I went to stand, she threw her arms around my neck, squeezing tight. I returned the hug, soaking up the affection of this little girl who'd carved herself a special place in my heart.

"Bye, Ransom," she whispered before pulling back and falling into line beside the other kids.

I hurried through the rest of my goodbyes, worried my emotions would bubble over and embarrass me. Then Taylor and I walked in silence to her car.

"So, that was a pretty special moment."

I looked into her beautiful blue eyes. "This weekend was full of pretty special moments."

Her cheeks grew pink, and she looked away as a shy smile spread across her face. "Yeah, I guess it was."

"Maybe we could have a few more," I asked.

She opened her car door before replying. "Maybe we can. See you at work, Ransom." Then she got in the car and started it up.

I watched as she pulled away from the curb and drove down the street, hoping we were heading in the same direction.

Chapter Twenty-Four

TAYLOR

The fire pit at the Yard always made everything better. So what if Manny threw up a few feet away from me at work today—thankfully into a nearby trash can—and then I had to run out of the room so I didn't vomit too? So what if Harry had gotten mad when I'd left the room full of children unsupervised? Most of them were old enough to watch themselves and their younger siblings anyway.

He hadn't exactly appreciated that defense, but he'd quickly softened when he'd seen how pale I was and decided it was best to go into the room himself to clean up and take care of whatever other disasters I'd unknowingly run from. I did feel bad about it considering Harry still had a lot on his plate, but not bad enough to clean up vomit that wasn't mine.

Second to a hot shower, which I'd taken immediately after I'd gotten home, the fire pit made me feel refreshed. Something about the crackling of the flames and the smell of the burning wood felt meditative. The weather had just started getting cold enough to wear a coat, but thinking the warmth from the fire would be enough, I hadn't brought one with me, and I was colder than I wanted to admit.

Ransom pulled me against him, his large hand rubbing over the sleeve of my sweater. "Here, take my sweat shirt," he offered. "You're still cold."

"I'm okay."

Ever since our babysitting gig last week—or more specifically, the mind-blowing sex we'd had—I'd been overthinking everything that happened between us. Every touch, no matter how innocent, the drink he'd bought me earlier, his offer of a sweat shirt. Somehow all of it meant more than it probably should've.

I liked Ransom. There was no denying that. He was sweet and funny, and we made a good team at work and when we'd taken care of Cindy. Ransom was comfortable, familiar in the same way as a favorite pair of sweat pants. You loved the way they felt but couldn't exactly commit to living in them completely.

Before I could refuse the sweat shirt again, Ransom was taking it off and handing it to me, and I was putting it on, amazed at how huge it still felt even over my sweater.

"Woohoo," Aamee called. "Take it off."

I glared at her, my jaw tight.

"What?" she asked innocently.

Aniyah glanced between us and then over to Toby and Carter, who looked just as confused. *Maybe I shouldn't have reacted.* I'd drawn attention to the very thing I'd been trying to keep under wraps.

"What'd we miss?" Carter asked.

"Ransom's striptease," Aamee answered, grinning from ear to ear. "It was quite a show." She said each word as if it were its own sentence before leaning back into her Adirondack chair and taking a sip of whatever orange drink she was holding.

"Does your mom know you've been sniffing the permanent markers at work again, Aamee?" Sophia asked, bless her loyal heart.

"First of all, I only sniff Crayola Silly Scents. They smell like jelly beans, and they remind me of my childhood. Second of all, I don't work at my mom's company anymore."

"Ouch," Sophia said. "Your own mother fired you? And after only a few months? That probably won't look good on your résumé."

"She didn't *fire* me. It was a mutual parting."

"That sounds like something someone would say after they got dumped," Toby told her.

"You don't even know what it's like to be dumped because that would involve someone wanting to actually date you in the first place. So maybe stick to things you know, like . . . the planets and anime porn."

Toby probably realized it wasn't worth arguing with her, so unfortunately, he let her continue talking.

"Didn't Brody tell you I'm moving back here in two weeks?"

Judging by most of our expressions, Brody had *not* told anyone. She'd been coming up on weekends more frequently, but this was the first I'd heard about her moving back. I turned to Ransom.

"Don't look at me. I had no idea."

"Really?" Aamee seemed shocked. "I mean, when I told him, I asked him not to mention it, but it's Brody, so I figured acting like it was a secret would ensure he'd tell everyone so I didn't have to. He really didn't tell any of you?"

"Nope," Carter said, and the rest of us shook our heads. "I think that's something we'd remember."

"Seriously?" Aamee craned her neck and looked toward the bar like a turtle searching for food until she spotted Brody. "Brody! Brody!" she yelled before he'd even had a chance to answer. She waved her hand for him to come over, and when he was done serving the customer he was getting drinks for, he came out from behind the bar and jogged down to where we were sitting like a labradoodle hoping for a treat. She really had that puppy on a short fucking leash.

"What's up?"

"Uhh, you didn't tell anyone I'm moving back."

"Right. You told me not to, remember?"

"Yes, I remember. That's *why* I told you not to tell people. So you would."

Brody looked more confused than usual. "I don't get it. Did I do something wrong? You told me not to say anything, so I didn't."

"Since when can you keep a secret?" Aamee asked.

"Since Ransom asked me not to tell anyone he was a stripper." He seemed proud for a split second before the reality of what he'd said sunk in. "Shit! I mean… I didn't mean… Sorry, man."

Shaking his head, Ransom laughed. I wondered how long Brody had known. "It's all good. Aamee kinda outed me already anyway a few minutes ago."

"Aamee? How did she know? I swear I didn't tell anyone, even her."

"Yeah. I know you didn't. I ended up getting booked for a bachelorette party that turned out to be the one Sophia's sorority sisters were throwing for her."

Brody turned back to Aamee, appearing just as surprised as the rest of us. "You didn't tell me that."

"Well," she said, sounding prouder of herself than she should have. "You're not the only one who can keep a secret. For a little while," she added.

"Okay, so does everyone know now?" Ransom asked.

"Drew doesn't," Sophia said. "I didn't know how he'd feel about me seeing your . . . *you* . . . like that. Plus, it's not my business to tell. And I guess Xander doesn't know either."

"He knows." When we all looked to Aniyah, she added, "I texted him as soon as Brody said it."

Aamee looked around at the group. "Okay, so is that it for the secrets, then? We're not gonna find out you two fools are dating each other or something, are we?" she asked Carter and Toby.

"Well, if that's the case, it's a secret from us too," Carter joked.

He and Toby laughed awkwardly, and I couldn't blame them. Aamee really knew how to put people on edge.

"I'm gonna go to the bathroom," I said. "Soph, you wanna come with me? We can stop at the bar to grab another drink and say hi to Drew on the way back."

We both got up, and after hitting the restrooms, we made our way through the crowd to the bar where Xander and Drew were working.

"Can you tell Brody to come back when you get a chance?" Drew asked. "We're swamped here."

Sophia texted Brody, and he was back in a minute, overly apologetic and mumbling something about Aamee that none of us could decipher.

Drew came back over a couple of minutes later with our drinks, and before we headed back to the group, Sophia asked, "So what's up with you and Ransom?"

I hadn't told her about what happened between us, but I knew better than to lie about it. Besides, she already knew something was going on, or she wouldn't have asked. And she was asking about more than the sweat shirt he'd loaned me or the fact that he'd been rubbing my arm to warm me up. She was asking about feelings. And I didn't know if I had an answer for that.

So I did the best I could to fill her in on the time we'd spent together, how . . . domestic, how right all of it had felt. And I told her about the sex, keeping only a few details for myself. She listened to all of it without saying much of anything until I felt like I'd told her all I could.

"Wow. That's . . . a lot," was all she said.

"I know. When I moved here, I had zero intention of getting involved with another guy. Not after Brad."

After I'd told Ransom about the picture Brad had sent, Sophia was my next stop, and she'd been equally concerned, though she definitely wasn't as visibly angry. She seemed to understand how much the situation with Brad broke me and that it would take more than a hot ex-football player to make me whole again. I needed to make *myself* whole before I could share any part of myself with someone else.

Which was why it surprised me when Sophia said, "Well, you don't have to make any final decisions right now. Just do what feels right and see what happens."

It seemed like simple enough advice, but the ambiguity of it left too much open for me to fuck up. If I decided to begin something real with Ransom, I risked getting myself in too deep too quickly, and if I decided not to be with him, I risked losing out on something that I felt had the chance to make me happy. Really happy.

And if I just waited to see what happened, like Sophia suggested, I risked dragging both myself and Ransom along until I eventually broke both our hearts.

I took another sip of my drink before suggesting we get back to the rest of the gang. When I arrived, I sat back down in my chair next to Ransom and put my phone on the large armrest.

Somehow, I still managed to knock it over onto the grass. Ransom leaned over to retrieve it, but as he brought it up toward me, the text on the lock screen glowed in the dark like a neon sign on a desolate Las Vegas highway.

Miss you, babe. See you soon.

When he handed it to me, his face fell. There was no doubt he'd seen the text too, even if he hadn't meant to. And though I was sure he wanted to ask about it, I was also sure he wouldn't.

Brad.

"That's not what it looks like," I offered as an explanation, albeit an extremely poor one.

"What is it, then? *Who* is it?"

"It's not... not anyone important," I settled on, feeling somewhat satisfied that at least I hadn't lied.

Ransom was quiet for a moment as he focused on his hands, which were clasped in front of him as he leaned forward onto his thighs. "So is that someone you're talkin' to or... ?" he asked, bringing his gaze up to me.

"No."

"Taylor, come on. I think I deserve more than that—"

"Deserve? Really? And just what is it you think you deserve from me, Ransom?" Brad had thought he'd deserved things from me—more than I'd ever wanted to give.

Ransom looked around at our friends, obviously wanting to make sure we didn't garner an audience.

I didn't want that either, but I kept my eyes on him, waiting for his answer.

"Look, if it's someone else you're dating, I just want to know," he finally said.

"Someone *else*?" I scoffed. Like I had time or energy for that. This annoying man in front of me had taken up all the mental space I could spare for weeks, and now he was accusing me of dating other people and not giving him what he felt he deserved? Well, screw him. "I'm not even dating you, let alone someone else."

"Wow," he said, the word holding more sadness than anger.

He leaned back into the chair, silent. And against my better judgment, my eyes followed his movements.

Rigid.

Detached.

I regretted that my comment had hurt him, and I did my best to control my urge to leave when Ransom's beautiful face seemed to break in front of me. But that only made my need for distance grow. *I did that to him.* I made him feel like . . . I didn't want to think about what that made him feel like. I was too concerned with my own feelings, which consisted mostly of panic with a splash of fear.

Okay, maybe more than a splash.

And sitting here, witnessing the internal monologue I

knew was happening inside his head did nothing to help my own.

The rest of our crew were still sitting with us, but they'd been debating whether it would be more embarrassing to fall up the stairs or down them, so they thankfully seemed oblivious to the tension. Well, maybe everyone except Sophia. And even though she knew better than to interject, I still felt exposed in a way that made me feel like ants were crawling beneath my skin.

"Can we go somewhere more private to talk about this?" I finally said, my voice low and intentionally calm.

Without saying a word, Ransom stood and followed me from the Yard and to around the front of Rafferty's. I sat down on the small brick wall that bordered the entrance, and Ransom took a seat next to me.

"I didn't mean we were technically dating," he said. "I know we never put any kind of label on . . . whatever this is, and that taking care of a kid and a bunch of dogs doesn't actually count as a date." He sighed heavily, and his shoulders slumped as he gripped the edge of the brick beside him, causing his usual confident posture to deflate like a day-old balloon. "I guess it's only on my end, but I felt like we were more than . . ."

He seemed stuck for a word, so I supplied it for him. "Nothing?" I was quiet for a moment before I continued. "We were."

When he looked up at me, his eyes seemed to ignite with a flame of hope I didn't want to put out. "*Were?* As in we're not anymore? Just tell me if there's someone else. I'd rather know if you're seeing someone—"

"I'm not," I cut in abruptly. "Seeing anyone else." Shaking my head, I lifted my phone from where I'd been holding it on my lap. "That was Brad."

"What the fuck? I thought your dad handled it. This motherfucker's got some real balls to keep harassing you after your father—"

"He didn't do anything," I blurted out quickly. "I told him not to."

"You what?" Ransom's tone was noticeably harsher now. "Why would you tell him that?"

"He was talking about me going back to school and finishing out the year on campus if Brad was out of the picture, and—"

"And you told him not to do anything to this fucking kid because you didn't want to have to give your dad a reason not to go back? Jesus, Taylor, this isn't some bullshit high school drama that has no bearing on real life. This guy might be dangerous. He's obviously here. Or he *was*. And he's planning to come back."

"Thanks. But I don't need your lecture," I said dryly as I began to stand.

"It seems like you do," Ransom shot back. "This isn't about your ego and proving to your dad you can handle yourself and you're an independent woman who doesn't need his help. This is bigger than that."

"No," I said sternly. "It's really not. That's exactly what this is about. If Brad were going to do something, he would've done it already. He's a coward. He's sending these texts because he wants to fuck with me, and I'm not gonna let him. I can take care of myself."

"Well, can we talk about how you lied, then? You told me your dad was going to handle the situation, and you had no intention of letting that happen."

"I did that to protect you."

"Protect *me*? I'm not the one who needs protecting. *You* are. And keeping me out of the loop does nothing to help either of us."

"I'm sorry I lied. I am. But this conversation isn't getting us anywhere, and I'm not in the right mindset to have it right now, so can we just table this for another day?" I started to get up.

"So we're just gonna go back and hang out with everyone and act like everything's fine?"

"No. You can do whatever you'd like. I'm gonna call an Uber and go home."

"Not by yourself, you're not. I'm coming with you." It sounded like a directive, but I knew his request stemmed from fear, so I let it go. I had more on my mind than picking a fight over semantics.

"I'll be fine."

"You don't know that."

His concern radiated off him like some sort of aura he couldn't leave behind even if he wanted to. And before I got trapped in that bubble of panic with him, I needed to get out of here.

"And you don't know I won't," I said before walking away.

RANSOM

I didn't know what to do with myself after Taylor left. I knew I couldn't follow her home, even though there was nothing I wanted to do more than make sure she was okay.

I'm sure she's okay.

Then why did it feel like my limbs were amped up with adrenaline like an eight-year-old waiting for recess to start after too much sugar and a morning full of worksheets and sustained silent reading?

I couldn't sit still, so there was no way I was going back to the group. I'd have to text Brody later since we'd all had plans to hang out late tonight after the guys got off work. Though I was sure Sophia would tell him Taylor was upset and left, so I went with her. There was no doubt she picked up on Taylor's mood and the tension between us.

Fuck.

I sat back down on the wall where I'd just been with Taylor and tried to figure out what to do next. I wasn't sure if that made me seem like a lunatic or a caring... I guessed *boyfriend* wouldn't be the correct term, but I didn't really have a better one right now.

A few more people came and went as I stared out into the dark parking lot. And in the reflection of the streetlight on the white Ford Raptor parked in front of me, I looked pathetic. If Taylor wanted to be with me, she would, and I had no right to suggest that the way she'd handled the situation with Brad had been wrong. It was her life and her decision. I was beginning to understand there was no right or wrong in any of this. Just feelings and more feelings that felt messy and confusing. And who was I to judge anything?

I'd spent enough time overthinking all of this for one night, so I stood and headed toward the steps to the Yard. Maybe I'd enjoy the rest of the night with my friends after all.

But before I got one foot on the wood, an empty feeling in the pit of my stomach stopped me. It took me a moment to realize that my body must have sensed it before my ears had heard it. Or my subconscious had somehow recognized what I could barely make out.

A faint voice in the distance, muffled but somehow still clear in the night air.

A scream. Then another.

Taylor.

And then I was running, faster than I knew my legs were capable of taking me. It was when the screams began to fade that the adrenaline carried me toward them. I didn't want to lose them. I couldn't.

Against my instincts, I stopped, waiting for a sound. Any sound.

And when one didn't come, I spun around and around, my breaths coming out in heavy puffs of fear.

"Taylor!" I was frantic. Looking down driveways and into dim parking lots. "Taylor!"

As sick as those screams had made me, I prayed silently that I'd hear them again. They were my only link to where she was—where *he* was. I knew it was him before I turned the corner into the skinny alley between the organic food store and the nail salon Taylor and Sophia had gone to a few times.

Why the hell did she even walk this far? It had only been a couple of blocks, but she'd said she was going to call an Uber.

"Taylor!" I called once more, my voice echoing between the surrounding buildings until it died completely.

I heard a rustling at the end of the alley that I hoped wasn't just some animal looking for dumpster scraps.

It wasn't. But it was another kind of animal. The kind that held an innocent woman by the throat against the hard stone of a building while he covered her mouth with his hand.

"Fucking piece of shit!" I yelled as I grabbed him by his

hair, yanking his head toward me before letting it go so my other fist connected with his face.

And like the pussy he was, Brad immediately let go of Taylor and brought his hand to his eye to comfort himself. He stumbled back a few feet when I followed with a quick jab to his stomach. He coughed—hacked, really—as I laid into him, but he didn't go down without a fight.

He swung wildly at me, partly because he could barely see and also probably because he had never been in a real fight.

I let him get close to me only so I could grab his head and bring my knee to his face. Blood spewed from his nose, and I was sure some landed on my shirt.

Once Brad hit the ground and stayed there, I ran over to Taylor.

"Are you okay? Are you hurt? Did he hurt you?"

"No. No. I'm okay."

I held her face between my hands and brought my thumbs to her cheeks to wipe the tears that had fallen. She was shaking, but otherwise didn't seem injured. *Thank God.*

I glanced over at Brad, who was starting to stand, and this time, I walked toward him slowly. "How does it feel?" I asked him.

His lip turned up as he rubbed at his jaw. When he tried to laugh, it came out as a mouthful of blood.

"How does what feel?"

"Being powerless, helpless like you made Taylor feel for so long. You feel like a big fucking man *now*? Because from where I'm standing, you're about a foot shorter than me, though that could just be because you're still doubled over."

"Listen—"

"No, you fucking listen! You're gonna find your way out of

this alley and this town, and I'm never gonna see or hear about you again. *Taylor's* not gonna see or hear about you again. You disappear from her life, or I'll make you disappear for good."

Even in the dim light, I could see the rigidity in his jaw as I spoke. He wanted to say something back, but he knew better. I wondered if his eyes always looked this beady, or if it was because the flesh around them was already beginning to swell.

"I'm so sorry," Taylor said, still sobbing. "I'm so sorry. I should've let you come with me."

I turned enough that I could see her without taking my eyes off Brad. "Don't apologize. It's okay," I said, pulling her into me. "*We're* okay."

I glanced over at Brad, who was still nursing his wounds and had all but given up. He spit a little blood in our direction, but he couldn't even do that correctly.

"You know who's not okay, though?" I said to Taylor. "Our boy Brad here could use some medical attention. Probably a good idea if you get yourself to a hospital. In another city, of course."

"Fuck you!" He was sitting on an old crate with his back against the stone wall of the nail salon.

"No, Brad. It actually looks like this time *you're* the one who's fucked."

Chapter Twenty-Five

TAYLOR

I woke to Ransom's hand running over my back gently, affectionately, but I could also recognize the cautiousness in it. His touch was light, almost like he was worried he might break me.

"Did you sleep here last night?" I didn't remember falling asleep and was surprised I'd slept so well, especially in someone else's bed.

"Where else would I have been? It's my apartment."

"No. I mean, did you sleep in bed with me?"

"I did," he answered, his voice low and raspy from the morning. "Would you rather I hadn't?"

I shook my head. "I'm glad you did. You make me feel safe." I rolled over so I was facing him, and I couldn't help but trace my thumb along the scratch that spanned from his temple to the middle of his cheek. "Is this the only place you're hurt?"

"Mm-mm," he whispered. "I hurt everywhere last night. Seeing what he did to you . . . How he grabbed you."

Ransom looked so sad, like the memory of it alone might

make him cry, and I couldn't be the reason for that.

"None of this is your fault. And as much as I want to blame myself for it because I should've just listened to you, I know there's only one person to blame for what happened, and I don't think he stuck around. Not after knowing you're in the picture now."

A smile crept slowly up Ransom's lips, and I smiled too, knowing I'd put it there.

"Is that what I am? 'In the picture now'?"

"Only if you wanna be in it," I teased. Our faces were closer now, but I didn't notice how they got there or who moved first. One second there was a comfortable space between us, and then suddenly we were right there—against each other, wondering when the distance disappeared. "I mean, you *are* pretty photogenic, so in my opinion, pictures always look better with you in them."

I kissed him first, an innocent but slow meeting of our mouths that barely allowed our lips to separate.

"Just to be clear, the picture thing's a metaphor, right?"

"Totally."

I went to kiss him again, but he hesitated. "So we're dating, then?"

"Yes, Ransom," I said, rolling my eyes at him playfully.

"I think I'm gonna need to hear it," he teased. "Just to be sure."

"Stop talking." I put a finger to his lips.

"I'm gonna need to," he said, my finger muffling his voice as he spoke.

"We're dating," I said, removing my finger from his lips so I could put my mouth against them again.

When we pressed our lips together again, it was Ransom

who deepened the kiss and began undressing us both until we were two warm bodies against each other—exposed, vulnerable, but no longer uncertain of what we had together.

We were done talking. From now on, we'd just feel. And my God, did that man give me something to feel.

XO

We allowed ourselves to get lost in each other for a little while before getting up and continuing the morning with breakfast—pancakes and bacon that Ransom cooked—and coffee on the balcony.

"I miss this apartment building," I said, bringing my feet onto the chair so I could pull my legs close. Even with the colder weather, it was still so relaxing to sit outside and look at the scenery. The only scenery my current place had was shit no one wanted to see.

"You know," Ransom said, "you can stay over sometimes if you want."

"I don't want you to feel like I'm using you for your luxury apartment." I said it as a joke, but part of me was serious. Plus, one night would become two, and then three, and before either of us realized it, we'd practically be living together.

"I could pretend you're using me for sex if it would make you feel more noble."

"Shut up," I said, laughing. "I like what we're doing."

Ransom reached to put his hand over mine. His palm was warm from his coffee mug. "I like it too."

I put my coffee down when my phone dinged with a text I knew was probably from Sophia. She'd texted last night to make sure I'd gotten home okay, and though I'd replied with a *yeah*, I hadn't said anything else. She was probably texting to get the details on my argument with Ransom.

When I lifted my phone, I saw she'd sent a link to a local article.

Only a few blocks from Rafferty's!!!
Crazy, right? Promise me you'll never
walk home alone again. Xoxo

Clicking into the article, I tried to read every word at once, but it felt more like trying to make sense of a shaken Scrabble board.

Victim... Beaten... Unidentified...

Each word triggered a flashback I'd hoped never to replay. But it wasn't until I read more of the article that my heart really began to race, and I could feel the moment the adrenaline released and spread rapidly through my body.

And Ransom must have sensed something was off too because I had no doubt my face was a sickly white.

"What is it?" he asked.

My eyes remained glued to the phone for a few more seconds, and even though it was open, my mouth seemed unable to form any words. Finally, after Ransom called my name twice, I forced myself to look up at him.

"What is it?" he said again.

"It's... Brad," I choked out.

"You're fucking kidding me! He texted you again?"

"No." I shook my head at him. And I wondered how long it would take his anger to turn to fear when I spoke again. "He's dead.

Also by
ELIZABETH HAYLEY

The Love Game:
Never Have You Ever
Truth or Dare You
Two Truths & a Lime
Ready or Not
Let's Not and Say We Did
Tag, We're It

Love Lessons:
Pieces of Perfect
Picking Up the Pieces
Perfectly Ever After

♥

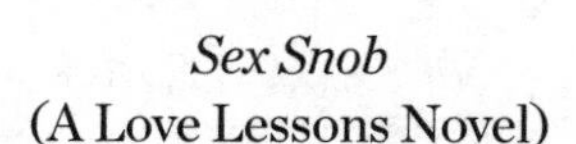

Sex Snob
(A Love Lessons Novel)

Misadventures:
Misadventures with My Roommate
Misadventures with a Country Boy
Misadventures in a Threesome
Misadventures with a Twin
Misadventures with a Sexpert

Other Titles:
The One-Night Stand

Acknowledgments

First and foremost, we have to thank Meredith Wild for allowing us to achieve our dream of writing a rom-com series. This has been a cathartic experience for us, and we'll always be grateful to you for this opportunity.

To our swolemate, Scott, these books wouldn't be what they are without you. Thanks for giving us room to push boundaries while reeling us in when it's necessary.

To Robyn, thank you for managing our writing lives—haha. We're honestly not sure how we made it this far without you.

To the rest of the Waterhouse Press team, you simply kick ass. Thank you for everything you do to help us be as successful as we can. You're an amazing group of people, and we're lucky to have the honor of working with you.

To our Padded Roomers, we don't even know where to begin to express how amazing you all are. You're funny and crazy and supportive and crazy and fierce and crazy, and... have we mentioned crazy? You make this process all the more enjoyable because we get to share every success and setback with you. Thank you for everything you've done for us, such as posting teasers, sharing links, reading ARCs, writing reviews, and making us laugh. We don't deserve you, but we're damn glad to have you.

To our readers, there's no way to accurately thank you for taking a chance on us and for your support. Thank you for letting us share our stories with you.

To Stephanie Lee, thank you for coming up with the name Ransom. It's perfect for him.

To Google, thank you for providing the means for us to research things including, but not limited to, fraternities, sororities, marketing degrees, alcoholic drinks, dean responsibilities, business class topics, college codes of conduct, Gen Z lingo, and popular clothing trends.

To our sons for inspiring the last names of our main characters. Our lack of originality strikes again.

To Elizabeth's daughter for being a spitfire and inspiring the way she writes female characters.

To our husbands, we know it's not easy. Thanks for hanging in there. We honestly don't deserve you.

To each other for pushing one another forward when we stall. The ride hasn't been easy, but it's sure as hell been a lot of fun. On to the next.

About ELIZABETH HAYLEY

Elizabeth Hayley is actually "Elizabeth" and "Hayley," two friends who love reading romance novels to obsessive levels. This mutual love prompted them to put their English degrees to good use by penning their own. The product is *Pieces of Perfect*, their debut novel. They learned a ton about one another through the process, like how they clearly share a brain and have a persistent need to text each other constantly (much to their husbands' chagrin).

They live with their husbands and kids in a Philadelphia suburb. Thankfully, their children are still too young to read their books.

Visit them at AuthorElizabethHayley.com